In the Forests of Serre

Ace Books by Patricia A. McKillip

THE FORGOTTEN BEASTS OF ELD
THE SORCERESS AND THE CYGNET
THE CYGNET AND THE FIREBIRD
THE BOOK OF ATRIX WOLFE
WINTER ROSE
SONG FOR THE BASILISK
RIDDLE-MASTER: THE COMPLETE TRILOGY
THE TOWER AT STONY WOOD
OMBRIA IN SHADOW
IN THE FORESTS OF SERRE

In the Forests of Serre

Patricia A. McKillip

ACE BOOKS, NEW YORK

IN THE FORESTS OF SERRE

An Ace Book
Published by The Berkley Publishing Group,
a division of Penguin Group (USA) Inc.,
375 Hudson Street, New York, New York 10014.

First edition: June 2003

Library of Congress Cataloging-in-Publication Data

McKillip, Patricia A.
In the forests of Serre / Patricia A. McKillip— 1st ed.
p. cm.
ISBN 0-441-01011-3
1. Princes—Fiction. I. Title.

PS3563.C3815 2003
813'.54—dc21

2003041928

PRINTED IN THE UNITED STATES OF AMERICA

10 9 8 7 6 5 4 3 2 1

For Lauren and Rachel and Jackson and Arleigh,
With a cauldron full of love

ONE

In the forests of Serre, Prince Ronan crossed paths with the Mother of All Witches when he rode down her white hen in a desolate stretch of land near his father's summer palace. He did not recognize her immediately. He only saw a barefoot woman of indeterminate age with an apron full of grain, feeding her chickens in the middle of a blasted waste full of dead trees and ground as hard as the face of the moon. It was the last place Ronan expected chickens. He did not notice the cottage at all until after the hen pecked its way under his horse's nose. It flapped its futile wings and emitted a screech as a hoof flattened it. Startled, Ronan reined in his mount, blinking at something unrecognizable even as suitable for a stew pot. The prince's following pulled up raggedly behind him. A few feathers flurried gently through the air. The woman, one hand still outflung, golden husks clinging to her fingers, stared a moment at her hen. Then she looked up at the prince.

His following, a scarred, weary company of warriors, guards, servants, standard-bearers, a trumpeter or two, seemed suddenly far away and very quiet. The young prince felt the same stillness gather in his own heart, for with her in front of him, he had nothing else to fear. As in all the tales he had heard of her, there was the ox-bone pipe in her apron pocket, the green circular lenses over her eyes, the knobby, calloused feet that broadened to an inhuman size when she picked up her cottage and carried it. There, behind her, stood the cottage made of bones, some recent and still bleeding marrow, others of a disturbing size and indeterminate origin. A single circular window, its pane as green as her lenses, seemed to stare at Ronan like a third eye among the bones. The door stood open. Never, all the tales warned, never go into the witch's house, whatever you do . . . Who, he wondered incredulously, would choose to enter that filthy pile of bones?

She smiled at him, showing teeth as pointed as an animal's. Her face, which could be sometimes so lovely it broke the heart, and sometimes so hideous that warriors fainted at the sight of it, looked, at that moment, ancient and clever and only humanly ugly.

"Prince Ronan." Her voice was the hollow sough of windblown reeds.

"Brume," he whispered, feeling a twinge of fear at last.

"You killed my white hen."

"I am very sorry."

"My favorite hen."

"I wasn't watching for chickens in this part of the forest. What can I do to repay you?"

"Bring the white hen into my house," she answered, "and pluck it for me. I will boil it in a pot for supper, and you and all your company will drink a cup of broth with me around my fire."

He swallowed. Never, never . . . Those strong pointed teeth had sucked the boiled bones of warriors, so the tales said. "I will do anything for you," he said carefully, "but I will not do that."

Her eyes seemed to grow larger than the lenses, and disturbingly dark. "You will not pluck my hen?"

"I will do anything for you, but I will not do that."

"You will not bring your company into my house to drink a cup of broth with me?"

"I will do anything for you, but I will not do that," he repeated, for the third time was the charm.

She raised her lenses then, propped them on her wild hair, and looked at him with naked eyes. In that moment, her face nearly broke his heart. He would have melted off his horse, followed that face on his knees, but now it was too late.

"Then," she said softly, "you will have a very bad day. And when you leave your father's palace at the end of it, you will not find your way back to it until you find me."

She dropped the lenses back on her nose, scooped the bloody mess of feather and bone into her arms, and walked into her house. The chickens, clucking in agitated disapproval, followed her. The door slammed shut behind them.

The house levitated suddenly. Ronan saw the powerful

calves and huge, splayed feet below it as the witch, carrying her cottage from within, began to run. Motionless, mesmerized, he watched the little house of bone zig-zag like a hen chasing an ant through the stark bones of trees until the silvery shadows drew it in.

"My lord," someone said tremulously. He looked around to find his entourage in chaos. She had shown the men all her faces, Ronan guessed. Wounded warriors, white and sickened by the loathsome sight, slumped toward servants and guards who were no longer beside them; they had already dismounted to trail, mindless with vision, after the woman who had, for an instant, reached into the prince to hold his own heart in her hand like a sweet, ripe pear.

He brushed a pinfeather off his knee and managed to turn them all toward home.

The prince was a tall, burly young man with troubled, watchful grey eyes and long coppery hair. Scars underlined one eye, limned one jaw; a fresh wound along his forearm was trying to seam itself together as he rode. He had gone impulsively to war with the army his father had sent to quell a rebellion in the southern plains of Serre. Returning bruised but victorious, they had met the king's messenger half-way across Serre. The message was accompanied by a troop of guards to make sure that Ronan did not disregard it. Come home, it said tersely. Now. Ronan was impressed with its restraint. He had not consulted his father before he joined the army; some part of him had not intended to return. Having failed to die, and too weary to fend for himself, he let fortune, in the shape of the king's guards, bring him back.

Fortune, appearing suddenly under his nose in the shape of the depraved witch Brume, baffled him. He tried to remember childhood tales. Did her predictions come true? Or were they only random curses that she tossed out according to her mood, and would forget as soon as she had added the white hen's bones to her roof? His mother would know. Maye would have known. But Maye was dead. He felt his heart swell and ache unbearably at the memory of his young wife lying so still among rumpled, bloody linens, with their child, impossibly tiny, the size of Ronan's hand, too delicate even to take in air, a soap-bubble child, a moment's worth of wonder and then gone, vanished like hope. Ronan had burned his heart with them. Then he went to court death as he had courted love, ignoring the fact that he was his father's only heir. The queen had failed, even with the aide of common lore and folk witchery, to conceive others. Ronan, understanding his father better as he got older, sympathized with her. Who would want to bear the ogre's children?

He pushed the terrible memories from his mind, and found again the Mother of All Witches, staring at him behind her fly-green lenses. The idea that she might have been waiting there for him was disturbing. But nobody took their chickens to feed in that benighted place. Even the insects had abandoned it. Long ago, tales said, some lovelorn maiden had drowned it with her tears and then cursed it barren as her heart. With some effort, he pushed aside the witch on the waste, too. If, he reasoned, he was to get lost after leaving his father's palace at the end of the day, then once he got home, he would simply not leave. As for having a bad day, he doubted that the witch herself knew how bad a day could get.

"My lord." A guard had quickened pace to catch up with him. "Lord Karsh has fallen."

Ronan's mouth tightened. The warrior had been dangerously wounded, but he had refused to stay on the plains. "Dead?"

"It seems so, my lord."

So it proved, when Ronan investigated. But his death was not unexpected. The surprise was that he had endured the journey so long. His body was wrapped in blankets and placed in a supply cart. Later, when the cart lost a wheel, the stiffened body had to be taken back out and balanced precariously over his horse's saddle. They left the cart there in the forest with the driver trying to reset the wheel. Not a good day, Ronan thought. But not impossible, and nothing out of the ordinary. Except the witch.

There was not much day left by the time the endless trees parted around them and they saw at last the ancient palace of the rulers of Serre. Part fortress, it seemed carved out of the crags on which it stood. Ribbons of water on both sides of it caught fire from the lowering sun, poured down steep walls of granite to the broad valley below. The riders quickened their pace. Even Ronan, who had no doubt that his father was furious with him, breathed more easily when they reached the road carved into the stone face of the cliff. Ronan, gazing up at the thick walls and high towers, saw a minute scratch of light across the dark, like the path of a falling star. From very far away, he heard the trumpet speak, announcing their return. Within the formidable walls would be food and wine, hot water and fire, aid and comfort for those who had ridden in constant pain from unhealed wounds. It seemed, at that moment, a fair exchange for what awaited him.

An hour later, he was home.

The king did not waste time sending for him. In his chamber, Ronan splashed water over his dusty face and hair, and stood dripping while a servant unbuttoned his travel-stained tunic and drew another over his shoulders. The door flew open suddenly. The King of Serre said, "Get out." Ronan's servants abandoned him hastily. His father swung a hand hard and scarred with battle and slammed the heavy door shut behind them; turning, still swinging, he slapped Ronan. The prince, surprised, stumbled against the washstand. The basin careened, spilled water over his boots. He caught his balance, his head ringing like the brass on the stones. The king waited until the basin was still, until the only sounds in the room were the endless thunder of water over the sheer cliff just beneath the open casement, and Ronan's quickened breathing.

Then the king said, "She will be here in three days. Her messengers arrived this morning."

Ronan let go of the washstand cautiously, touched his bruised mouth with the back of his hand. "Who?" he asked warily, mystified.

"The woman you will marry."

Ronan stared at him. He and his father were much alike in their height and strong build, though the king, massively boned like an ox, stood nearly a head taller. Ronan had also inherited his coppery hair. The king let his grow in a fox's pelt over his mouth and jaws. He had lost one eye and one front tooth in battle long ago. The scar seaming his face from his brow had pulled his upper lip open in a perpetual snarl. But it was the puckered, empty skin where his eye should have been that was more chilling. It seemed, Ronan had decided long ago, as though he had a hidden eye there, that could see into secrets, thoughts, invisible worlds. His visible eye was a deep, fuming black. He had been born on a battlefield, tales said, and had spent his life there, in anticipation when not in deed. In the last few years he had been attempting sorcery to make himself and his kingdom even stronger. Occasionally, to strengthen his son's defenses or to let Ronan know he was displeased, the king would conjure an explosion out of the air and fling it at Ronan. This time the explosion was silent, and Ronan, dazed, thought he must have swallowed it. He felt the shock of it finally all through his body, as something jagged and drenched with color burst where his heart had been.

"Marry." He was shaking suddenly with rage, with pain, with grief. "I can't marry."

"You will marry." His father's powerful voice had a deep, feral resonance; it drove the words into Ronan like an ax into wood. "In four days. The youngest daughter of the King of Dacia has been travelling toward you through much of the summer—"

"I will not marry!" The force of the shout tearing out of Ronan startled him; he did not recognize his own voice. But the king only matched it with a shout of his own.

"How dare you?" He was suddenly too close to Ronan, dangerously close, turning the puckered eye socket toward his son; it seemed to search mercilessly into his most private thoughts. Ronan stood still, too furious even to blink. The king did not touch him, but his voice roared over Ronan like wind or water, held him in the grip of some elemental storm. "How dare you pretend to fight battles for me while you try to kill yourself? Your life is mine. How dare you even dream of stealing it from me? I made you; you belong to me and to Serre." He moved abruptly again, crossing the room to fling the window wide. Ronan had chosen the chamber, in a tower flanking one of the foremost corners of the outer wall, after his wife and child had died. It overlooked the exact place where water as clear and silent as blown glass fell off earth into air and roared down a thousand feet to the ground below. Ronan had cast himself over the falls countless times in thought. His father's words seemed to bellow at him out of the surging water. "I will call up your drowned ghost and curse it every hour if you leave me with no one to inherit my kingdom when I am dead. The princess from Dacia will be here in three days; you will marry in four. The negotiations were completed, the documents signed and sealed even before you began your journey home from the south. Her name is Sidonie. Love her or hate her, you will give me heirs for Serre. Dacia is tiny, nothing. It would be lost within the forests of Serre. But it is wealthy, and its kings have been renowned for their sorcery. Your children will inherit the vastness of Serre and the powers of Dacia. My kingdom will be invincible." He reached out, in another swift, unpredictable move, and closed the casement; the wild, urgent voice of the water receded. "Get dressed. You will not spend another night listening to this. You will be under guard until your wedding." He came very close to Ronan again, laid a hand on his shoulder. What might have seemed a gesture of reconciliation weighed like stone on Ronan's shoulder, weighed like the rough, massive walls of the tower itself, as the king summoned his private strength. Ronan yielded finally, loosing a cry of despair as he fell to his knees. Hands clenched, head bowed to hide tears of fury and humiliation, he heard his father cross the room, open the door, then stop.

Someone spoke a word or two. Ronan raised his head slightly, recognizing the soft, mourning dove voice. The door closed again; his mother, Calandra, crossed the room quickly, knelt in front of Ronan.

He felt her hands frame his face, coax him gently until he lifted it finally, showed her his angry, defeated eyes. He saw the stark relief in hers, and realized that she had not expected him to return.

But, he thought, getting wearily to his feet, he did not seem to be good at dying. He had offered himself in battle and, beyond a scratch or two, had been rejected; a witch had invited him to become her next meal and he had refused. He began, clumsily, to push buttons into loops down the front of his tunic. His hands shook. The queen drew them into hers, kissed them as though he were still a child.

"Let me," she said, eyeing the haphazard hang of hem. "You started wrong."

He watched the braids of chestnut and gold crowning her head drop lower, button by button. Her hair had begun to lighten since he had seen her last, lose its rich lustre. But the ghost of her fine, delicate beauty still haunted her: the memory of what she had been before she realized what, in marrying Ferus of Serre, she would become. When Ronan was very young, she had still known how to laugh. He remembered her fury more easily, her tears, her cries of outrage and pain. Those, like her laughter, had become less frequent in later years, when Ronan grew old enough and strong enough to decide for himself what he could bear. In his early years, after his father had driven them both to tears, she would hold him in her arms and tell him stories.

He remembered that now. She turned her face briefly, to look at him, working at the last of the buttons. He whispered numbly, "He wants me to marry."

"I know."

Still his voice would not sound. "He can't see—he can't see that it is impossible."

"No." She reached the hem and straightened. She was quite tall; her gaze was almost level, grey and still like an autumn sky. "He can't see." She touched his face again. "You came back. I didn't think you would."

"I wish I had known," he said more clearly, "what I would be coming back to." He glanced around at the tower walls, searching blindly for some way out, some way around; memory struck him again, and he gave a faint, bitter laugh. "I have to give the witch her due; she does know a bad day when she sees one coming."

"Witch?"

"Brume. I met her in the forest this morning. You used to tell me tales of her; that's how I recognized her."

The queen raised a slender hand, pushed a knuckle and

her wedding ring against her mouth. The mingling of fear and wonder in her eyes startled Ronan; he had never seen that expression before. She whispered, "Brume."

"I ran down her hen. Does she really see the future?"

"Her white hen?"

He blinked. "Yes. Why? Does it matter?"

The door opened again; the captain of the guards stood on the threshold. He said, bowing low to the queen, "Your pardon, my lady. The king commands your presence in his chambers."

Her mouth tightened; the bleak sky descended once again. "I will ask him," she murmured to Ronan, "if we can talk privately later." She kissed his cheek quickly, took her leave. The guard stood aside for her, then returned to the threshold where he caught Ronan's attention with his silent, stubborn waiting.

Ronan sighed. "A moment."

A moment for what? the man's eyes asked. The door stayed open. Ronan's attendants scattered quietly through the room, began to carry his belongings away.

He wandered to the casement, causing a stir within the chamber. But it was only to stare out the window, blind again with grief and memory. Across the grey-white water, within the trees blurred together beyond his tears, an odd banner of fire rippled and soared, spiraled sinuously into itself, then bloomed again, casting ribbons of crimson everywhere within the green. He blinked, felt tears fall. He saw it clearly then: a bird made of fire, its eyes and claws of golden fire, drifting plumes of fire down from the branch where it perched, so long they nearly touched the water.

He swallowed, stunned. It was, he thought, the second most beautiful thing he had ever seen in his life.

Then it changed, became the most beautiful thing. The bird's long feathers swirled about it, hiding its long, graceful neck, its proud flowing crest, its eyes. Then the flames parted again, revealing amber eyes, fiery hair tumbling down toward the water, a face carved of ivory, with cheekbones like crescent moons, a smile like a bird's wings angling upward, taking on the wind. The woman who was a bird who was fire seemed to see him. Her enchanting smile vanished. Feathers of gold and fire hid her face. Wings unfurled; their reflection flowed across the glassy water like outstretched hands.

Ronan moved. He left by the door, not out the window, which caused the guard leaning against the walls, waiting for him, to follow his quick steps at a more leisurely pace. He spiralled down the tower stairs, glancing out at every narrow window for a glimpse of the magic within the trees. He saw the bird; he saw the road beyond the gate; he saw the inner courtyard; he saw the woman, beginning to reappear now that she felt no longer seen. The door at the foot of the tower opened directly into the outer yard. Walls and towers rose around him there; he could not see the trees beyond it, nor the water, gathering such power into its calm, smooth flow that it echoed across the valley as it fell.

But it was the sun Ronan saw first, not the forest, as he walked impatiently across the drawbridge to the road. It hung just above the distant mountains, red as a hen's crest, and round as the lens over a watching eye.

He stopped dead, heard the pebbles settle under his boot.

Behind him, the yard was eerily silent. No steps followed across the bridge; he heard no voices. Wind blew a light spray from the falling water across his face. He stood, uncertain and unprepared, not daring to look behind him, and finally, not needing to look, knowing that the road began where he stood and ended at the bone that marked the threshold of the witch.

TWO

Earlier that summer in Dacia the scribe Euan Ash, translating a poem out of a long-dead language, was lulled by bees and the scent of sun-warmed roses into a dream of the poem. His eyes closed. The ragged breathings and scratchings from dozens of noses and pens, the occasional curse let loose as gently as a filament of spiderweb, faded around him. He walked down a dusty road in a strange dry landscape, eating a handful of stones. In that land, stones turned to words in the mouth. Words tasted like honey, like blood; they vibrated with insect wings between the teeth. He spat them out after he had chewed them. Bees flew out of his mouth, birds circled him, bushes took root in the parched ground and flowered; he was speaking a landscape to life . . . Then something he spat out took shape in the distance where the road narrowed to a point. A dark, rectangular object, like a column or a book, travelled swiftly to meet him, casting a shadow over the dream. It had no face or mouth, but it towered over him and spoke a word like a book slamming shut.

Euan woke with a start and saw the wizard.

Sightings of him were quite rare, and the sleepy scriptorium, a curve like a question mark at the end of a long hallway in the king's library, was the last place Euan would have expected to see him. He stared, still drugged with dreaming. The wizard who called himself Unciel spoke softly to Proctor Verel, who was nodding vigorously, looking, to Euan's dazed eyes, like one small ball rolling on top of a much larger ball. The wizard, around whom legends swarmed and clung, each more fabulous than the last, seemed worn by the burden of them. He was tall and spare, his lined face honed to its essence of muscle and bone, his cropped hair dead white. He was the son and the grandson and the great-grandson of a long line of powerful sorcerers, and he had become the most powerful of them all. That was one rumor Euan had heard. Another had him born in a land so old all but its name had been forgotten; he had tutored the first King of Dacia in the magical arts. He had wandered everywhere into the known and the unknown. According to most recent tales, he had overcome some great evil, some fierce, deadly monstrosity that had challenged his strength and power beyond endurance. But he had endured, and had returned to peaceful Dacia to recover. He did not look injured, but the weariness that emanated from him seemed almost visible to Euan; it must have come out of his heart's marrow.

The wizard stopped talking and turned his head. Every pen had stilled, Euan realized; everyone was staring at the wizard, whose light eyes, cloudy with fatigue, were gazing back at Euan. The scribe woke completely then, with a jerk that shook his high, slanted desk and tipped the inkstand over onto the poem he had been transcribing. Black welled across the parchment, eating words as swiftly and irrevocably as fire.

Euan righted the ink hastily, tried to dam the flood with his sleeve. He heard snickers, a sharp, impatient breath from the proctor. Then a hand touched the paper. Ink seeping into Euan's sleeve vanished. Words reappeared, lay across the dry landscape of paper as neatly and clearly as footprints down a dusty road.

He froze, his eyes on the parchment, not daring to look up. "This one," he heard the wizard beside him say. "What is your name?"

Still rigid, he managed to remember. "Euan." How, he wondered wildly, were wizards addressed? He cleared his throat, gave up. "Euan Ash."

"My name is Unciel. Come to me when you are finished here."

The scribe glanced up finally, incredulously. But the wizard had gone. Everyone stared at Euan now, even Proctor Verel. If he could, Euan would have stared at himself. He scratched his head instead. So did the proctor, riffling at his bald head and looking mystified.

"To work," he said briskly, then wandered among the desks to see the paper touched by magic.

Euan, still stunned, asked warily, "What does he want with me, Proctor?"

Proctor Verel shrugged his plump shoulders and shifted Euan's inkstand farther from his elbow. "He needs a scribe." He studied the scribe's neat, graceful writing, no more or less neat and graceful than that of a dozen others. "Why you, I have no idea. Especially since you chose that moment to spill ink all over everything." He tapped the paper where Euan's last word trailed down the page. "And you fell asleep," he added reproachfully. "In the middle of one of Laidley's poems."

"It was not the poem," Euan assured him. "My head was full of bees."

The young man at the next desk snorted. The proctor said dourly, "Start over."

"How did he do that?" Euan wondered suddenly, intently. "How did he separate the spilled ink from the words? How did the ink recognize the words?"

"One was liquid; one was dry," the scribe beside him suggested, too intrigued by the question to observe the rule of silence. "One had form; the other was chaos."

"But how," Euan persisted, "did he speak to the ink? What language did he use to make it listen?"

Proctor Verel raised his voice irritably. "Another word in any language, and you'll all be seeing midnight in the scriptorium." He added to Euan as he returned to his desk, "Ask him."

An hour or two later the scribe found the wizard, not in a

tower as he had expected, nor in a secret chamber beneath the palace, but down a busy side street beyond the palace gates. COME IN, said a wooden sign hanging on the door. The cottage looked much larger within than it should have. Worn flagstones led to more closed doors than seemed possible. Herbs and flowers hung drying on smoke-blackened rafters. A one-eyed cat slunk around a corner and disappeared at the sight of Euan. A raven perched on a small, cluttered table near the door. Stuffed, Euan thought, until it fluttered abruptly, raggedly, like black flame to a stand in front of a line of open casements. The windows, diamonds of thick glass framed in brass, overlooked a garden. Like the house, the garden seemed to wander beyond possibility; the far wall might have crossed the next street. The wizard's gardener knelt in the late light, a torn straw hat on his head, picking seeds slowly, painstakingly out of one trembling hand with the other, and dropping them into a crumbled patch of earth. Some ancient, beloved retainer, Euan thought. Then the raven squawked hoarsely beside him, and the gardener straightened, glancing toward the windows. Euan, recognizing that seared gaze, gave a hiccup of surprise.

The wizard gestured, and Euan found the door leading into the garden.

Unciel stood with an effort, one hand closed around the seeds. He took the hat off, dropped the seeds into it, then wiped at sweat, his movements slow, precise. He studied Euan silently a moment, like the raven had. Even the color seemed to have been drained from his eyes, along with his strength. Euan saw only the faintest shade of blue beneath what must have been the paler ash of memory. The scribe, who was lanky as a scarecrow, pallid from working indoors, and habitually terse, wanted to melt into a shell like a snail and politely close the door behind him. He still wore the long black robe that absorbed stray ink. In the hot light he felt sweat trickling through his dark, untidy hair. His lean, somber face grew rigid beneath the scrutiny; his eyes, green as cats' eyes and as reserved, widened and slid away finally, dropped to study the wizard's bare, calloused feet.

Unciel said gently, "I need a scribe to copy my papers. My writing grew illegible years ago. The librarians will give you leave for a time, and I will pay you twice what they do now, to compensate for the amount of work and the lack of company. Do you mind?"

Surprised, Euan stammered. "No. I don't—I dislike most company, anyway."

"Then we will suit each other. In return for borrowing you, I have promised the librarians a portion of what you copy for me. Come into the house. I'll show you what needs to be done."

Inside, he opened one of the closed doors along a hallway like a stalk that sprouted short passages and doors at random. The room was empty except for a dark wooden chest, whose arched lid was filigreed with delicate patterns of paler wood. Unciel murmured something and the lid sprang open. Euan stared at brimming piles of unbound sheets and scrolls that must have held countless decades of spells, notes, tales of travels to distant places that perhaps no longer existed, recollections of a long life governed by rules and forces beyond most human comprehension and experience. He asked impulsively, "Why can't you copy them with magic? You found the poetry within the ink."

"That was a simple spell of undoing. This would be far more complex, and I am very tired. I would rather garden." He closed the lid, held a hand over it. "Go," he said, and the chest vanished.

"Where did it go?"

"I wouldn't expect you to work in this windowless place. Come."

Euan didn't move. Caught in a sudden tangle of curiosity and longing, he saw himself as an ornate wooden chest full of papers. It could not comprehend or appreciate being touched by magic, and yet it had been filled and moved by the wizard's power. Move me, he thought confusedly, urgently, and expression, swift, nebulous, slid through the wizard's eyes.

His fingers closed lightly on Euan's arm. "Now," he said after a moment, "you can see out."

They had not taken a step, yet the room was suddenly full of light. The sun was lowering beyond the casements, igniting rainbows in the small prisms set here and there among the panes. This room held a vast table, a chair, a carpet, and the chest, open again, crammed with words and waiting. Euan, blinking at a rainbow in his eyes, said blankly, "I didn't feel—"

"You did feel." The wizard's breath had grown ragged; his hand gripped Euan's arm as if for balance. "So here we are."

Euan looked at him, saw his bloodless face, the sag of his shoulders, as though he had borne the scribe on his back and run. Euan pushed the chair around, eased Unciel into it.

"Why," he asked incredulously as the wizard caught his breath, "was it so difficult? I thought I would be as simple for you to move as that chest."

"I already carry," the wizard said haltingly, "all the words in that chest in my head. That makes it easier. I don't know you."

"Then why did you do that for me?"

"Because you are so full of wonder. After what I— After—" He gestured, his eyes hidden; deep lines ran down his cheeks like claw-marks. "That seems very precious to me now. How could I not give you such a small thing?"

Words collided with wonder in Euan's throat. He swallowed, watching Unciel, his set expression quelling amazement, curiosity, horror, anything that might disturb the infinitely frail and powerful wizard. The sun slipped behind the garden wall. The prisms on Euan's sleeve, in the wizard's hair, vanished. Unciel's face took on a healthier shade of pale; his breathing steadied. He stirred finally, glancing out at the dusk.

"I must finish planting my seeds. Come back tomorrow. The proctors will not expect to see you for some time."

For a lifetime, Euan thought the next day as he drew papers out of the chest and began to sort through them. The wizard had provided him with pens, ink, and a stack of vellum as high as the casement. Euan scanned the prickly lines, picked out what he could. "Forest" he recognized, and "interminable." Then what looked improbably like "chicken." "Brume" he found. Broom? And then "Serre" and the trees in his head multiplied immeasurably, climbed towering, frozen peaks, spilled toward bright plains. He wandered to his chair, engrossed now, beginning to make his way more easily through the cramped, spiky letters. The wizard had once come across a formidable witch in the forests of Serre . . .

He grew quickly content, watching the wizard's astonishing life form out of his pen. Days flowed past, each greener than the last. The one-eyed cat began to nap among the papers on Euan's table; the raven greeted him by name each morning. He and the wizard met at midday to eat together. Unciel, preoccupied with his garden, spoke of little else. Euan did not question him, unwilling to tax his strength or trouble him. But the wizard changed shape daily in his head. The fragile gardener in his tattered hat had counseled kings, matched wits and powers with monsters. He had lived in lands Euan knew only as names on dry parchment in the scriptorium. The range of his powers and experience became disturbing; it was a measure, Euan realized starkly, of the terrible power that had drained and nearly destroyed him. The scribe sensed that the living things which the wizard coaxed daily out of the ground and into bloom shielded him from memory. Gazing into fiery petals, picking grazing beetles off leaves, he looked neither forward nor backward; he was trying to bury his past under the roses.

Finally the wizard, who read Euan's face, or his mind, or heard the questions piling up behind his back teeth, said briefly as they ate, "Ask me. If I can, I'll answer."

Euan felt his face warm with more than light. He said haltingly to his bowl of vegetable stew, "If there are—If you wrote about your last battle, I don't have to ask."

"No. I didn't."

"Do you—Can you tell me—"

"No."

Euan nodded, lifted his spoon, and swallowed a lump of something. "Then you can't. I won't ask again."

The taut, strained note left the wizard's voice; he repeated more easily, "I will answer what I can. I know you must be curious."

Euan, struggling to pick through a lifetime of marvels, managed only the simplest. "That witch—Brume. Does she really eat people?"

Unciel's face smoothed; he gazed back, unblinking, at something beyond pain. "Brume," he murmured. "Never underestimate the power of a tale. What you put aside as fantasy in one land can kill you in the next. As far as I know, she eats anything. Like death, she is always hungry and too much is never enough. Like love."

Euan blinked, startled. But that tale, he told himself, would likely be among the wizard's papers, and so he did not ask.

The afternoon seemed hot enough for the sunlight burning in the prisms to ignite the parchment on Euan's desk. All the windows were open. In the garden he could see Unciel digging so slowly to unearth the roots of weeds that they probably expired naturally before he got them out of the ground. For the hundredth time, Euan tried to imagine the fearsome evil Unciel had faced that had left him too shattered even to wither a thistle by magic. The evils he had written about seemed nasty enough, ranging from the bloodthirsty Brume, who could be baffled by a charm, to the subtle and devious mage Ziel, who had counseled a king nearly to his death so that the mage could seduce his queen and rule his kingdom. Strand by strand he wove his invisible web toward that end, with no one seeing except one young wizard who had no reputation then, and little experience, and who was a stranger in that land . . . Engrossed in the tale, Euan scarcely noticed a blast of trumpets from the street. The sound seemed to come from the battlefield on which the king fought his most loyal and completely bewildered knight, who would be the unwilling weapon Ziel would temper with his magic to murder the king. But the mage found himself thwarted, again and again, by the bumbling and exasperating stranger who kept getting in his way . . .

The front door flew open. The raven rattled feathers and squawked. Euan's head snapped up; his jerking hand invented an unknown letter. He caught a glimpse of a disturbance crossing the quiet cottage and banging out the garden door. Euan went to the casement, leaned out, squinting at the brightness. Unciel, digging down to the end of an apparently endless root, had no time to rise before the whirlwind was upon him.

It was a young woman. She seemed, in the drenching light, to be made of gold, honey, cornsilk; bees, drawn to her scent, clung to the fat braid down her back. She covered her face with her hands, shook her head violently. Drops of gold fell between her fingers. The wizard started to rise, became unbalanced between a pair of prickly rose trees. The young woman dropped her hands abruptly and stooped, catching his elbows and guiding him carefully to his feet. Then she resumed weeping, noisily and passionately. The wizard turned her gently toward the house, gesturing, and Euan felt as though a passing sprite had snatched the breath out of his mouth.

He had glimpsed the youngest daughter of the King of Dacia only twice. The last time she had been two feet shorter and placid, riding with the royal entourage through the city after her oldest sister's wedding. Now she was nearly as tall as Unciel, and trying to wring a storm out of the clear summer sky, and she was coming into the house. Euan, panicked after weeks of solitude, moved piles of separated tales from the carpet onto the one-eyed cat on the table. Its eye startled open. It yowled a protest and poured itself onto the floor and out. Euan, following, shut the door and leaned against it, trying to hear. The wizard opened the door abruptly, pulling the scribe, still clinging to the latch, into the hallway under the princess's swollen gaze.

She stared at him; he stared back at her. A great peace seemed to float through him. He felt his mind open like one of the wizard's peonies. Her tears hung suspended on her flushed golden face, clung to her eyelashes; fair tendrils of hair curled like petals around her face. In all that gold, her violet eyes seemed astonishing. Within the silent, elongated moment, Euan felt all the poems that he had never written welling up in him, trying to find their way into words.

Her eyes loosed him, flicked to the wizard. Euan let go of the door handle and bowed his head awkwardly.

"Euan Ash," he heard Unciel say. "A scribe I borrowed from your father's library to help me. Euan, the princess Sidonie needs details about my travels in Serre. It seems she will be journeying there herself, to marry the king's son. Will you search my papers and copy what you find?" Euan, remembering Brume, threw him an appalled glance. "Whatever," the wizard amended, "seems appropriate."

Euan heard vague, disturbed sounds from the princess. A tear flashed through the bright air; he would have sworn it reflected a prism as it fell. "I'm not going," she told them fiercely. "I am not leaving Dacia to marry some stranger in a barbaric country whose king does nothing but make war. How can my father do this to me? He let all my sisters marry in Dacia. He let my sister Cythera marry for love. What can he do to me if I refuse? Roll me up in a carpet and bundle me off to Serre in the back of a cart?"

"You will be Queen of Serre one day," Unciel reminded her. "Your children will rule it."

"I don't want to be Queen of Serre! I would rather marry a humble—a humble—" She glanced around distractedly; her eye fell on Euan. "—scribe and live in a cottage in Dacia than be forced to leave everyone I have ever—"

"I will," Euan said breathlessly. She only burst into tears again. He felt the wizard's hand on his shoulder.

"There is wine," the wizard said a trifle shakily, "in the kitchen."

"I don't want wine. Do you know what the King of Serre wrote?"

"I cannot imagine."

"He wrote that his beloved son Ronan had become melancholy from his grievous double loss of wife and heir, and that the king judged it both expedient and merciful that he should marry again as soon as possible. Expedient! It's not as though he had fallen off a horse! And merciful to whom? You must come and talk to my father. You've been to Serre; you must make him see that this is impossible. I would rather stay unwed for the rest of my life than leave Dacia to marry a melancholy prince still in love with his dead wife!"

The wizard was silent. She gazed at him desperately, her hands, long-fingered and oddly calloused, winding around one another, flashing tears and gold. Marry me, Euan thought wildly. Here. Now. No one could send you away then. He opened his mouth, heard a trumpet cry out of it, and closed it, confused. Someone flung the front door open and announced as sonorously as the trumpet,

"The King of Dacia."

Euan felt the wizard's hand grow heavy on his shoulder. Unciel's other hand rose with underwater slowness, pulled at his gardening hat, and dropped it on the floor. Euan heard his unsteady breath. Arnou King of Dacia entered, looking grim, harried. His eyes went to his daughter, who folded her arms and matched his gaze. The king was shorter than she, so she could not raise her chin far in defiance; instead, she stepped to the other side of the wizard.

"I will not go. Unciel will speak for me."

The king's eyes went to the wizard, whose face had grown milky in the light. "Get him to a chair," he said sharply to Euan, "before he falls."

The princess put a hand to her mouth, watching them. "What is it?" she breathed.

"He has been badly—" the king began.

"I tire easily."

"I am sorry," Sidonie said, her eyes filling again. Dew, Euan thought dazedly as he settled the wizard. Dew on violets. No, rain. The king, who was square and brown beside his daughter's wheatstalk grace and coloring, went to her, took her hands. Her face crumpled.

"How," she demanded, "can you send me so far away from you? What have I done wrong?"

"Nothing." He put his arms around her neck; she had to stoop a little into his embrace. "Nothing. I will miss you more than any of your sisters. But I need you for this. Dacia needs you."

"But why?"

The king was silent a moment, his face set, struggling. Unciel raised his head, watched the king expressionlessly, the lines furrowing deeply into his face. "It is," the king said finally, softly, "the last thing I want. Have you seen a map of Serre recently?"

"No. Why should I have? It meant nothing before today."

"There are no recent maps of Serre. Since King Ferus has extended his boundaries to the north and the south, no one is certain anymore how large it has grown. His most recent battle gave him claim to a swathe of desert twice the size of Dacia."

"Desert." She straightened, her brow creased. "That's far south of us."

"There is a single mountain range between Dacia and Serre."

She opened her mouth, closed it. Then she whispered, "A very high mountain range."

"Very high. But for a man who conquered ice palaces in the north and princes who follow the sun in the south, no mountain border is too high. He will marry Dacia or he will conquer it. I would guess that only rumors of Dacia's gift for magical arts gave him a second thought about attacking us."

He turned questioningly to the wizard, his brows raised. Unciel answered slowly, "From what I have seen of Serre, you may be right. I have not been there in years, but the Kings of Serre throughout their history have had little knowledge of sorcery and a great awe of it."

"So you see," the king said to his daughter. "You must understand. I have no choice. If you do not go to Serre, the King of Serre will come here. And I do not know which of us would wear the crown of Dacia after that battle."

Euan saw the princess swallow, muscles in her long throat sliding beneath her skin. He felt his hand fill with that smooth, shifting warmth and closed his eyes.

He heard her say, after a long silence, "Will you come with me?"

Euan opened his eyes. But it was Unciel she asked, her eyes dry now, and distant, seeing beyond the wizard's house and into a troubled future.

The wizard shook his head wearily. "I cannot. I am very sorry, because there are things about Serre that I loved, and I could protect you from those that are dangerous. But I can barely—As you see, I cannot bear anything much more strenuous than breathing."

"What dangers?" the king asked, his brows pulled harshly together. "Beyond Ferus himself?"

"The land has its own sorcery. It conjures unexpected things, like dreams do. Unlike dreams, you cannot wake from them; if you are challenged, you must act."

The princess's face lost some of its burnished color. "I thought you said there was little sorcery."

"In its rulers. The land itself has peculiar powers; they are unpredictable and not always safe. You never know, in Serre, when and where a tale will become true."

"Please come with me," she pleaded hollowly. "Please try."

"I would not survive the mountain passes," he said simply. "I would not be with you in Serre, where you would begin to need me."

"No," the king said abruptly. "Of course you can't go. But there must be someone. Some mage or wizard you know who can guard her."

Unciel did not answer immediately. The wizard's eyes grew very distant, as though he were gazing at the world through all his memories, and the ashes of his deep weariness, his lost powers. His face did not change before he spoke, and Euan knew that the name must have already been at the surface of his thoughts, perhaps for a very long time, until the moment came to say it, like the beginning of a spell.

"Gyre. A young wizard I met on my travels a few years ago. He is formidable and clever; he should enjoy matching wits with Serre. The princess will be safe with him." He dropped his head against the chair back, murmured as his eyes closed, "I will send for him. He owes me a favor."

"Thank you," said the King of Dacia, and took his daughter's hand. Euan gazed helplessly at the straight back, the golden braid framed in the open door against the street. Then the king's guard closed the door behind her and the warm light faded into twilight, and the scribe thought with wonder and rue, I will never see you again except in poetry.

THREE

The wizard Gyre was sitting in a tavern in the back streets of the ancient city Thuse beside the Yellow Sea negotiating a price for his services when he received the summons from Unciel. The tavern was noisy, flea-bitten, not a suitable place in which to meet a messenger from Prince Frewan. But the messenger was in disguise. They always were, Gyre knew, and they chose such places in order to disguise the message. Which was always the same, Gyre knew, in those lands along that part of the sea. A loose scattering of constantly bickering princedoms lined the coast; the princes were always in need of this or that, something made or done in secret, about which Gyre must pledge not to breathe a word.

Patiently, he ran through the list of things he would not do for anyone, for any amount of gold, as much as he could have used it. He was a dark-haired, sinewy young man, with calm eyes that hid an edge of restlessness as he spoke. Invisible weapons, this prince would want, or the walls around his palace made impregnable before he goaded a neighbor into attack. A secret tunnel built before dawn; a spy in the shape of a falcon to listen to conspiracies plotted on horseback in the middle of a meadow where no one could possibly hear. The wizard was more than familiar with such requests.

Gyre was simply dressed; nothing about him proclaimed any particular powers. He had been born in those noisome streets to an itinerant tinker from across the sea, who performed magic tricks for his children when he was drunk. The child Gyre, trying to imitate the tricks, realized quickly that they were not. The sodden tinker had a genuine spark of power within him, and Gyre found himself wanting it, with passion and beyond reason. When his father ran out of things to teach him, he looked elsewhere. He nosed magic like a dog in those poor, crowded, colorful streets, where strangers constantly wandered in from the sea. One day he followed a stranger out of the city, beyond the sea, to a place where others like him gathered to be taught the astonishing magic in the color orange, in the shape of an orange, who peeled away the rind to discover the mysteries hidden within the wonder of the visible.

Leaving that place a penniless wizard, he had wandered hither and yon, finding work where he could, until his path led him back to Thuse, perhaps to wait for another stranger to give him direction. He was still hungry; he woke at nights, wanting and not knowing what he wanted. He only had to wait and recognize it when it came. He thought he had found it once before, when he had first met Unciel, in a distant land full of the memory of dragons. He had found, he thought, the dragon's heart: the power, the fierce strength, the indomitable beauty of it. But it had disappeared, melted away in Thuse. He had been mistaken; it had been nothing alive.

So here he sat, preparing to perform a series of tricks for as little as the prince who hired him could get away with offering him. Still, this prince might lead him to others, wealthier and more powerful, who could challenge his skills, use him for something other than those interminable petty feuds. He was listening with his usual imperturbable expression, treating the request with all the gravity with which it was made, when the image of a folded sheet of parchment slipped among his thoughts. It unfolded, revealing a handful of brightly burning words.

I need you in Dacia. Unciel.

He was on his feet without thinking; so Unciel had helped him once, when he was in dire need.

"I'm sorry," he told the surprised and aggrieved messenger. "I must go." The man made an inarticulate protest. "I promise," Gyre assured him, "that your secret will be safe with me."

Flying north from the sea in hawk-shape, he had only a map in his head to remind him where Dacia was. He had never been there. Rulers of Dacia were their own sorcerers. Rumors of their power kept the land untroubled; conquering armies tended to veer away from it. The rocky, wrinkled land beneath him flattened, after several days, into broad river valleys, placid and richly green. On a hunch, the hawk dropped straight as a plumb line to a valley floor, where a farmer guided a donkey dragging a harrow across dark, crumbling soil.

The farmer stopped to stare as the hawk landed on a furrow and the young man emerged from its shadow.

"Where am I?"

"In my beet field," the farmer ventured, still amazed.

"I mean what country?"

"Oh. You're in Dacia. East of Serre, north of Fyriol, west of—"

"Thank you," Gyre said. He glanced around vaguely, as though the groves of trees and peaceful fields might conceal a city. He guessed at several things in that moment: that Unciel had sent as much as he could, that he was still weak from his strange ordeal, of which Gyre had heard even as far as Thuse, and that exactly where he was would be so obvious that he would not need to waste effort to send yet another word. Gyre waved a gad-fly away from his face and addressed the farmer again.

"Which way is the king's city?"

The farmer loosed a rein and pointed. "That would be that way. Saillesgate, it's called, after the first king. The one who brought magic into Dacia."

Gyre nodded, remembering the name from his studies. The uneducated warrior Sailles had conquered the land, and then, curious and fiercely determined, had hired a wizard to teach him to read and write. Words sparked magic within the king as they had within the tinker in Thuse. The king's children inherited his formidable gifts. Beyond that scrap, Gyre knew little of Dacia. It was small, wealthy, and rarely threatened. A good place for a drained, exhausted wizard to rest.

He reached Saillesgate one of several twilights later, in the shape of a ubiquitous pigeon. He changed shape somewhat wearily in a convenient shadow. Rather than send his name silently through the city and force Unciel to use his depleted powers to answer, Gyre questioned a few shopkeepers. The wizard was easily found, the third told him. He had not kept his presence hidden. But there was no use asking him for anything. Something terrible had befallen him; he had barely the strength to move his bones and breathe; he had nothing left to give . . .

Gyre found Unciel waiting for him beyond a door that said COME IN.

The wizard might have just opened his eyes after a nap, or he might have been awake and waiting for days. His eyes startled Gyre, who remembered them as the light, burning blue of a high mountain stream. A bleak, impenetrable mist had settled over the blue. His voice was a tendril of itself, frail and slow. There were no visible wounds, nothing unhealed, that Gyre could see. But the wizard who had once helped him so effortlessly seemed barely to exist; there was only this husk closed protectively around the embers of his powers, which he stubbornly refused to let die.

Gyre asked the obvious, suddenly aware in that quiet cottage of what might lie beyond the known. "What happened to you?"

"It's dead," Unciel answered, simply and implacably. "I don't want to talk about it."

They were alone, Gyre sensed, but for a startlingly observant raven and a cat dreaming somewhere within the cottage.

"So are you," he breathed. "Nearly dead."

Unciel did not answer, only gestured at a chair, and Gyre sat. He was silent, waiting for Unciel to speak, keeping his own thoughts as tranquil as the twilight garden, with its stakes and lattices rising like peculiar growths among the patches of seedlings. At least he tried for tranquility. Horror and curiosity bubbled beneath it, throwing up shapes, intimations of power that he could only guess at. Again and again, questions tried to form; against Unciel's stubborn silence, they scattered into unfinished words, left question marks hanging in the air between them.

Unciel said slowly, forming each word as painstakingly as a spell, "I will tell you what I need. And then I will make supper."

"Don't—" Gyre began, but Unciel raised a palm.

"I like to cook. It is like making magic, and far easier for me these days." He paused as though hearing another unspoken question; they both let it die unremarked. "The King of Dacia has pledged his youngest daughter, Sidonie, to the son of King Ferus of Serre. Serre being what it is, and as immense as it is, she will need a guardian and a guide. She must leave as soon as possible. It will take a few weeks of human travelling, perhaps most of the summer. The king will pay you well for guarding his daughter. Have you been to Serre?"

Gyre shook his head. "I have heard that its magic is primitive and it is full of trees."

Lines deepened along the sides of Unciel's mouth; it was, Gyre realized after a moment, the haunting memory of a smile. "All magic is primitive. It is the oldest language of the heart. Serre's heart is ancient, wild, and very lively. I would go myself if I could. I cannot, so I thought of you. I think that such a journey will test and broaden your abilities, and add a dimension to your understanding of what it is you want most." This time he took note of Gyre's silent response; the seared, veiled eyes meeting Gyre's seemed to look at him from very far away. "Which is what we all want, of course, for it is the nature of a wizard to want power."

Gyre felt his answer before it became the word. "Yes."

"The scribe I borrowed from the king's scriptorium has gathered together my writings about Serre. Some, which are toothless, we will send to the king, to reassure him. The rest you should read. If you can get through my handwriting." He separated himself from the chair slowly, bone by bone. "The cat is sleeping on them. Read a little before you decide."

Gyre followed the flickering thread of cat-dreams, and found the scribe's desk. He read for a long time, incredulous but intrigued, while in the kitchen knife debated with chopping block, and pot-lids commented. The magic of Serre seemed patched together out of children's tales, Gyre decided. Its king was by all accounts a force greater than all its magic. He had forged an immense, formidable kingdom, and the princess Sidonie would one day become its queen. A young woman useful to know, and certainly in need of a wizard, to whom she might have cause, if Gyre kept her safe, to be grateful. The rest—witches, ogres, trolls—he consigned to a streak of eccentricity in Unciel, who seemed interested in anything, even cooking. Gyre had dealt with such small magics before, mostly witches' spells, which frayed like spiderweb under a word of wizardry.

It seemed a simple matter, this journey across Serre with the princess. He owed Unciel far more than that. So he said, when the smells of hot bread and lamb stew drew him into the kitchen, "Of course I will go."

"Good."

Unciel ladled stew into bowls with mesmerizing slowness, the ladle shaking constantly. Gyre watched him, guessing that he would refuse help. Little enough he could do, now . . . Again the intimations of something powerful and terrible, beyond all Gyre's imagination, swept through him. If he could have envisioned it, it might have forced itself into shape then and there between them in the wizard's tidy kitchen. Unciel let drop a final mushroom from the lip of the ladle, and put it back into the pot. "Tomorrow," he said, trying to pick up both bowls at once, "I will take you to meet the king and Sidonie."

"Let me—" Gyre murmured hastily, taking the bowls from him. "I prefer not to eat off the floor."

Again he glimpsed the forgotten ghost of a smile. Unciel found a couple of goblets in a cupboard, and a dusty crock of wine. He blew at the cobwebs on the label. "Pear? Or could it be pea?"

"No."

"Then it must be pear." He left it for Gyre to uncork, and carried a couple of spoons to the table. "I haven't been here long; this place still has surprises for me. The widow who owns it told me that her son liked to experiment with different—"

"What happened to you?" Gyre demanded, standing with the wine in one hand, gazing at Unciel, while the dark pushed against the window behind him and tapped at it with urgent, invisible wings. Gyre felt his own bones willing to shape themselves into an answer, to reveal the deadly, perilous face of what must have been the opposite of Unciel. "What did this to you? And why did you fight it alone?"

For a moment, he saw Unciel's face shift, its stark, rigid lines flow into the reflection of what he had fought. The vision was gone in an instant, but it took Gyre's breath with it; he felt the hoarfrost form, cold and heavy, on his bones. Unciel took the crock as it began to slide, and set it with some effort on the table.

He said gently to Gyre, "It seemed a simple matter at first. I was mistaken." He touched the young wizard's shoulder, and Gyre could move again. He drew his hands over his face, caught a shuddering breath, feeling the ice still in his fingers. "It was very old," he heard Unciel say. "And now it's dead. Some day when I'm stronger, I will be able to speak of it. But not now. Not now. Let it leave us in peace for now."

"You became what you fought."

It was a moment before he realized he had spoken aloud. But it didn't matter, he thought dazedly; Unciel would have heard the thought in his heartbeat, in his marrow. Unciel set bread on the table silently, a knife. Then he wandered into the middle of the floor, stood looking vaguely for something, and Gyre saw his eyes, stunned and bright with pain.

"I'm sorry," Gyre whispered, shaken again, and reached out to grasp a trembling hand, guide the wizard out of his memories to the table. "I am sorry. I wish I had been there with you."

"You were," Unciel said, so quietly that Gyre made nothing of the words themselves, only of their echo, which he heard some hours later when a nightmare without a face loomed across his dreams and spoke his name.

FOUR

The princess's first glimpse of Serre was an eagle's dizzying view from the highest point of a pass through the mountains. Their stony pinnacles vanished into cloud so far above the slowly moving entourage that, Sidonie thought, to a mountain's eye it must resemble the long, bulky, furry insect she had found inching its way across her cot one morning. By the time she saw Serre, she had become resigned to the wildlife that crept and fluttered and fell into her food. Only farmers lived in the high, rocky meadows between Dacia and Serre, above their animals in small cottages that stank and whistled in the howling winds. Not suitable, she was told, and had to make do with a gaudy pavilion slanting down the slopes that strained against its pegs and threatened to fly away at night. Appalled by the endless expanses of granite and wind, her attendants hid themselves in the evenings behind their own rippling walls, braiding one another's hair against stray insects and whispering stories. Sidonie, faced with the wasteland of an empty marriage, longed for a cottage full of bellowing cows in the crook of a peak so high that its shadow ran like a dark river through the valley floor below.

The wizard Gyre, who had a startling ability to change shape, had found their way through the mountains with an eagle's eyes. One midsummer evening, while the guards and servants pitched pavilions and cut wood, and the cooks put their heads together over what the hunters had brought them that day, the wizard dipped on outspread wings down an angle of sweet twilight breeze, landed at Sidonie's feet, and turned into himself.

"Come and see," he said. He was a brisk, lean young man with calm dark blue eyes. As far as Sidonie could tell, he viewed the world with a great deal of curiosity and no fear whatsoever. He gave the princess a rare smile as she hesitated. "It's just over those rocks."

What was? Sidonie wondered as she followed him to the edge of the meadow where they camped. Something wild, she guessed dourly, with teeth. Peering over a boulder beside the silent wizard, she did not understand at first what she saw. It lay beneath the pale sky like night; it ran everywhere, up distant mountains, to the edge of the far horizon; it tried to climb the slope they stood on. Then the vision named itself and she swallowed dryly.

"The forests of Serre," the wizard said softly. He leaned over the boulder, his face turned away from her toward the silent, murky blur below. He pointed across it where, on the other side of the world, something the size and shape of a child's tooth rose above the trees. "That's where we're going. The summer palace of the Kings of Serre sits on that cliff."

She felt suddenly dazed, sick with terror at the sight of it: the place where her life would stop, all she knew would vanish, an unknown woman would wear her face like a mask. She straightened suddenly, fumbling at the clasp of the chain she wore around her neck. "I'll pay you," she said wildly.

"What?"

The clasp broke in her shaking grip; she dropped gold and its pendant into her palm, and offered it to him. "Just let me go. I'll find my way back. You take my shape so they won't search for me—"

He stared at her incredulously, then looked at what lay in her palm. He stirred it with one finger. "What is this?"

She blinked at it: a nut, a red feather, and a black snail shell, strung together and tied to her gold chain. "Oh."

"It looks like a charm."

She sighed. "It is." Her voice stopped trembling. "Auri—one of my attendants—made it for me. Her mother was born in Serre, and told her stories. It's supposed to protect me from witches."

He snorted. "The witches of Serre would eat it, shells and all. Are you really so afraid of marrying Ronan of Serre?"

"Yes," she said tightly. "I am used to being loved."

She felt his attention, cast hither and yon, pull itself out of the vastness of Serre, the camp noises behind them, the scents on the wind, and the rising moon, to focus entirely on her. His face was absolutely still. Startled, she felt as though he were seeing her for the first time; she wondered what, during the past weeks, he thought he had been looking at.

He told her. "When Ronan inherits, you will be Queen of Serre. Your children—"

"I know," she said impatiently. "I know. Meanwhile I will live with a man who will expect me to occupy his bed but not his thoughts. All to keep his father from attacking Dacia and killing my father."

She turned away from him abruptly before he could answer. "Where are you going?" he asked, beside her suddenly as she strode back across the meadow.

"To shoot something."

She sent an attendant running for her bow and arrows. In the darkening meadow, away from horses and people, she shot furiously at the face of the moon, at implacable slabs of granite, at a raven that watched her silently from a distant tree. She almost hit the raven; it leaped off the branch with a squawk, dropping a feather as it flew away. Spent finally, hungry, she wandered toward the fire outside her pavilion. Someone took her bow; someone else slipped a mantle over her shoulders against the evening chill and unfolded a leather stool for her. She ate what she was handed. Hare, she realized when she began to taste what she was eating. Again.

The next day they began their descent into Serre.

The forest, closing around them as they left the mountains, became another season: something warm but capable of harsh shadows that seemed to burn on the sunlit ground. The trees were huge, ancient; they smelled like some rare incense. The hard ground, the constant slope of the mountains had changed to a soft, spicy pallet of dried needles, on land that rarely varied. Trees were all Sidonie saw. Far above, a hawk, and trees. A thrust of rock, a tumble of boulders, and trees. A silvery web of streams. Trees. Their branches grew so high up the trunks, seeking light, that riders could pass beneath them without bending their heads. Seed pods of gold, like fingers, grew among the broad, lacy boughs. They fell occasionally, making a noise like a comment as the entourage passed.

They had chanced into a timeless place, Sidonie felt as she sat at her fire one night. Into a place that would never change and never end. The trees hid even the changing moon. Gyre sat with her, or his shape did; his thoughts were far from her, prowling, she guessed, through the dark, quiet forest around them. She watched the bright, flickering wings of the fire trying to illumine the night within the forest. It did little more than burnish a tangle of roots, a couple of massive trunks, the gilt-edged doors of her pavilion. Water in a shallow stream flowed endlessly through the dark, out of nowhere, into nowhere. Wild things crept past them to drink from it; now and then she heard a stray panting, a thump or a scurry. Around other fires, wash-water simmered; water slopped and echoed hollowly as pots were scoured. Servants tossed dice, mended harness; guards oiled weapons; hunters whittled arrows and fletched them with black and gold, and the rare flame-red feathers dropped from birds that were never seen. As always, Sidonie's attendants had hidden themselves. The pavilion beside hers was tightly closed. She could see their silhouettes flung by lanterns on the walls; they sat as closely massed as flowers in a bouquet, mending torn seams and speaking nervously, breathlessly. Others waited for the princess in her pavilion; three heads bent closely together while a fourth, most likely Auri, told a story.

"Brume," Sidonie murmured thoughtfully, remembering one of the stories. The wizard did not move so much as an eyelash at her voice. But she felt his attention gather out of the forest around them, come to her. It was as though he had suddenly become visible.

"Brume?"

"She haunts these forests. She entices people into her cottage and boils them in her cauldron for stew."

He stirred slightly and did not smile, which made her vaguely uneasy. But he only asked, "Who is telling you these tales?"

"Auri. Her mother told them to her and says they are all true. Her mother's brother lost his heart to a woman who lived in a deep pool beneath a waterfall in a forest just like this. The woman came to him among the reeds, and lured him into her watery cave and he drowned."

The wizard grunted. "Auri's mother probably floats flowers in bowls of milk and leaves them outside her door in Dacia to placate the goblins of Serre."

"She does. I also read accounts of the wizard Unciel's travels through Serre, before I left. He mentions the milk and the flowers. But nothing with teeth. I suspect he left out a few things." She tossed a seed cone at a squirrel eyeing the fluttering doors of her pavilion. It changed its mind, bounded away. Unciel's bright cottage with its brilliant garden, the shy, awkward scribe seemed a dream, a lifetime past.

Gyre did not comment. She glanced at him, found an odd open, rueful expression on his face, as if he were looking inside and found himself lacking. It was unusual, she thought; his confidence seemed always unassailable.

"No one is unassailable," he said, shifting a branch in the fire with his bare hand. Then he turned his head quickly to meet her cold eye. "I'm sorry. My thoughts were drifting; they floated into yours."

"Anchor them," she suggested drily.

"I will try."

She wished, immediately, that she had that ability to pry into his thoughts without bothering to question him. She tilted her head back and saw, beyond the pinnacles of trees taller than the towers of Dacia, stars as cold and beautiful and incomprehensible as Serre itself poured across the black. "Have you known Unciel long?" she asked, suddenly curious. He had opened a door, with that expression. "He said you owed him a favor."

"He helped me once, when I was in trouble in a land south of Dacia. He did not know me at all, but he rescued me."

"From what? A monster?"

"Something like that." He did not look at her.

"Something like what? An ogre?"

He smiled a tight, spare smile, asked in her direction, "What do you know about ogres?"

"Nothing. What exactly are they?"

"An ogre is a grotesque monster, hideous in appearance, with a taste for human flesh."

"Does everything eat people in Serre?" she wondered, fascinated and appalled.

"You should stop listening to Auri's tales. Anyway, ogres are very stupid, and terrified of princesses."

"You laugh now," she said darkly. She shifted closer to the fire and spread her hands to it. She wished suddenly for an ogre, a witch, a goblin, anything out of Serre's unpredictable heart, to loom at them out of the dark, send them fleeing for their lives. She would find an abandoned hermit's hut, live like one of the skittish, unwashed recluses of the forests, eat nuts and berries, keep a pet crow for company.

"I will not," she heard from within the crackling, fuming flames, "let anyone harm you."

She lifted her eyes to the wizard. But his own eyes were lowered; he seemed to be listening again to the trees, the animals, the wind, perhaps the stars. His lashes were black as embers against his fire-flushed skin. His dark hair, neatly trimmed at the beginning of the journey, hung loosely to his shoulders. He sat so still he scarcely seemed to breathe; she wondered what he heard.

"How long," she asked him abruptly, drawing comfort from his familiarity, "will you stay in Serre?"

He looked at her. Again she had the sense of thoughts hidden, words unspoken. But he answered simply enough. "Your father told me to use my own judgment. You should go in. I'll send your guards to you."

"I'd rather watch with you."

"I can see the dark better in the dark," he told her, and leaned down to sculpt the fire with his hands until it burrowed into itself, pulsing instead of flaming. He would climb a tree, she guessed, and watch with the owls.

"How long?" she heard herself ask again, though she did not want the answer. "Until we get there?"

"I don't know. I'll fly ahead tomorrow and count the days."

Days, she thought, chilled. Once it had been half a season. She rose reluctantly. One pavilion was dark; in hers, the young women sat slumped and yawning on the cots. Seeing her move, they rose and opened the doors for her. One left with a pitcher to fetch warm water; others helped her undress.

"Tell me," she said to distract herself from her thoughts, "the story Auri was telling you."

Auri, barely more than a girl, with a thin, pointed face and constantly disheveled hair, looked at Sidonie out of the corners of her eyes. She was busy tipping a candle into the shadows, searching for wildlife.

"My lady," another protested. "It's not suitable."

"I'm going to be married," Sidonie said wryly, remembering what her sisters had told her, "to a total stranger. Surely nothing could be more unsuitable than that."

In the dark, they whispered a tale involving a poor widow, a beautiful daughter, and the King of Trolls. Serre, she thought, seemed to be full of ravening nightmares who killed what they loved and ate what they didn't. But it was the faceless prince in her dreams, not the troll, who woke her abruptly in the night to stare sleeplessly at the dark until dawn.

She did not see the wizard at all the next day until sunset, when a crimson light spilled through the trees, and the weary entourage gathered to a ragged halt beside the grassy banks of a slow, deep river. They could bathe, she saw with relief. Guards were already marking pools with their pointing fingers, deciding where to hang rugs for the princess, while the horses were led downstream to drink. She heard a splash downriver; someone, dusty and sweating, could not wait.

Beware, she warned him silently, the water-woman in the reeds.

Then an eagle plummeted through the stained light at her feet, and Gyre appeared. She waited, watching as the fierce thoughtless scrutiny melted out of his eyes; gold and black became a familiar shadowy blue. Like everyone else, he looked exhausted, though his voice held its usual briskness.

"Five days," he told her. "At the most."

"Five days?" Her heart was in her throat suddenly, fluttering like something trapped. "Only five?"

"We've been travelling half the summer," he reminded her gently. "I will send messengers ahead to tell the king that we are nearly at his doorstep. They will travel a day or so faster alone." He paused, touched her for the first time, his fingers linked lightly around her wrist. Her face felt icy, drained of all expression. "You are saving your father's kingdom," she heard him say. "Perhaps his life. If you can't find any other reason for being in Serre, remember that."

She swallowed dryly, not seeing him, not speaking. His fingers tightened and she lifted her head. His gaze, in that moment, seemed to contain all the wild things of land and air that he had ever shaped, as well as all the powers that controlled them.

"I won't leave Serre," he said softly, "until you tell me to go."

She blinked, oddly shaken. He loosed her wrist, his eyes changing again, familiar, imperturbable, at once clear and secret. He waited silently until she found her voice.

"Five days, then. Thank you." She raised her skirts and walked blindly, carefully past him, as though she had already entered the stone walls of the summer palace.

They had camped within a day of the palace when she finally saw something of the magic of Serre.

She had wandered away from the noise and confusion of the camp being set up in an unexpected clearing along the river, which had decided to accompany them east. She took her bow with her, in case there were ogres, and walked into the clearing, a little meadow rich with late summer grasses and wildflowers. In the middle of it she stopped, staring upward at what the parting trees had made visible. On a crag, a dark, blocky mass of walls and towers rose between two slender ribbons of water that fell a long way from the top of the cliff to vanish into the tops of the trees. The water burned like light on a blade. The setting sun illumined a brief nick of road pared out of stone, impossibly high and slanted, leading into the massive fortress. Summer palace, Gyre had called it. It had as much to do with summer, Sidonie thought incredulously, as a mausoleum.

She bent her head, feeling visible, and moved across the meadow beyond sight of the dark palace. Within trees again, she shot a few arrows in desultory fashion at tree boles and cones until the sunlight faded. She stood uncertainly, bow cocked, looking for one more target before she was forced to yield to the fact that one more day had inevitably passed and tomorrow there would be none left.

Something crashed out of the trees behind her. She whirled, heart pounding, bringing the bow up and aimed at whatever troll or witch had crackled into shape out of the underbrush. But it was only one of the guards, she thought confusedly. No. One of the hunters. He stood with his arms raised, showing her his empty hands; he was panting, as she was, and just as startled. Not a hunter, she amended; they slept and bathed with their knives, and there was not a weapon to be seen on this man. An ogre, maybe, in disguise. He looked strong enough, broad-shouldered and muscular. His long copper hair was tangled and matted with bracken; there was an otherworldly look in his grey eyes. His clothes were torn; so was the skin on his face and wrists, as though he had run through brambles.

Her bowstring had slackened a little, she realized. She tightened her grip, pointed the arrowhead at his heart. "Show me your teeth," she demanded. If they were pointed like an animal's, she would know what he truly was.

He ignored that. "Did you see it?" he pleaded. "Did it fly this way?"

"Did what fly this way?"

"The bird made of fire."

She lowered the bow after a moment, aimed cautiously at his foot. He must be one of the forest's eccentrics, she decided. Newly eccentric, for his tunic, though torn in places, was of fine dark silk, embroidered at the sleeves and hem. His boots were scratched, but neither worn nor cracked.

"Auri," she said coldly, "never mentioned a bird made of fire. Neither did Unciel."

He drew breath, loosed it in a weary shudder. He glanced around them into the still trees, his shoulders slumped. When he looked at her again, his eyes seemed less fay-ridden.

"Who is Unciel?" he asked.

"A great wizard."

He took a step; her bow came up. "Can he help me?" he asked, his face taut, desperate. "I must find the bird. And the witch."

She swallowed. "Unciel might help you," she said carefully, in case he grew mad again, and attracted the witch. "But he is far away in a cottage in Dacia, and too weak to do much besides garden."

"Dacia?" He stood very still, not breathing, looking at her so strangely that she backed a step. So did he, abruptly, reeling away from her, it seemed. "Who are you?"

"I am Sidonie of Dacia," she said very clearly, indicating dire consequences if she were eaten by magic in Serre. "I have crossed two lands to marry Prince Ronan of Serre. My guards are setting up camp behind you; my hunters are close around us, armed and—and hunting."

She heard his quick breath. "They must not shoot the bird!"

"We cannot eat fire for supper," she reminded him reasonably. "Anyway, we never see the red birds. Only their feathers, now and then. They must be very beautiful."

"They are," he whispered. And then something pulled his face awry; he clenched his teeth. She saw the blood flush around his eyes, and the terrible, stark expression in them, as though he were about to weep. She let the bow go slack in her hands.

"What is it?" she breathed. "What's wrong?"

He saw her again, beyond the frozen sheen in his eyes. His hands clenched; he fought for air, struggling against whatever sorrow held him in its terrible grip. "I must find the witch," he told her finally, and she felt her own hands grow cold.

The witch and the bird had driven him mad, she thought. But if he grieved, then he had lost, and loss she understood. She went to him impulsively, pushed the bow and arrow into his hands. "Take these, if you're going witch-hunting. You have nothing to help you in this place, and I have an entire village to take care of me."

He gazed at them a little incredulously. Witches, she realized then, must use arrows for toothpicks in Serre. But he didn't hand them back. He studied her again, his expression calmer now, and unfathomable. She felt suddenly like a pampered child who had handed a starving beggar her gold shoe-buckle.

"I'll come home as soon as I have found the witch," he said incomprehensibly. And then she saw his face shed grief and confusion, along with all memory of her. Wonder and longing filled his eyes, blinded him, so that he did not even see her as he stumbled past her into the trees.

She turned and saw the firebird.

She saw nothing else, heard nothing, as it flew silently

through the twilight, its wings trailing plumes and ribbons of flame, its tail covered with jewels of fire. Its claws and beak and eyes seemed of hammered gold that melted into fire and then hardened again into gold. It sang a note. She felt the sound fall through her heart like a pearl falling slowly, with infinite beauty, through liquid gold.

After a time, she felt the hand above her elbow, holding her to earth, she guessed, keeping her from running after the dream of the bird when the bird itself had vanished. She felt the wizard's presence before she looked at him; they had been together that long.

"Did you see that?" she whispered, still searching for it within the darkening forest.

"Yes."

"No wonder he follows it . . . I never asked his name. Did you see him?"

"I saw everything," he answered simply. He was gazing into the trees as though he could still see, with his magical eye, the luminous bird and the man with his heart outstretched to follow it. "I was here watching even before you finished turning and saw clearly what you were aiming at."

"How—"

"I felt your terror. You moved me in a breath." His light grip opened; he moved her with the suggestion of a touch. "Supper is ready and you are missed. Come back to the world."

The next afternoon, beyond all possibility, she found herself riding up that final paring of road so high above the valley floor that she did not dare look down. She kept her eyes on the road until it passed behind one of the falls and out again. Then she raised her eyes to the dark palace. There were airy, glinting banners along the walls, she saw with surprise, and trumpeters to greet them. The road ran up to the drawbridge and ended; the gates stood open. Guards in black leather and silk lined the road, the sides of the bridge, the inner courtyard. Sidonie, riding numbly between Gyre and the captain of her guard, watched a man detach himself from the stiff, silent gathering, and walk across the yard toward her.

Gyre reached over, pulled gently at the reins in her lax hand. Her horse stopped. The stranger held one blunt hand up to her. She looked down into a broad, scarred face, with its hairy upper lip lifted and snarling over a missing tooth, the eye above it lost behind crumpled, puckered skin. The other eye was the iron-black of the walls around them, and as hard.

"I am Ferus King of Serre," he said. His lost eye seemed to move behind its scars, still trying to see. She felt herself freeze like an animal under the hunter's eye. "Welcome to your home."

FIVE

It was after midnight before Ronan remembered the Princess from Dacia. He had followed the firebird to the moon. He had run across luminous, barren plains, over empty crystal mountains, down ancient river beds, dry and white as bone, where the pale stones reflecting passing fire ahead of him flushed the color of garnets. The bird sang as it flew. It patterned the black sky and the moon with a starburst of sounds, each more brilliant, more haunting than the last. It drew farther and farther from Ronan, finally no bigger than a shining tear across the face of the moon. When it had vanished and he fell, choking on glittering shards of moondust, he heard it sing again with a woman's voice that should have melted mountains, drawn water out of the harsh landscape. She would not show him her face; the bird would not change while he was watching. He crawled to his feet after a while, and followed her singing, trying to come upon her unexpectedly. But he fell to earth before he saw her.

In the forests of Serre, he leaned against a tree and stared up at the moon, transfixed, waiting for that tear of fire, of blood, to cross its face again. The moon only grew cold, distant, gathering its stars about it, wandering away into some darker realm, leaving the forest black around him. A burning star within the trees brought him to his feet again. But he smelled it before he moved: charred trees bleeding pitch. Human fire, he thought, and remembered the princess.

At the time, she had seemed little more than a daydream, a bit of story, appearing out of nowhere like a talking bird or a crone, to give him something and then vanish again. Now, in a lucid moment, he saw her more clearly: a young woman in a strange land who had no idea, when she entered the walls of the summer palace, what morass she would be walking into. His father, faced with the absence of a marriageable son, would be in no mood to return her to Dacia with a polite apology. Ronan couldn't just leave her there to fend for herself against the ogre. Wherever "there" was. He couldn't marry her, any more than he could fly or turn himself into a fish. The idea was preposterous. He had died with Maye and their child; his heart had turned to ash; the dead do not marry. He had to free the princess somehow, persuade her to go back home. Surely she would want nothing else, after a few days with his father. But Ronan had slipped into a sideways world, where the summer palace did not exist. He could not even see the waterfalls. Nothing—no trail of crumbs, or jewels, or drops of blood—marked his path home. The forest was the world; the firebird held all its truths and secrets. Following such beauty, he left all pain behind. Within the bird lay the greatest mystery of all: the woman who made him forget. He would follow her all his days, all his life. But first he had this one small thing to do: he must find Brume and persuade her to show him his way back into the world. And then he would help the princess, who seemed innocent and kind, and who certainly did not deserve to be shut up in the bleak walls of the summer palace with his father. And then he would flee from that barren world, back into the forests of the firebird, follow it until he found her.

A waft of something fallen into a firebed and slowly cooking knotted his belly. He had forgotten about food. He still carried the princess's bow slung over one shoulder; he had forgotten about that, too. The arrow still rode at a slant in his belt, pushing against his ribs. He stood up slowly, clinging to the tree when the world spun. He was dizzy with hunger suddenly, gnawed with it. He couldn't see to hunt in the dark. But he could see fire. He would forage for the forgotten morsel searing itself in the coals, if nothing got to it before he did. But the other animals were afraid of fire; he alone was in love with it.

He steadied himself, walked across the little meadow beyond the trees.

The forgotten morsel turned out to be an entire hare skinned, spitted, and charring above the embers. He knelt beside the fire, ate the hare with his hands, tearing pieces off the spit, burning his fingers and his mouth; he did not care. He scarcely saw the horses tethered nearby, or the wagons hung with cooking pots, the silent pavilions lining the river. The man beside the fire seemed to shape himself out of the sudden flames leaping up to lick at the fat dripping between Ronan's hands. First an eye was illumined, unblinking and remote as a star. Then a tendril of lank, dark hair. A jawline, lean as a fox's and faintly shadowed. Ronan, putting the pieces together, felt himself go still as a hare under a hawk's stare.

But the man only said softly, "Go ahead—eat. I cooked it for you. You looked half-starved."

After a time, Ronan managed a word. "When—"

"I saw you with the princess. I'm travelling with her. My name is Gyre. I guard the camp at nights; I sensed you out there, awake and hungry. I was curious about you. So I threw a scent in your direction and you followed it."

Ronan, still scenting it, tore off a few more bites. The man disappeared again, back into the fire, maybe. Ronan dropped the bones of the hare into the fire, reached for the cloth left on an old stump. He wiped his hands, looking at the half-loaf of bread and the cup of wine that seemed to have appeared when he wanted them. Like magic, he thought, reaching for them. So the man appeared again, like magic, when Ronan had turned the bread into crumbs, and swallowed the last of the wine.

Then he wanted to do nothing but sleep, which had not occurred to him before, either. Perhaps, in his dreams, he would see the firebird.

But the man, Gyre, had begun to talk again. "The princess told you her name, and that she is to be married to Prince Ronan."

"Yes," he said indifferently. They were characters in another story, the prince and the princess happily wed, not in the life he led.

"Do you know him?"

"No."

Gyre was silent, his cool eyes remote again, revealing nothing. "I saw the firebird," he said finally. "It is more beautiful than anything I could imagine."

Ronan's hands clenched; above him, star fire blurred and spun. "How could you see her," he whispered, "and not want to follow?"

The still eyes spoke finally, of wonder, before the man did. "Her?"

"There is a woman hidden within the bird, even more beautiful than it is."

He heard Gyre's indrawn breath. "How strange . . . And the witch? You said that you would return home after you found the witch. Will she help you find the bird?"

"She'll help me find my way home."

"Which is where?"

"No where. Nowhere in this world."

"And the witch? Where is she?"

"In her cottage made of bones."

Again he heard the man's breath, and the name that flowed out of him, almost inaudibly, as though to keep her from hearing. "Where will you find her?"

"I don't know. Perhaps in the waste where I first saw her. She warned me then that I would have to find her to return home. But she did not foresee the firebird."

"Aren't you afraid of the witch? She sounds very dangerous."

Ronan shrugged. "It doesn't matter. I have been trying to die for some time now."

Again Gyre was silent. He leaned forward abruptly, stirred the fuming cinders with his bare hand, and flames danced between his fingers. Ronan blinked, struggling with the image. Mage? he thought. Magic? He heard a hollow, desperate plea for hope, a night-bird's cry; was it in himself or within the trees? But Gyre was still again, so still he could not have moved; Ronan could not have seen what he saw.

He had a single, coherent thought before he saw the firebird again. "You must not let the princess enter my father's house."

He did not hear Gyre's reply. The bird hovering above the meadow, trying to catch stars in its beak, turned its head and looked at him out of one melting, golden eye. It caught his heart in its beak and he followed it thoughtlessly, helplessly, forgetting burned bones and princesses, the mysterious Gyre, the possibility of magic.

Dawn stranded him, bone-weary and empty, somewhere within the forest. He slept curled like an animal in the hollow trunk of one of the ancient trees. At noon, he stirred, brushed the bracken from his hair, and went in search of the witch.

He found her a night or three later, under a shrivelled moon, in the barren patch of forest where they had first crossed paths. The bones of her cottage glowed eerily, brighter than the moon. The round green window watched him like an eye. He had no fear left. He walked up to her door, pounded on it with his fist. The cottage seemed to shift, startled out of sleep; what sounded like her entire flock of chickens began to squawk. If she invited him in, he thought, he would go in. If she invited him to drink a broth made of his heart's blood, he would. Anything to end the endless confusion of worlds, of longing and loss, anything to rest.

He pounded again, heard her voice like wind blowing hollowly through a bone. "Go away!"

Fist cocked, he stared incredulously at the door. "You brought me here. Now tell me how to find my way home."

"It's the middle of the night."

"What night?" he demanded bitterly. "In what world? And why do you care? You would open your door to anything with a beating heart."

"You're dead," she said succinctly. He brought both fists down against the door, and then his face, pushing it against the hard, dry bones.

"Please," he whispered, terrified at last. "Don't leave me out here. Tell me how to find my way home."

"It's late and you have wakened all my chickens. Come back another day."

"No!" He pried at the bones of her door with his fingers, then threw himself against them. It was, he thought, like trying to batter at his father's implacable will. He sank down finally, leaned against the door. "I will sit on your steps outside the door until you open it. I'll ride your house if you run. I'll wake your hens every hour with my shouting. You won't be able to leave your cottage without tripping over me. I will cling to these stinking bones like a carbuncle until you answer me. Tell me how to find my way home."

The third time was the charm. The door opened abruptly; he tumbled backward into a darkness smelling of hens and rotting marrow. A thin, plain, knobby woman with her grey hair in a bun and her sparse brows arching adjusted her lenses and peered down at him.

"Why," she asked distantly, "are you suddenly so eager to return home? You hate it."

"I don't intend to stay." He was reluctant to bring up the matter of the princess. But the witch already knew what questions to ask. He had no idea what else she might know, and he dared not lie to those wide, unblinking eyes behind the fly-green lenses. "I must go back to help someone."

"Who?"

"A young—a princess, a stranger. She should never have come to Serre. I fear for her, in my father's house."

The witch sniffed, wiped her long nose on her sleeve. "A princess." Ronan, chilled by a tone in her voice, gazed up at her silently, wondering which of the two Sidonie might find most incomprehensible: the witch or his father. But Brume only commented, "You can't expect me to bother myself with all this."

"I warned you," he answered recklessly, "what a bother I will be if you don't. You warned me that having left my father's palace, I would not find my way back until I found you. I have found you."

"Indeed." Her lenses slipped down her nose; she studied

him over them, groping with one hand in a pocket for her ox-bone pipe. She lit it with a flick of nail, puffed something that reeked worse than the house. "You're a clever and troublesome young man. Such a clever man would know to bring me something worth your trouble."

He felt the utter weariness seep through him, as though the barren land around him were leaching him of life. "Such as?" he asked without hope, knowing that whatever she wanted, it would be innocent and alive.

"You killed my white hen."

"Yes. You have already punished me for that."

"You refused to pluck it, or to bring even one of your warriors into my house to drink a cup of broth with me."

"Even one was one too many."

"Then bring me this, to replace my white hen. Bring me the firebird in a golden cage, and I will set you free."

He stared at her wordlessly. She puffed a billow of foul smoke, levered him off her threshold with a broad foot under his shoulder, and slammed the door. The cottage, rising under him, shook him off the steps and onto the moon-parched ground before it stalked away to find a quieter corner of night.

SIX

Euan Ash's pen encountered Gyre's name for the first time toward the end of an endless summer day. The pen stopped on the curve of the first letter. Gyre, the scribe thought curiously, and then remembered the name spoken on the day he had seen the princess. He saw her again, vividly, as he sat with his pen poised to begin the name: standing in the wizard's garden with her hair like coils of braided gold, and the bees braiding their erratic golden paths through the light as they followed her scent. Now Unciel's seedlings had grown tall, vines and stalks offering a confusion of color and scents that caused other flashes of color to hover and dart through the corners of Euan's attention. He shifted the pen just before the bead of ink in its nib welled and dropped. How long had she been gone? he wondered, and then realized, with surprise, how much of the summer had passed. She would have reached Serre, begun the long journey through its forests weeks ago. She might, beginning a longer and even more hazardous journey, have already married.

He frowned down at his paper, ruthlessly pulling his attention out of memories, colors, the intimate, throbbing voices of the mourning doves on the garden wall. He could hear the wizard Unciel working in the kitchen, tying herbs to dry, cooking up odd ointments for bunions and spider bites. Euan dipped his pen again, finished the name finally: Gyre.

"In Fyriol, a harsh land south of Dacia, I met a young mage called Gyre . . ."

He heard the wizard's breathing then, and turned. Unciel, his fingers green from tearing herb leaves, leaned against the doorway, panting slightly. He had used magic to move, Euan guessed, recognizing the pallor, the weary slump of shoulders. He made a questioning noise, wondering if the wizard needed help with some disaster in the kitchen. But Unciel, his breath calming, only looked at Euan quizzically a moment before he spoke.

"Why now?" he asked, then made himself clearer. "Why that tale now?"

Euan shrugged slightly, baffled. "It came next out of the chest."

"Oh."

"I can copy it later," Euan offered, stifling interest. "Or not at all. I haven't read it."

"I know." He explained, as Euan blinked at him, "What you write wakens memories. They are, after all, my words."

Euan put the pen down, gathered papers. "Then you tell me when to do it."

But the wizard lingered in the doorway, gazing, it seemed, at the wall at the back of the garden. Even in the warm light, his eyes looked the color of ash. He said finally, mildly, not seeing Euan at all as he made his decision, "As you said. It came next." He drew himself slowly off the doorpost to walk back to the kitchen, and added, "I had forgotten that I wrote about it."

Euan listened until he heard a murmured greeting; the raven, answering, spoke the wizard's name. Moments later, a lid clattered in the kitchen. Euan, unable to quell a curiosity that must have made itself palpable even in the steamy air above the boiling pots, dipped his pen and went on with the tale.

"In Fyriol, a harsh land south of Dacia . . ."

Fyriol, he learned that afternoon, was a hot, parched land whose fierce winds laid bare the bones of hills and sculpted them into high, eerie shapes of colored sand and granite. Dragons had once lived there, tales said, and had left the land unfit for human occupation. But the seventh son of a king who was also a seventh son had gone looking for a land of his own to rule, and had claimed Fyriol. As there were only a few nomadic wanderers occupying it at the time who soon drifted north to fairer climes, no one argued with him. Other adventurers, disinherited, dispossessed, and otherwise frustrated, joined him to wrest their fates out of the difficult land. The king, building a palace out of the colored sandstone, unearthed a vein of gold. With that, he paid a wizard to tame the unpredictable and ruthless storms. The wizard died of his work, struck by a recalcitrant claw of lightning—the ghost, some said, of a dragon-king. But the weather did improve. Wanderers stopped there and settled, raised their flocks on hardy grasses and scrub. As years passed, the kingdom grew rich on gold and oil from the fruit of gnarled, twisted trees that thrived on arid ground and light. The aging king, wanting to protect his fledgling kingdom for his own sons, sent word to more civilized lands that he would hire another mage or sorcerer or wizard to pursue any rumors of dragons still living, and to mark the borders of his land with signs of magic to discourage other kings' sons with nothing else to do from casting an eye toward his domain.

A fledgling wizard by the name of Gyre, seeking to establish a reputation, responded to his request.

"I was," Unciel wrote, "passing through Fyriol out of curiosity, on my way to Dacia, when I heard a silent, desperate cry for help."

In his dreams that night, Euan tried to continue the tale. A dragon flowed out of his pen. Many dragons stirred in their stony haunts, forgotten fires smoldering at the interruption of their sleep. A band of brutal thieves posing as nomads found the young wizard alone on the borderlands and forced him to use his magic to draw unwary travellers into trouble. The King of Fyriol himself, furious at some wizardly ineptitude, had locked Gyre in a tower and thrown away the key. Gyre, his throat raw, his voice dead from shouting, had cried out silently for help, pounding at the door. Euan, startled out of his dreams, opened his eyes and still heard the pounding. He tried to cry out in the dark; his voice would not come. Then he recognized the drunken laughter at his door. It was a pair of pretty scribes who had cast their eyes earlier that summer at the lanky, cat-eyed Euan, challenged by his shyness and reserve.

"Come out with us," they called, their bangles ringing brightly against his door. "Euan. We haven't seen you for weeks, and our eyes have grown desolate. Come and play."

Someone across the narrow street drew attention to the sinking moon and bellowed for silence. Euan, motionless on his bed, pretended he was not there. The lowering moon, full and milky, shed light on his uncluttered, meticulous life: the water jug there, pens and ink so, manuscripts of favorite poetry stacked neatly here, shoes aligned in suspended motion beneath the window, at the end of a journey, or the beginning of another.

"Euan," the door whispered. "We know you're in there. Summer's almost over. Come out before the leaves wither and the sun grows pale. Euan."

Euan rolled over and dragged his pillow over his ears, wanting to find his way back into the strange, dragon-haunted tale where the mysteriously imperiled wizard cried out wordlessly for help. But he still heard the laughing, coaxing voices, even after the young scribes had gone and he had fallen asleep again.

"I followed the silent cry to its source," he wrote the next morning, trying to keep his curiosity from outrunning his pen as he copied. "In a cave along the rocky northern border of Fyriol, I stood in the heart of the cry. There were bones in that cave. I recognized them: the huge triangular jaws, the backbone running the length of the visible cave, stretching back into the utter dark. The teeth were jagged, and blackened with the dying fires of its last breaths. It had been dead a very long time, perhaps centuries. There was no danger from it. And yet the silent cry for help seemed to echo against the walls of the cave as it pulsed out of my heart. It came, I guessed finally, out of the dark deep within the cave."

Invisible, soundless, able to see in the dark as easily as day, the wizard Unciel followed the trail of helplessness and terror through the winding corridors of stone.

"That it was another wizard in trouble I already knew: the power of his cry, reaching so far across the desolate land to find me, told me what he must be. I sensed something else, beyond his power, that I could not define. It seemed at once small and vast, here and elsewhere, vulnerable and yet absolutely implacable. I could find no name for it. And so I came at last to meet Gyre, in the dark under earth and stone, caught with his hand in a gold casket inside the coil of the monstrous backbone of yet another dragon. Its ribs, collapsed under the fallen weight of backbone, spilled in a ring around him. The gold, filigreed casket itself was a small treasure. He could carry it easily out of the cave into the light. It belonged to no one any longer; why should it not belong to him? So he must have thought."

What Gyre saw becoming suddenly visible in front of him was left unwritten. What Unciel saw was a young, very helpless man lying on the ground within a spill of bones, one hand locked under the lid of a casket, which seemed to have bitten down on it like a live thing. His wrist was bloody; on his free hand the nails were broken and bleeding from tearing at the lid. His lean, dirty face was hollow with hunger and pain. Unciel, accustomed to noting such things, saw that the earth beneath the casket was black, hardened. Something once there had left its shadow of blood and fire, which, hardening through the centuries, had sealed the casket to the ground as though it were gripped in stone. The young wizard opened his mouth at the sight of Unciel and croaked like a raven. He had worn his voice to nothing; only his heart could speak.

"I told him my name, and felt it reverberate in his thoughts, in recognition and in hope. But I was not so sure of myself. I did not tell him that. I knelt beside him and told him what I saw. 'The casket has been hidden within stone, in the dark within the stone, in the dragon within the dark, in the heart within the dragon. What, I wonder, is within the casket?'

"He had wondered, too, his rueful thoughts told me. He had glimpsed something, but the casket had slammed over his hand when he touched the secret it held. His name was Gyre. He had been hired by the King of Fyriol to seek out any dragons left alive in the kingdom. The only life he had found in that cave was the hinged jaws of the little casket.

"To open the casket, I told him, I would have to persuade it that it recognized me. Gyre had already guessed that. He had lain there in that changeless night saying every name he had ever learned in his life. Even in a young wizard's life, that is a great many names. I tried a few; the casket refused to open. So I did what I had to do. I reached into the casket with my mind to encompass the power hidden within it. Masked in that power, I would reflect like a mirror whatever lay within, giving the illusion that the casket belonged to me.

"I brought all my thoughts, all my powers, to focus upon a nightmare.

"I withdrew as soon as my thoughts had touched it. It was like becoming death. But in that instant, when I became the power within the casket, it opened to me, freeing Gyre. Its lid dropped back, revealed its secret: a small, faceted ball of black crystal. An odd jewel, it must have seemed to Gyre, looking neither very beautiful nor very valuable. But it must be both for someone to have hidden it so completely.

"We both knelt there, staring at it. Gyre seemed perplexed, and still curious. I could not speak. My heart had changed shape for only an instant, a sand-grain of time, but I had glimpsed what I did not know had ever existed. Such dark power. Such evil. I recognized the thing for what it was, but not whose . . .

"'Remember the tales you have been taught,' I said at last, rising. 'Within a dragon-ridden land there is a cave; within the darkness of the cave there is a dragon; within the dragon's fiery heart there is a casket. Hidden within the casket . . . ' There is a heart, he finished silently. 'Yes. Kept in secret far from its owner, whose body cannot be killed until the heart is found and destroyed.'

"I heard Gyre's thoughts again, untangled finally from his wonder: It must be centuries old, as old and dead as these dead bones. I turned away, sickened by the thought that whoever claimed it had existed at all. 'Leave it,' I told him. 'It is well buried here.'

"I heard the casket close, and then Gyre's uncertain steps

behind me. It never occurred to me that, having been trapped for days in the dark with a casket gnawing at his wrist, he would risk putting a hand back into it. But that was Gyre, and that was his mistake. But I had opened the casket for him; I had persuaded the heart within that it had recognized itself, that it belonged to me.

"That was my mistake."

The tale ended there, at dusk on a summer's day. Euan sat silently, gazing down at the last word he had written. The kitchen, he realized slowly, had grown as silent, as though Unciel were listening for Euan's first coherent thought. He felt it before he thought: a chill prickling through him, even in that tranquil warmth. The nightmare that Unciel had glimpsed had been very much alive, and it had come looking for its stolen heart . . . That was the untold tale, the one left unwritten, only glimpsed between the lines of an earlier tale, where, for an instant, something powerful enough to leave a fragile husk of a wizard in the wake of its death had opened an eye in the dark and looked at him.

But Gyre had taken its heart. Gyre must have been there when Unciel had fought his nightmare. The young wizard had escaped unscathed; he must have run—

"No."

Euan had not heard the wizard enter. Unciel stood beside him without speaking again for a moment. He touched the paper gently, the blank inches beneath its final line. Euan saw his hand tremble.

Then he continued, "Gyre never saw whose heart he had stolen. I began to hear terrifying tales that haunted me, that roused memories of what I had glimpsed so briefly in the cave. I knew that whoever had lost its heart had begun to search for it. I found Gyre and took the heart from him without telling him. Nothing I could do would destroy the heart, and I felt its owner's power focussing on me, searching now for me. So I took the heart far north, to lure the danger away from all the worlds I knew. I thought such an ancient thing would be easy to destroy. If I had known, I would never have gone alone . . ."

"Does Gyre know what you fought? And that you rescued him?"

"I never told him. We spoke only of Dacia and Serre when I sent him with the princess. He knows that I fought something deadly, and he might have guessed what, but I refused to let him question me. It exhausts me to remember."

"I'm sorry," Euan said shakily. "I didn't mean—"

"I could have stopped you."

"Why didn't you?"

"I wanted to test my own strength," the wizard answered slowly. "And because that was the tale that found its way out of the chest into your hands. Like water, tales find their own paths; they go where they are needed. Perhaps I need to remember."

Euan gathered the sheets of parchment, put them in order: two tales in two different hands, one hasty, careless, nearly illegible, the other neat, clear, nothing in its straight lines and even words indicating that the scribe had been moved by anything beyond the shape and flow of letters. He tapped the two piles straight, said tentatively without looking at the wizard, "Maybe you should finish it. Tell it to me. I'll write it as you speak."

He waited, but the wizard did not answer. Turning, he found himself alone.

The next morning, having begun a less harrowing account of the mishaps of a ruler's son attempting to study magic with Unciel, the scribe was startled by the sudden cry of the raven in the quiet house. Unciel was among the tidy rows in the garden, picking beans. The visitor, too impatient to wait, pushed open the back door and went out to him. Euan, watching, saw the king's livery among the bean rows. A paper passed from messenger to wizard. Unciel read it, folded it again slowly. Euan couldn't see the expression beneath the shadow of his hat. He said something. The messenger nodded briefly, came back in as quickly as he had gone out; Euan heard the front door close behind him. Unciel came in far more slowly. Euan was back at work, with a prince under his pen who had just set a carpet on fire, when he heard the wizard behind him.

He turned. Unciel, untying the apron full of pockets he wore to harvest, said, "I'll need your help."

Euan put his pen down and rose. Unciel, he saw with some apprehension, did not look pleased. His face, set, colorless, did not look anything at all. If the messenger from the king had come with news of Sidonie, Euan guessed, it was not to report word of a marriage accomplished, happily or unhappily, after all those weeks.

"Is something wrong?"

"That is what we must find out. The king wanted to know if I had heard from Gyre. He has had no word from anyone since the princess and her entourage reached the forests of Serre. Gyre was to have passed me word of any trouble, which he could do quickly, by various ways—water, crystal, even thought, if he felt strongly enough. I heard nothing, so I thought that all was well. Gyre was also to have sent word to me when Sidonie finally reached the summer palace safely."

"Maybe," Euan suggested, "it took longer—"

"Maybe. But the king's patience will not stretch longer. He asked me to speak to Gyre."

Euan scratched a brow with his thumbnail, gazing doubtfully at the wizard. "Will it be difficult?"

"Anything," Unciel sighed, "beyond chopping cucumbers is difficult. Some ways are easier than others. I will start with the simplest, but even for that I'll need you."

Euan nodded. He glanced vaguely at his work, dipped the pen nib in water to clean it. Then he heard his own voice again, bringing to light unexpectedly what had been lurking beneath the threshold of his thoughts. "Why did you send Gyre with the princess? He was careless of you after you helped him—he should have known what happens when you steal a heart."

"Yes," Unciel said, and left the matter there. "He'll never hear me with all this light," he added incomprehensibly, and took Euan's arm. "Come."

SEVEN

It was not until supper, that first evening in the summer palace, that the princess noticed a lack of bridegroom.

The wizard Gyre, who had last seen the prince haggard and half-mad, crouched over a fire in the night-forests of Serre and tearing into a spitted hare with his hands, did not expect him to appear among the curious, whispering courtiers in their flowing silks. Sidonie, seated beside the silent queen, seemed too dazed by what she saw to remember what she had not. The massive hall, with its low dark ceiling and dizzying view of the valley below, might have been hewn out of raw stone like a cave. Pelts covered the cold floor; the horned skulls of animals hung everywhere on the walls, between long narrow ribbons of tapestry that depicted, from what Gyre could recognize, witches and trolls and birds whose singing came out of them in spiralling threads of gold. Gyre, seated to King Ferus's left, watched him take the ragged bone of a haunch of beef off a platter and toss it over the dais table to the hounds below. It seemed a calculated gesture; the cold black visible eye of the king's profile challenged the wizard to blink.

But Gyre, who had blinked at many things in his life, had already sensed the dangerous intelligence in the King of Serre. It was the princess, on the king's blind side, whose mouth slipped open and hung indecorously, as the hounds tore at the bone and quarrelled over it, their deep rumbling voices sounding akin to the king's. Her attendants, seated by rank among the courtiers below, seemed as astonished. Sidonie, recalling some childhood admonition, closed her mouth and straightened her spine. Ferus, who had gotten his teeth around the bone of wizardry in Dacia and was worrying it, to the neglect of queen and guest, asked Gyre, "And the present King of Dacia, Arnou, of course has inherited his father's great gifts for sorcery?"

Gyre had no idea. "Of course," he answered smoothly. His knowledge of Dacia was still perfunctory; it had not interested him until now.

The row of arches along the far wall of thick, unpolished stone opened their casements to endless forests smoky with twilight, and across them to the jagged, very distant peaks between Dacia and Serre, still visible in the lingering flush of light from the wake of the sun. What a princess could cross, so could an army, Gyre mused. Ferus could see that even out of his blind eye. His fear of sorcery must have stopped him; his fascination with it must have inspired the alliance and marriage. Well and good, Gyre thought as

Ferus stopped his questions long enough to finish a quail stewed in cream and honey. Even then there was no such thing as true silence in that place; water weltered and shouted through it constantly, as though the king's summer court floated. Well and good. But how could there be a wedding without a bridegroom?

He felt the shock in her mind as Sidonie finally noticed the prince's absence. He understood: they had been travelling together for so long that she had grown used to Gyre's company. Struggling with the sudden foreignness of her world after the calm, predictable forests, she had forgotten to question his presence in the place of the man she was to marry. He watched her bend her head toward the pale, still queen.

"But where is Prince Ronan?" She might have thought the falling water would cover her words. But her voice, sweet and passionate, did not know how to hide anything. "Does he care so little about who he is to marry that he does not even want to meet me before the wedding?"

She might have stood up and shouted for the moon. Courtiers' voices faded; their faces turned to her, some calculating, others uneasy, no one perplexed, Gyre saw, but she. The king's profile, blunt and craggy, lifted above his plate, but he refused to turn anything more toward her than a blind eye. Beside him, the queen, her own head lowered, seemed to be searching for answers among the patterns of a few bird bones and some scattered leaves.

"You will meet my son when you marry," the king said. "Meeting him now will change nothing. The documents are sealed; you are here; you will wed."

"I would like to meet him now," Sidonie persisted, despite the seamed eye staring at her. "I have come so far—"

"You have come so far that another day cannot possibly matter," the king muttered testily, and turned his seeing eye to the proffered dish of a huge fish crusted in scales of orange and lime.

Gyre saw the queen shift, felt the princess's surprise as a hand touched hers. In warning? he wondered. In sympathy? "Please—" Sidonie began.

"Enough!" The fish was flying suddenly; the muttering had become a full-fledged roar that brought the hounds leaping nervously to their feet. The fish landed in the flickering shadows behind Sidonie's attendants, who had loosed a bevy of cries and ducked. The hounds took off after it. Ferus turned both eyes, visible and invisible, at the princess. "You will see him when you see him! Until then you will begin to learn to wait in silence, without question, as he has learned—"

His voice seemed to pour over her stiff, shocked face with all the force of the water plunging over the cliff, with all the ceaseless, relentless noise of it. Still, something of him triggered the sudden recognition Gyre saw in her eyes: the broad, high bones of his face, perhaps, his long, still-bright hair, his single-minded intensity. She caught her breath in a deep, audible suck of wonder, as though for a moment she had been drowning.

"Oh," she whispered and rose, her hands to her mouth, staring back at the one-eyed king. "You don't know where he is."

Ferus stopped shouting. It was as though one of the falls

had run dry. She had riveted even Gyre; he had no idea what she might say. She dropped her hands and said it. "Well, I do. Your son is running wild in the forests below, searching for a bird made of fire. It seemed to me, when I saw him, that marriage was the last thing on his mind." What Gyre could see of the king's face had flushed purple. Sidonie's voice shook badly, but she continued, "You have no bridegroom; there can be no wedding. I am going home."

She gestured to her attendants and turned. Flocking around her, they stunned the court with the sight of their backs turned firmly away from Serre. The princess and her entourage, resolutely following a startled servant with an empty platter, nearly found their way to the kitchen stairs before the king began to bellow.

The guards from Dacia were nowhere to be seen; they had been neatly buried between water and rock in the lower chambers of the palace. Gyre, beside the princess in an instant, made Ferus blink when the king caught up with her. His own guards were crowding through doors, ringing the frightened group. Some of the young women had begun to weep with terror. One or two, getting a close look at Ferus's seamed, snarling face, had fainted.

Sidonie flung a look like a cry at Gyre. He said quickly to the king, "If you will permit me to speak to the princess alone—"

The black eye rolled at him, acute and fuming. "You do not need to ask," the king said flatly.

"No," Gyre answered softly, after a heartbeat. "I do not need to ask. But I am in the service of the King of Dacia, and what he wants for his daughter, I must want."

Ferus considered him silently, a vein in the scarred eye-socket swollen and throbbing. "Then you must help me," he said tautly. "Go with her. I will send for you shortly. If I don't find you both still here, I will march across the face of Dacia until the magic it takes to defeat me hammers it flat and barren as the southern deserts of Serre."

He strode back to the hall. Sidonie stared after him, her own face moon-white. Gyre turned to her. She closed her eyes, bowed her head until it came to rest, lightly and very briefly, against the wizard's shoulder.

He took her to his own chamber, a quiet room in the back of the palace, overlooking the point where the broad river separated into the twin strands of silver that had carved the rocky island on which the palace stood. He expected a certain amount of crying and pleading before she could be persuaded to listen to him. But she surprised him again. She walked across the room, stumbling a little over the broad, fanged head of some skinned animal, and stood at an open window, gazing out until she finally stopped trembling. Then she drew a deep breath and turned.

"I can't let him war against Dacia. My grandfather, Ursal, was the last great sorcerer-king of Dacia. He might have sent Ferus running back over the mountains. My great-aunt Tassel, Ursal's sister, is still alive, but she inherited only a portion of the family powers. Unciel is so weak that he can barely battle the weeds in his garden."

"And your father?"

"My father has tried very hard to make magic, but he only makes messes. What the King of Serre fears is truly not much more than a legend. My great-aunt Tassel might toss a few obstacles in his path, but she could never stop an entire army."

"And you?"

She paused, gazing at him out of eyes the color of the twilight above her shoulder. "I have no idea," she said, surprised. "No one ever asked. But I doubt it. My older sisters have no talent for sorcery; why should I?"

"There's a difference," he said, "between sorcery and magic. Magic is inherent everywhere, in everything; it cannot lie and it cannot be deceived. Sorcery can lie, can twist, can delude. It may be that you have a gift for one but not the other."

"I hope," she answered grimly, not really understanding him, "that you have gifts for both. For whatever you need to rescue the king's son from the magic in Serre, and bring him home." She held his eyes with her own magic that the twisted forces in Serre would soon enough turn to sorcery. "You saw the prince when I did. He looks very much like his father. You didn't recognize him?"

"No," he said, feeling his own way into sorcery, and let her see his surprise. "Of course I do now. So that was Prince Ronan. Out chasing birds when he should have been here to welcome you."

Her wheat-gold brows pulled together a little. "I told him my name."

"Yes."

"I suppose—I suppose he might have been running from me as well. Though he seemed obsessed with the bird." She sat down on the casement ledge, pondering. "He said," she added, inspired, "something about a witch. Do you remember? He had to find the witch as well as the bird. He would come home, he said, as soon as he found the witch. It surprised me then that he seemed to think it was important for me to know. Now I understand why." Her voice trailed away. She studied the dusty, indifferent eyes of the white pelt splayed at her feet. Gyre touched candles to light with a thought, watched the firelight glide down her slender, golden throat. She was looking at him again suddenly, as though she had read his mind. But she only said, "He doesn't seem anything like his father. I think—I think I might be able to marry him without fear. Even though he is in love with a bird. Will you find him?"

Which was, as Gyre had anticipated, exactly what the King of Serre said to him a little later when he sent for the wizard. Guards escorted the princess back to her chamber, and Gyre to a room in a tower. It hung dizzyingly between valley and sky, just above the smooth curve of river dropping over the cliff. Torch fire on the walls above rippled on water that flowed like black silk under the night sky. As he waited for the king, Gyre watched the fiery reflection move with the water, try to fall, pull itself whole again. Weapons of every description hung on the walls around him: massive seed-pods of iron dangling from chains, ancient blades worn nearly transparent with age, long bows taller than the king, ornately decorated with painted, inlaid wood. The weapons of giants, the walls intimated, skilled and invincible. The king entered finally, pulled the circle of gold off his head, and hung it on the handle of a crudely whittled club that might have come out of a giant's den.

He poured wine and drank it, eyeing the wizard

somberly over the cup. He put it down empty, and said, "Find my son. Bring him home."

Gyre nodded. "It seems the only thing to do." He turned to watch the water again, and the reflection of the king's face in the little panes of bevelled glass. "I sat late around a watch fire last night, in the forest below. A young man came out of the trees to my fire. His fine clothes were torn and dirty; his hair, the color of yours, was tangled and full of bracken, as though, if he slept at all, he had crawled under a bush. He took the hare off my spit with his bare hands, as though he were starving. He would not tell me his name."

The king, staring at him, swallowed. "Is it true?" he demanded hoarsely. "What the princess said? He is pursuing the firebird?"

"Yes," Gyre said steadily. "And he mentioned a witch as well, someone who lives in a cottage made of bones."

The king's face turned the color of one of his skulls. "Brume." He looked, to Gyre's amazement, almost helpless for a moment. "The queen told me that he said he had met her, on his way home from battle a few days ago. He killed her white hen."

Gyre asked tentatively, "Is that—"

"Yes. Very bad. So my wife seemed to think. A thing for which the witch exacts the most dangerous payment before she forgives. If." His mouth tightened. "But she is an ancient hag who lives with her chickens and eats the unwary. You are a wizard trained in all the arts of sorcery and magic. You could break her like a bone between your fingers, free my son from her snares. Find him first and drag him home before he finds her; then you can deal with her.

He'll marry the Princess from Dacia with bracken in his hair and his eyes full of firebirds if I have to chain him to a pillar for his wedding. You must break that spell as well. Witch and firebird, so that he'll sleep in a bed at night and give me heirs, instead of under a bush dreaming of a bird."

Gyre drew breath, loosed it noiselessly, his eyes on the reflection of the ruthless, harried king. One eye, one heir, he thought. Lose either now, and Serre would be adrift like a leaf on that water . . . He saw the single eye begin to narrow at his silence, and he turned. "It would help me to outwit the witch if I knew something about her. She might find me before I find your son."

The king opened the door and shouted for a servant, then poured himself more wine, "Ask my wife," he said, and emptied the cup again. "She knows all the tales."

Later, Gyre wrote on parchment in letters so ancient only a wizard as knowledgeable as Unciel or a scribe trained in abandoned languages would have been able to decipher his thoughts: "I have opened the casket. . . . I have not yet touched the heart." He paused, his cool eyes unblinking, reflecting candle light as he remembered the cave in Fyriol. When the silence and the terrible, unrelenting blackness became unbearable, he would ignite the air, and then see the ring of bones around him, his own blood slowly pooling on the crystallized remains of dragon-heart. The memory of the wizard appearing out of the bleak, empty northlands of Fyriol to help him could still melt his heart. But Unciel was far away in Dacia now, digging in his flower beds. "And I," Gyre wrote, "am beyond help. I have fallen in love with a land. Its magic is extraordinary, unpredictable, so beautiful it can destroy past and future, so terrible you must reach beyond language to describe it. The king has some crude understanding of sorcery; his heart sees less than his missing eye. His son and only heir is lost. His queen is a ghost of what she must once have been. A pale woman with a perpetual twilight in her eyes, who rarely speaks. But within her silence, she carries like a rich treasure the tales of Serre. She told me all she knew of the peculiar witch Brume, and warned me of this and that: bridges, lonely mountain paths, deep, still pools. There, she said, stories begin. She was the third, between dusk and night, to beg me to find Prince Ronan.

"And so tomorrow, I will go looking, for a suitable time, until I can return without him and persuade them all that he is irretrievably lost within the magic of Serre."

EIGHT

Sidonie heard the mad King of Serre shouting at her all night long. Some time near dawn words changed to water, flowing endlessly past the summer palace, flinging itself to freedom in the valley below. Sleepless in the silvery light, she contemplated what she had left behind when she had ridden through the gates of the palace. On one side of the gates she had been free; riding under stone and shadow, she had—No. She tossed restlessly. She had left freedom behind in Dacia on a bright summer's day when she had stopped running away from what her father had told her. No. Her father and the King of Serre had signed away her freedom long before that. No. History had consumed her freedom as greedily and mindlessly as the hounds in the king's hall had gnawed at their bones. King Ferus was swallowing the world; her father had not inherited the weapons he needed to fight the threat to Dacia. She had lost her freedom even before she had been born.

She rose, looked out at the quiet trees in the wood across the river. If she leaned out of the casement, she could see the place where the water vanished, turned into sky, space, nothing. A high crook of road emerged from behind the falls, angled sharply and disappeared from view. Perhaps Gyre was walking down it at that moment. He had told her the night before that he would leave at dawn to search for the prince. But why would a wizard walk or ride when he could fly? She looked up, saw a bird wheeling through the vast emptiness beyond the palace. A blazing finger of light illumined it, colored its red-gold feathers. Gyre? she asked silently, with wonder.

It answered, or it seemed to, or her own wishes answered her: If you need me, I will know. I will return as soon as I can.

As soon as you can, she thought dourly. As soon as you find the witch, the bird, the prince. And here I am, trapped like a bird in a cage in the house of the King of Trolls. On what should have been my wedding day, she remembered ruefully. Her life was held in abeyance by creatures out of Auri's tales. Such things never happened in Dacia.

At mid-morning, she watched the king and a dozen guards file around the steep elbow of road visible from her window. Then they disappeared completely. Ferus would badger the forest to give him back his son, she guessed; he would scar the trees with his huge sword, scare the crows with his roaring. Her attendants crowded around her, not wanting to be separated, mending torn lace and hems, and speaking wistfully of Dacia. Her wedding dress hung over a mirror, a billow of gold cloth and pearls. Empty shoes stood beneath it. Going nowhere, she noted morosely. The chamber door opened abruptly; Sidonie, looking up with apprehension, found the Queen of Serre in her doorway.

There was a flutter; needles fell, tugging floating lace behind them, as heads bowed, skirts wafted into deep curtseys. Sidonie, raising her head again and taking a second look at the still, colorless face, felt as though she were looking into a mirror. Fear, sorrow, loss, the mirror said, and she swallowed a sudden burning in her throat.

"Leave us," she said impulsively and her attendants filed out reluctantly, abandoning her to the empty wedding shoes, the incessant noise of water, the silent queen.

Calandra slid her fingers together, clenched them, and said stiffly, haltingly, "I came to tell you that my—that Ronan is nothing like his father—"

"I know." Sidonie's own hands had found themselves, fretting around one another anxiously as she studied the tall, somber woman. Expression touched the frozen eyes.

"How do you know?"

"He spoke to me when I saw him in the forest. He didn't tell me his name. But I recognized the color of his hair—his face—in—in the king." She stopped, swallowed drily at the memory of the indescribable supper.

"Yes. They look alike."

"The prince seemed very sad. But not—but not unkind."

"Cruel."

"Cruel," Sidonie whispered.

The queen's eyes flickered past her to the window as

though Ferus might have heard the word falling with the water half-way down the cliff. "It is difficult to speak in this place," she said wearily. "I never know how much he can hear. Did my son give any reason for pursuing the firebird?"

"Only that it was beautiful." She saw it again as she spoke, opening in her mind like a flower of fire, blinding her to time, sound, the stones around her.

"You saw it too," someone said and Sidonie blinked. "Your eyes are full of it."

"What is it?"

The queen shook her head a little, her mouth tight. "Many things, I think. To Ronan, it must have been what he followed to flee from his life."

Sidonie looked at her wordlessly. The queen's hair was a braided crown of chestnut and gold and silver; her eyes were the cold color of dawn at the end of a sleepless night. Her son had inherited those grey eyes, Sidonie realized. And that heart.

"I know," she said with difficulty, "that your son still grieves for his first wife and their dead child. Was it his wedding he fled from?"

"It was life," the queen said simply. "He keeps trying to leave it."

Sidonie's hands slid over her arms. She started to answer. Then the gold of her useless wedding dress filled her eyes and she found herself crying instead, noiselessly, mutely, staring at the queen and shaking, holding herself tightly so that what was trying to come out of her would not overwhelm them both.

The queen's face changed, expression melting through

the set, icy cast of it. She touched Sidonie's wet cheek. "I can't remember," she murmured, "the last time I cried." She eased Sidonie onto the cushions and furs in the window seat. Then she stood beside the weeping princess, gazing at the world beyond the stones, one hand resting on a trembling shoulder. Her voice ran in and out of the sound of tears and water; now and then an image surfaced, flashed alive. "The firebird is what you follow to change your life, and every tale of it is different. But in every tale it is inevitably the heart's desire. Once there was a great king who heard it singing in his garden by moonlight, and he fell so in love with its beauty that he promised to marry his youngest, fairest daughter to any man who could capture it for him . . . The young man who pursued it left everything he knew behind and entered a world where animals gave advice, where horses flew, where not even death was the end of the story, for the singing of the firebird could wake the dead. He won his heart's desire. The firebird, which in the end eludes all capture, escaped from the king and flew away into another tale . . ."

Sidonie, quieting so that she could hear past her own sorrow, said hollowly, "That is not very comforting, when the heart's desire of the man you are to marry is his dead wife and their child."

"No." The queen sat down beside her, took her hand. "His heart's desire is the firebird now; he goes where it takes him."

"I wish I could."

"The king will never let you go," Calandra said softly. "Even if Ronan does not return. Ferus will force your father to come for you, force the powers to Dacia to challenge the magic of Serre. He wants Dacia; he thought it would be easy."

"It should have been. It should have been as simple a matter as putting on that dress. Not a matter of warring sorceries." She fell silent, gazing again at the confection of gold and lace, with its overlay of tiny pearls like a web whose threads ran everywhere. Her eyes followed a single strand along a sleeve; in her mind she held the strand in one hand, following it while it led her down a hallway, down stairs, into shadowy, unwatched places within the palace. Surely there was a way . . .

"There is no escape," the queen said, reading her thoughts. "I have tried."

Sidonie, her eyes dry now and seeing more clearly than ever where the vagaries of history had stranded her, answered simply, "Your son escaped."

At dusk, she watched the dark, powerful figure of the king, in black leather and chain mail, appear again at the sharp angle of the road, and disappear behind the falls as he rode toward the gates. His guards followed. Sidonie studied each figure carefully before it vanished. The bright-haired prince was not among them.

She braced herself for another unnerving supper, full of flying fish and bones. But the king did not appear, and the summer court, suspended between a wedding and a funeral, not knowing whether to celebrate or mourn, spoke in subdued voices of an uncertain future. Sidonie retired as soon as she could with her attendants, relieved at the absence of the obstreperous king. As soon as she reached her chamber, he sent for her.

His guards took her to a high tower room above the falls. They left her alone there, hanging between air and stars, breathless at the bird's eye view of the darkening fields and forests a thousand feet below her. The river, barely wider than a knife blade, caught light from the rising moon, turned a liquid silver as she stared down. She closed her eyes, backed away from the casements, and nearly bumped into the king as he entered the room behind her.

She smelled leather and sweat as she veered hastily away. Still lightly armed, dusty from the road, with a twig or two caught in his hair, he eyed her dourly, chewing on something that, she guessed, had once had a hoof or a claw attached to it.

He swallowed and said, "Your father must have a room like this."

"My father," she answered dizzily while the king stuck his head out a window to spit, "is not a mountain goat." Then she took a closer look at it.

It did resemble the room her grandfather had taken her into when she was small, where she watched him float fire in water, and call birds out of the air to perch on her fingers. Later, her father had tried such things in that chamber full of books and beakers, scrolls written in letters resembling twigs and bird-claws, jars and stoppered pots, pet toads, owls, crows, mirrors, cauldrons, precious stones, crystals, flakes of gold, and an endless supply of candles. She had watched the King of Dacia set his boots on fire trying to light a candle, and erase his reflection in a mirror trying to make himself invisible. For several years, the castle rang with his shouts of frustration or sudden cries for help; it trembled now and then with random explosions; swathes of colored air fluttered out of the windows like windblown curtains. Abruptly, he gave up on magic. The last time Sidonie had seen the room, it had grown very dusty and all the animals were gone.

This chamber seemed more the lair of some mad witch. Ogre, she amended, watching the strong teeth tearing at the meat, the single eye above it rolling darkly toward her. This was the ogre's lair, with animal bones in the fire bed and a grinning human skull with a red, faceted jewel in one eye socket. His basins of water were cloudy with ash or blood; dried mushrooms, dead moths, desiccated birds were strewn across his tables. More lively, lizards flicked in and out of the casements; a poisonous toad, one leg cuffed and chained with a slender strand of gold, swelled and hissed at any movement. The mirrors were opaque, reflecting the ghosts of trees. No, she realized suddenly, the trees were real. High above the forests of Serre, the mirrors searched the night-ridden trees for the prince.

She was drawn to them, the magical eyes of the king. He watched her stand in front of a long oval mirroring the silent forest. She had slept beneath the canopy of those huge branches; she had watched the birds weave their colored threads of flight through them, and the small animals burrow among the massive roots. She stretched out a hand, remembering how time had stopped within those changeless trees, and how she thought she had been free. The king, his mouth closed motionlessly on a bite, seemed to be expecting some unfamiliar display of sorcery. Her hand touched cold glass, dropped.

He said harshly, "You must have inherited the powers of Dacia's kings. Why else would I have chosen you to marry my son? Show me how you would search for him."

She looked at him, her face expressionless, very pale. Words failed her. The whole idea was ludicrous, and he might very well toss her out of the nearest window along with his bone if she told him so.

Gyre, she hoped desperately, would catch her if he did.

Somewhere between laughter and terror, she began to babble, giving him the only magic she could remember: the fragment of a tale. "I cannot. I hid my powers in a secret place before I left Dacia, so that the wild powers in Serre would not sense it and seek to challenge it. The wizard Unciel gave me this advice. He is a very powerful wizard and has travelled many times in Serre. Gyre helped me. Unciel told me that I must never, ever, for any reason, tell anyone where my magical powers are hidden. When Gyre returns, he will get them for me." The king's eye, flat black and smoldering like a coal, seemed to bore through her, seeking what she hid. Beyond him, on top of a pile of books, the skull's eye glittered at her as though it laughed. Inspired by it, she added, "My magic is hidden in a jewel, in a locked box without a key. My voice is the key that will open it."

A guttural confusion of words snarled in the king's throat. He gave up on them, raising his hand instead. But it was the bone, not the princess, that he pitched out of the window, before he bellowed for guards to remove her from his sight.

NINE

Ronan sat in the dead of night listening to the firebird sing.

It clung to a branch high above him, dropping notes like a shower of fiery cinders that burned toward him, then cooled before they touched him. It sang to the rising moon, he thought, the way other birds greeted the sun. Either it was oblivious of him or had grown used to him, for now and then it showed the moon a woman's face. From a tangle of tree roots, Ronan watched, enraptured. He was turning without realizing it into some rare forest creature, with a pelt of bracken and tattered silk. Tiny spiders had woven webs across his torn pockets; great luna moths clung to the tarnished brightness of his hair. Mice had nibbled the threads of his buttons; magpies had stolen them. He had used a boot for a pillow one night, and then wandered off without it. He ate when he remembered, foraging for berries and mushrooms; he drank when he chanced across a stream. Now, as intent and thoughtless as a wild thing, he watched the face of the firebird shift slowly, unpredictably, from bird to woman and back again, her eyes full of moonlight, the song coming out of her like a lullaby. And then its eyes, gold as the sun, its song like flaked fire, falling and melting in Ronan's heart. And then again her. He was utterly content.

He barely remembered his own name; it had gone the way of his boot, so when the owl first spoke, he didn't recognize himself.

"Ronan." He saw a pair of round, bone-white eyes peering down at him from a low branch. The sound the owl made seemed harsh, pitiful through the liquid song of the firebird, and he didn't understand the word at all. "Ronan. Prince Ronan."

Above them the bird's face changed. The woman sitting on the branch smiled at the moon, her fiery hair tumbling down and down, an endless froth of curls in which stars were born. He didn't hear the owl again for a while. He heard only the woman, her singing gentle, tender, as though she sang a child or a lover to sleep.

Then she melted in the fire, and the bird, its voice a harp strung with gold, sang again to the moon.

"Ronan," the squat, dark oval of feathers cried, and pitched forward suddenly. It dangled awkwardly from the branch, its great, fierce eyes nearly level with Ronan's. "Prince Ronan!"

He blinked. An upside-down owl was hanging in his

face, trying to get his attention. "What is it?" he asked softly, so not to disturb the firebird.

"I'm caught in a snare. Please help me. Set me free."

A desperate impatience filled him. He did not dare move; he had no time for owls, and this one had a voice like the rasp of a handsaw. "Hush!" he told it, but it would not; it muttered and shook its wings and tried to bend double to pick at the snare. Above it, the firebird was beginning to shift shape again; he could tell by the husky, human overtones. He closed his eyes, clenching his jaw tightly, and got to his knees, feeling along the branch for the snare.

It had taken the owl by both claws. He snapped the loop of rotting leather easily and slid back down, holding his breath. She still sang above him, her voice unfaltering, undisturbed.

The owl fluttered, caught its balance in mid-air, and came to perch on Ronan's knee. "Ronan."

"What?" he demanded in a whisper. "Must you talk now?"

"I only wanted to thank you."

"You're welcome."

"And to give you this morsel of advice, in gratitude."

"Please," he breathed. "There's no need—"

"Don't put your trust in wizards."

The owl flew off, a silent glide of silver in the night. The firebird sang of inhuman beauty and incomprehensible desire to the blank face of the moon. For one moment, between notes, Ronan thought he understood what the owl said. In another note, he had forgotten even that he was human.

He remembered that much when he woke in daylight, a sprawl of bones among the hard roots, the sun trying to pry open his eyes with a blade. Before he opened them, he had a sudden, stark vision of himself: Prince Ronan of Serre, heir to the kingdom and a princess waiting to marry him, ragged and starving and talking to owls, spellbound by a witch, in love with a bird, and no idea how to get home except by capturing the thing he loved above all else and giving it to the witch for supper.

He loosed a small, helpless croak of a sob, struggling to separate his body from the bones of the tree. To his surprise, something croaked back at him. He rolled up painfully, settled himself against the tree trunk, letting the dazzling light in little by little. He saw nothing for a moment but a glare of sun and hot green shadow. He was hungry enough to eat the next thing he laid eyes on. Luckily for it, when his raw eyes finally cleared, the thing was speaking to him.

"Prince Ronan."

He blinked wordlessly at a lump beside his hand. Shadows rippled over it like water. He squinted, wondering incredulously how something no bigger than his fist could possibly see the prince in the tattered, exhausted man slumped like a broken puppet under a tree.

Then he wondered how a toad could talk.

"Prince Ronan," it said again, creeping a little closer to his hand. It was diffident and ugly, with a voice as rough as its nubbled back. "Please take pity on me."

"How do you know my name?"

"I recognized you. Something swooped down on me last night and carried me away from my pool. I struggled and barely escaped with my life, but in falling, I injured myself. I can barely move. Will you carry me back to my home? I can smell it, my long mosses and water lilies and the still green water, but I cannot get there. Please take me home."

Ronan sighed. He saw no reason not to help the toad when he saw no reason in anything, and besides that he was thirsty. He turned his hand on the ground and opened it. He felt the flaccid, trembling thing climb over his fingers, its webs spreading and clinging at every slow step, until it spilled across his palm and squatted there.

"Thank you," it said humbly. "Now, if you'll rise and turn your back to the sun."

Ronan, speechless, managed to get himself up without squashing the toad. Limping and hollow, he moved through the forest not much faster than a toad. He had long since parted company with the princess's bow and arrow, but perhaps the toad's pond would have a fish in it. He closed his eyes, laughing silently, glimpsing himself again and appalled.

"It's just ahead," he heard the toad tell him. "Just past those briars."

"A month ago I was in a battle trying to give away my life."

"You don't say."

"Now I'm wandering around the forests of Serre wearing one boot and carrying a frog."

"Toad," the toad corrected, but politely. "And I'm very grateful for the help."

Ronan felt it shift as the dank smells of damp earth, slick waterborn creatures, moss trailing eggs like bubbles, wafted over them on the breeze. He set the toad down on the bank and lowered himself wearily to drink. He saw his worn, harrowed face in the still water: shaggy-haired, crowned with twigs and water lilies, his eyes haunted and beginning to be afraid. Then he dropped his face into his reflection. Small fish darted away through the ripples. He breathed again, scooped water over his face and hair. As it dripped back into the pool, he heard the toad speak.

"I am very grateful. There is a wizard looking for you. He will tell you that he can help you but beware."

Ronan lifted his head above the water, got a toad's eye view of the toad sitting on a stone among the lily pads.

"What wizard? Beware what?"

But the toad only stared back at him, its senseless eye and mute, clamped mouth asking only what made him dream that toads could speak?

He wandered on, scavenging with the birds and the deer for food and searching through his mother's tales for a wizard. He stood for a while with his feet in a stream, trying to catch a fish with his hands, and to imagine what worse a wizard could do to him. Fish slipped through his fingers again and again until he was soaked with his own flailing and too weak to stand. Then, as his sight grew strange, water and sky merging into one flat grey plane, he felt a great fish brush through his hands and linger there. He fell over with surprise. The fish came with him, flying out of the water and landing on the bank, panting beside him. He turned his head cautiously, waited for it to call him by name and plead for its life. It said nothing. Its eye dimmed. He got up, grateful to it for simply dying, and began to gather wood.

He had finally found a stone to spark fire, twigs had finally sparked, the spitted, steaming fish had finally flaked into a bite which he was about to put into his mouth when he saw the wolf watching him silently on the other side of the fire.

She was lean and mangy; her hollowed sides showed ribs. Her muzzle and ears were grey with age; her eyes had grown cloudy. She did not speak. She did not need to. Ronan stared at her, his own belly whimpering with hunger. He yielded finally to the exigencies of his peculiar fortune, and broke the fish in two.

"Thank you," she said, and swallowed her half in a gulp, coughing a moment to settle a bone. She turned to leave as silently as she had come. Her muzzle swung toward him before she took a step.

"I know," he said, his mouth full of fish. "The wizard."

"No," she said, her voice slow and husky with age. "The firebird. I hear it singing just across the river among the trees."

She padded away, her sunken shoulders and haunches sagging on the bone. He dropped what was left of the fish and splashed into the water, his eyes already filling with fire, his heart emptying itself of all memory but the firebird's song.

Sometime in the night, long after the sun had set and the stars crowded out of the dark to hear the firebird, another voice troubled Ronan for his attention. It refused to be still.

It tugged at him as he sat entranced beneath the singing bird. It poked at him annoyingly like a stone; it whined like an insect in his ear. He seemed to fall through unimaginable distances, past stars pulsing with the firebird's music, down past the moon, through the massive, silent trees, down to earth. He felt his body shift. He saw the firebird far above him, luminous against the moon. Then he heard the voice again, and turned to see what forest creature needed him now.

He recognized the lean, composed face, the dark hair. The still eyes caught moonlight this time instead of campfire. It was the man who had drawn Ronan to his fire with the smell of spitted hare. He was very quiet, his eyes on the firebird. If it was not his voice that had dragged Ronan to earth, he was back anyway, in the confused, weary, constantly hungry body, half-prince, half-forest creature, and both halves utterly lost.

He whispered, "Can you help me?"

The man, who was leaning against the truck of the tree Ronan sat under, dragged his eyes away from moon and bird to look down at Ronan. With a murmur of surprise, he dropped down beside the prince. "I remember you," he said. "The first time I saw the firebird, you were there."

Ronan nodded. "You fed me at your fire."

"Yes." He paused, studying Ronan, then added slowly, "You look half-starved. And half-wild. Is it the firebird that torments you so?"

"It haunts me, yes. She." He put out a hand, gripped the man's arm as though one of them might vanish; he was not sure which. "Help me—"

"Yes," the man said quickly. "Of course. Tell me what I can do for you."

"I can't find my way back home. The witch has me trapped in a terrible spell because I killed her white hen. I can't see past this forest; most of the time I can barely see beyond myself. At first she said—she said I would not find my way home until I found her again. And so I found her again, in her cottage of bones. But she still will not set me free. Now the price for my freedom is the firebird. Bring it to her, the witch said, in a golden cage. Tell me how. Even if I stumble across a cage of gold big enough for the firebird lying under a bush, tell me how I could bear to capture all that beauty and give it to Brume? My heart would break even as she freed me. Please. Help me think. Tell me what I should do."

The man, whom Ronan held with both hands now, gazed at him out of dark, unblinking eyes for a long time without speaking, while above them the woman sang in her sweet, tender, unfathomable language. Some time during that endless moment, Ronan realized that his hands had fallen limply at his sides; it was the man who held him now.

Finally he spoke. Do nothing, it sounded like to Ronan, or perhaps just: Nothing.

Then Ronan was moving. Being moved. Trees were passing him. They tossed and pitched oddly, and were as oddly streaked with bars of gold. He tried to touch the gold, brush it away. He had no hands. His arms were feathers. Were fire. He opened his mouth to cry out; he could not make a sound. It was he who moved, he saw then, not the trees. The bars of gold were just that. He touched one; his fingers were claws of gold. A terrible sound welled through him. He tried to batter himself against the bars; he tried to eat through one with a beak of gold. But though feathers and plumes of fire melted out between the bars around him, he could scarcely move. He was caged in gold, within a body that made no sense. It was a dream, he thought desperately. He had been so obsessed with the firebird that he dreamed he had become the thing he loved.

Then he saw the hand above him, carrying the cage by a sturdy loop of gold. He stretched his long neck, pushed his head through the curved upper bars to bite at the human fingers, make them drop the cage. He drew blood; he heard a sudden exclamation. The world stopped swaying back and forth a moment, but the cage did not fall. The loop simply grew larger, the hand unreachable. A face turned briefly down to look at him. It was his own.

If he had been the firebird, he would have shaken stars loose with the sound of his voice. A crack would have marred the face of the moon. Beware, beware, the man who wore his face and body told him with the sound of every step. Beware. He could not find a single note within himself to cry terror, to cry rage, to cry his total bewilderment. He felt the gold beak open wide. Cries flooded through him, drained away into silence. After a long time, he slumped, numb and exhausted, against the bars of his cage. Plumes dragged in the bracken behind him, gathered needles and dust. He watched the moon set, the silent stars grow faint and cold.

In that dark hour, they came to the witch's house.

The man's steps faltered; his breathing stopped as he

stared at the bones. The bird stirred itself, tried once more to cry out. The man with the prince's haggard face, his torn clothing, his unsteady movements, let the cage drop to the ground and dragged it the last few steps to the witch's door.

He pounded on it. With horror, the bird heard his own voice.

"Witch." It was hoarse and trembling with weariness. "I have brought you the firebird."

The door sprang open. Man and bird gazed speechlessly at the toad-woman who appeared. She was massive, damp, and slightly green. Her long hair clung to her back like wet moss. She lifted the green lenses from her squat nose, propped them on her head, and stared with bulbous, hooded eyes at the motionless bird in the golden cage. Her mouth opened slightly; an impossibly long and narrow tongue flickered out as if to snag a fiery pinfeather.

Then she turned her dark toad's eyes to the man holding the cage. "It's very quiet."

"It's terrified," he answered heavily. "And most likely furious. I broke my heart to get it for you." The bird moved at that; a claw swiped through the bars, but missed. "Please. Let me go home now."

The toad-witch, neckless and hideously humped, could not bend, but she hunkered slightly to brush a wood chip out of a misty plume. "How beautiful it is. And how clever of you to find a golden cage in the forest."

"I did a favor for a fox. It told me where to find one."

"It pays to be kind to animals." She poked a fat, webbed finger through the bars, tried to stroke the bird's head. It ducked wildly away. "I'll hang the cage beside my fire, let it sing to me while I boil my bones for stock. I suppose you have earned your freedom, Prince. And I have no more use for you, now that I have a bird to replace my white hen. Go home. And let this be a lesson to you: stay away from my chickens."

She dropped the lenses back on her nose, hoisted the cage off the steps, backed into the cottage, and slammed the door.

Ronan, trapped in the dark that stank of rotting marrow and cooped hens, threw his bird's body against the bars; its wings and plumes flailed at the air. Its beak wide, it tried again and again to cry out. The witch hung the cage on a pot hook above the glowing coals in the hearth. She lit a candle or two, peered at the bird, fondled its flowing plumes.

"What a beauty you are," she murmured. "Even your eyes are gold. I'll feed you a bite of something, and then perhaps you'll sing. What, I wonder, do firebirds eat?" She glanced around her, then dipped into the pocket of her apron and pulled out a fistful of grain. "Try this, my lovely." She opened her hand enticingly just beyond the bars.

Ronan slashed at it with claw and beak. Grain spilled; the witch shrieked. She pulled the cage off the hook and, opening the door again, hurled it into the ragged end of night. "And there you'll stay," she shouted, as the cage flew, "until you're in a better temper. Then if I say eat, you eat, and if I say sing, you sing, or I will boil—"

The cage hit the ground hard. Its floor broke free from the bent bars. The firebird and the witch moved together, both with frantic speed. The bird worked itself free through the bottom of the cage just as the witch flung her enormous body upon it to catch it.

Ronan, feeling as though he had been hit by a barrel, struggled for air while the witch, on top of him and screeching like a hen in his ear, groped around her for feathers. Her hands locked on his human arms. She pulled back, staring at him. For an instant both their mouths opened; neither could speak.

Then she heaved to her feet, dragging the prince upright after her. "You!" She peered to one side of him, then the other. Then her face came very close to his, until her eyes were nearly crossed. Her nails dug into his arms like thorns; her hot breath stank of blood. "Where is my firebird?"

"There is—" He swallowed, still fighting for air. "There was no firebird. Only me."

"You." She searched behind him again. "You just left."

"That wasn't me."

"You aren't the firebird, and you aren't yourself," she ranted in sudden exasperation. "Who are you?"

"I killed your white hen."

She peered at him, first out of one lens, and then the other. "Prince Ronan," she said very softly. "Answer me this. Who was wearing your face?"

"I don't—" he began, and then he knew: the owl had told him, and the little toad. "He is a wizard who travelled to Serre with the princess from Dacia . . ." He felt the caged firebird's fury and terror again, at the wizard's inexplicable sorcery. "But why?" he whispered. "Was he hoping you would eat me?" Then he saw himself in the golden cage, along with all of Serre, forest and witch, firebird and king, swinging in the wizard's grip, powerless to cry for help. He felt his skin constrict with horror.

"It's him I'll eat," the witch said testily.

Ronan's hands clenched. "He'll wear my face into my father's court," he said raggedly, trying to chart the path of the wizard's sorcery through Serre. "He'll take my name, my place—he'll marry the Princess from Dacia himself. My father only has one eye and he only sees what he wants to out of that—Please." He reached out desperately before he remembered what he almost touched. "You must let me go home. I'll bring you a hundred white hens."

"You have not brought me even one firebird," she complained. "And why do you care if another man steals your life? You didn't want it anyway."

"I don't—I didn't—" His thoughts tangled; he paused, speechless at having to explain himself to a witch who would have boiled his bones for stew. Then, as he looked back at what had led him to that inconceivable moment, words came. "What I wanted," he said, his voice raw with pain, "was a reason to want it."

The witch gazed at him, her toad-eyes unblinking behind the lenses. Her long tongue flicked the air suddenly, as at a passing thought. "You killed my white hen and you've given me nothing in recompense."

"Let me go and I'll bring you every white hen in Serre."

"I don't want that. I don't even want the firebird now." Her tongue slipped between her lips again, out and in. "What I want is the man who can make a firebird. There is magic in the marrow of his bones. Bring him to me and I will set you free."

"Yes," Ronan promised between his teeth, not knowing how or where or when, only feeling in the marrow of his own bones the insidious threat to Serre. "But you must let me find my way home if you want him. That's where he's going with my face."

The witch gave an untoad-like snort. "You won't come back."

"I swear—"

"Words. Give me something you'll bother to come back for." She added, her voice thin as thread as he checked his hands for stray rings, and slapped his torn pockets for anything valuable that might have wandered into them, "Your voice. Your memory. Your eyes." His head rose abruptly; he stared at her, suddenly breathless. "You'd come back for such as those."

He was silent for what seemed a very long time in the soundless hour between dark and dawn. Then he offered her what of all such things he valued least, and would not miss if he did not return for it. "Take my heart. I'll bring you the wizard. Make what you will of his bones."

TEN

Euan Ash sat at his desk in the wizard's house, hunched over a blank sheet of parchment and staring as blankly at it. Now and then he would bring the dry nib to hover over it, as though to form a letter out of air instead of ink. Then the end of the pen would find its way to his lips, and his eyes would lose interest in the paper, wander towards the garden where the wizard knelt among his herbs, harvesting some of this, a little of that, more slowly than the insects chewed. It was the first morning Unciel had been able to leave the house after he had sent his magic into Serre to get Gyre's attention. The memory of that magic kept distracting Euan; gazing at the gardener bending unsteadily over the herbs, he did not see the wizard's frailty but his power.

"If I cannot go to Serre," Unciel had said obscurely, "I will bring Serre to Dacia."

They had spent a day and a half of a night in a windowless room. Things appeared and disappeared at random. Unciel sent Euan for water, for candles, for a book on a shelf beside the raven. Each time Euan returned, the room had changed. Shadows beyond the single candle stretched, it seemed, across the entire city. The wizard was making wind, stars. The air smelled of pitch, of earth, of water. Euan heard rivers in the black beyond the candle. He heard a hawk's cries, a wolf howl. The room had vanished, it seemed; Dacia itself must have vanished beneath the wizard's night. Yet when Euan was sent for something, he found the door latch always where he had left it, as though the door stood waiting on a boulder, or between two trees in some vast, wild land of the wizard's making. The house, the raven, Dacia itself were a step or two away across the threshold of a world.

Finally a restless night wind blew the candle out, stranded them in the soughing dark. Euan, blinder than he had ever been in the lamplit city nights, jumped when Unciel spoke.

"Gyre."

"I am here," the younger wizard's calm, even voice answered, and Euan's skin prickled. "You should have waited for me to send to you."

"The king could not wait any longer."

"Tell him that the princess is safe and well. The wedding will take place soon."

"You were to tell me when you reached the summer palace."

"We have only just arrived," Gyre explained. "I am sorry if the king was worried. There was nothing to worry him about. I will tell you when they are married."

"Did anything—was there trouble—"

"No. No trouble. Unciel, you are taxing your strength over nothing."

"Perhaps."

"I will send word to you very soon. Let go of the dark. Are you alone?"

"No."

"Good. Let go of me. Rest."

Unciel's breathing had become louder than the wind. For a moment longer he held the dark land around them. Euan heard him struggling to speak. Then the winds escaped, and the stars scattered, and Euan heard the candle fall over. He rose quickly, opened the door for light, and found the true night filling the house. The candle flared again. The light shook badly in the wizard's hand. Euan heard him groan.

He caught the sagging wizard before he fell, and took the candle. Unciel, trembling, could barely stay on his feet. Euan slid an arm firmly around him, still hearing the singing winds among the trees, still expecting a wilderness as he guided Unciel through the door.

He said inanely, to keep the wizard awake on his feet, "Then all is well. The princess is safe and the king will be relieved."

He had to listen for a long time before a rustle of leaf, of raven's feathers, answered him. "A no and a no and a nothing equals something. Especially in Serre."

If you did not trust him, Euan asked silently for the hundredth time since that night, why did you send him with her?

He finally had a chance to ask when he and Unciel ate together at mid-day.

Unciel, eating very little as slowly as possible, seemed to bring his thoughts back from another country before he answered. "I trust him with the princess," he said absently. "He would defend her with all his powers. I don't trust him with himself."

Euan brought a thumb up, scratched at his forehead. "What does that mean?"

Unciel gave him an oddly searching look. "Do you know yourself?"

Euan considered himself. "I think so. I always find my shoes in the same place. I always clean my pens."

"You fell in love with the princess."

Euan opened his mouth, closed it. He felt the blood flare into his face, as he remembered the hot, sweet, motionless light, the princess's hair the color of light, jewelled at the hair-line with little beads of sweat. "I didn't—That was unexpected."

"Do you remember how you felt?"

"Of course." He had to swallow before he continued, a trifle stiffly, "Are you expecting Gyre to fall in love with her?"

"Not exactly," Unciel said, "but if such an unexpected thing could happen even in this quiet cottage, then imagine what might happen to you in Serre, where nothing is predictable. How could you know what you might do until you do it?"

"How could anyone know?"

"And yet you say you know yourself."

Euan was silent. There was an answer to the riddle the wizard had presented to him, but it eluded him. He chewed a bite of stewed kale, asked tentatively, "But you can never know what will happen, so how can you know how you will react?"

"You act," Unciel said simply. "And then you know. Which is what Serre might ask you to do in as many different ways as it can dream up."

Euan sighed. "I don't understand anything."

"Then you understand something very important."

Euan shook his head to clear it. "But what has all this to do with Gyre? Why do you not trust what he told you? That there is nothing to worry about?"

"Because," the wizard said grimly, "I know Serre too well. It may be that Gyre simply could not speak freely at that moment. I will have to ask him again."

Euan swallowed a bite or two more before that sank in. He stared at the wizard, aghast. "You'll kill yourself. The king didn't ask you to do that. Why did you send Gyre? I've copied enough of your writings to know how many others you could have asked to guard the princess."

The wizard's face, after his recent weakness, seemed barely more than a mask over bone. Something of that night's power lingered in his eyes. They seemed clearer, Euan thought; the wizard might have been looking out of his kitchen window at the incomprehensible land of Serre. Or at Gyre.

"Gyre owes me," he answered and got up, his carrots and parsley calling him from the garden. Euan watched him helplessly. Words, he decided, were inadequate at best, impossible at worst. They meant too many things. Or they meant nothing at all. Later, seated at his desk again, he contemplated them bewilderedly. Where did the truth in them lie? If every word he spoke meant nothing more than itself, then how could that add up to a lie?

He whispered, "No and no and nothing equals something." He propped his chin on his fist, gazed morosely out at the wizard, who was dropping peas into an apron pocket. "What," Euan asked aloud, "if it simply equals nothing? Then you could go on gardening and forget about magic."

The wizard seemed to, for a few days. Once it rained from morning till night. Unciel sat in the house with the raven on his shoulder and the cat on his knee. He lifted his hand to stroke it now and then. Beyond that, Euan did not see him move; he barely blinked. He might have been napping with his eyes open. More likely, Euan thought uneasily, he was thinking. At least he was resting.

The next day Euan finished an account of Unciel's travels in a northern land, where he learned some peculiar sorcery involving fishbones, amber, and water pulled to its highest by the full moon. He took another tale out of the chest, sorted through the papers for a beginning, a middle, and an end. The hurried scrawl was difficult, the adventures absorbing. Euan wrote for hours before he realized that he had not seen Unciel at all that morning. The late summer day was cloudy; already leaves in the old vines were beginning to turn. But the rain had stopped, and Euan expected to find the wizard in the garden when he finally looked at midday. Hungry, he checked the kitchen. It was silent, tidy. One plate, one cup, and a cold meal of bread and beef and tomatoes lay on the table. Euan frowned at it, perplexed. Unciel rarely left the house; he could barely keep his balance among his quiet plants, let alone on the lively city streets. Most likely, Euan decided, the king had sent for him. He ate his solitary meal, still wondering, and went back to work.

He was making his way toward some dangerous sorcery the wizard had been asked to unravel when he heard a door open within the house. The raven gave a sudden screech that sent Euan's nib jittering across the page. He got up quickly without knowing why. He saw nothing in the hall. A door that had always been closed had unlatched itself. Nothing more. He went toward it, his breathing suddenly erratic. He heard the wizard's voice, inarticulate and very faint, from within the room. Euan slammed the door open and fell on his knees beside Unciel.

The wizard lay face down on the floor; Euan put an ear to his back to hear his heartbeat. One outstretched hand clutched something. The scribe took it from him gently, rolled him over. Unciel's eyes flickered open; he gripped Euan's arm.

"Bring it," he whispered. "Help me up."

"I'll help you to bed. Then I'll go for the king's physician—"

"No. I could never lie well. Just put me to bed."

"Maybe," Euan breathed as the wizard half-walked and the scribe half-dragged him, "you can't lie. But you can raise a fog of obscurity well enough when you want to." He pushed open the door the wizard indicated, and Unciel dropped onto his bed. Euan piled silk and skins on him, then stood anxiously a moment, listening to his breathing.

The wizard, his eyes closed, whispered, "There is a small amber jar in the kitchen."

He drank from it, when Euan brought it to him. Foxglove, Euan guessed, and who knew what else? It was only then, as he watched the wizard grow so still that he seemed entranced, that Euan remembered the thing locked in his left hand.

He studied it. It seemed nothing: a common, milky crystal the size and shape of a hen's egg, with a jagged streak of black through it. He laid it carefully down on the table next to Unciel's bed, beside the amber bottle and a small book with a pen marking its place. There was a jar of ink beside the book. Euan drew a breath, held it, adding book, pen, ink, and coming up with yet another tale. Perhaps, he thought with sudden, avid curiosity, there in that book was the one tale Unciel had never told anyone. Eyes clinging to it, he let his breath out again slowly. No. The price was too high. The wizard would never trust him again. He brought a pitcher of water and a cup from the kitchen, then drew a chair up to the bed and waited.

Unciel came alive again some time near evening. Euan, who had fallen asleep, felt a hand on his wrist. He pulled himself awake, blinking at the wizard. The one-eyed cat lay at the foot of the bed; the raven perched in a casement. Euan saw the darkening sky beyond it.

His mouth was a desert, he felt suddenly, and poured a cup of water. But he found himself holding it to the wizard's mouth, which was also a desert, he knew, because. Because, he thought confusedly, then enlightened himself. Because that was the way the wizard had asked for water. Unciel, his face the color of bone, his eyes cloudy, looked at him silently again, and Euan found a candle in his head.

He lit a couple of tapers, brought one to stand on the table between them. "What do you want me to do?" he asked gently. "Do you want a physician?"

No, the still eyes told him.

"Do you want me to stay with you?"

Yes.

"Do you want anything? Wine? Food? One of your potions?"

He found a pale crystal with a black lightning bolt through it in his head, and he picked it up from the table, let the wizard see it. The weary, unblinking eyes gazed into it for a long time, as though it contained worlds, mysteries, the answers to unanswerable riddles. He closed his eyes finally.

Euan, putting the stone down, ventured to ask, "What is it?"

No and no and nothing, he heard. And then, as the wizard slipped off a precipice into sleep, nothing more.

ELEVEN

The face and form of Prince Ronan of Serre returned to his father's summer palace very early in the morning, just as the moon slipped beyond the western mountains into Dacia. Gyre, who had shaped Ronan's gaunt, starved, magic-ridden body so completely he carried even the prince's hunger, had walked on foot up the granite face of the cliff. He had let his powers drain down into the deepest, most secret parts of his mind. He had buried his name where even Ferus's blind eye, with its intimations of omniscience, would never see it. The misused body, with one bare, blistered foot, was exhausted by the climb up the hard, winding road. He did not notice the guards on the wall staring down at the bedraggled, limping figure with its powerful breadth of shoulder and hair touched to fire by a last finger of moonlight. They raised a shout. The man sank down at the foot of the closed gates and went to sleep.

Later, he woke to find a scarred, snarling, pit-eyed creature looming over him. The wizard started, then remembered the savage face of the King of Serre. The single eye, black and fulminating like a thunderhead about to kindle lightning, studied the prince's face and grew less ominous.

"It's about time," he said roughly. He clamped a thumb and forefinger along the prince's jaws, turned his head this way and that. "You look sane enough. The queen said you had been bewitched by Brume. Are you free of her? Or is this another of her tricks?"

He loosed the prince, who shook his head slightly and pushed himself up. As though the room spun around him, he dropped his face in his hands. "I am free," he whispered. "I was—I have been running mad in the forest. It seems like a dream now."

"Are you hurt?"

"No. Only hungry." He let his hands fall, took a cautious glance at the unfamiliar room. There were no windows in it, just stone walls hung with bright ribbons of tapestry. It must be deep within the palace; he would have to open a wizard's ear to hear the sound of water.

"Good." The king's huge hand closed on his neck, one thumb pushing against his throat as if feeling for a vein, or a thread of breath. The single eye came so close to the prince's that it divided into two, both charred, unblinking. "No more running. You will wed by day's end or I'll toss you back to Brume myself and you can take a bath in her cauldron. Which is it?"

He said as clearly as he could around the probing thumb, "I will wed."

"Well, we can thank the witch for that much," the king said dourly, and loosed him. He opened the chamber door, said to the hovering servants, "Get him ready for his wedding."

He was bathed, shorn, fed, dressed without needing to utter a word, let alone assemble an entire sentence that might have been spoken by the prince. He was weakened, it was understood. He had barely escaped death in the shape of the witch, and madness in the beguiling shape of the firebird. That he had returned at all was a tribute to his strength and an indomitable will to live despite himself. He had come back to wed; he would give his father heirs for Serre. If he spoke strangely now, or produced an opinion not formerly held, or had trouble remembering things he had known all his life, that could be blamed on the vagaries of magic. No one, he suspected, would care what he said that day as long as he said yes.

At last, resplendent in black silk and cloth of gold, a ceremonial sword at his side that looked as ancient as a tree in the forests below and felt about as heavy, he was taken to meet the woman he would marry.

She rose as he entered her chamber. Her attendants clustered around her in pale silks and satins; clouds, his eye told him, in the wake of the rising sun. The tall, slender young woman in a gold gown webbed with pearls startled him. Surely that could not be Sidonie, who had nearly shot him in his raven's shape, who had tossed a frog out of her pavilion one morning as handily as any stable-boy. Something stirred deep within the hidden wizard. He had, Gyre realized suddenly, acquired a heart. It confused him; he had never had one before. Her courage moved him; so did her grave eyes, which, he suddenly saw, were the color of the hour he loved best, when the last haunting moments of day shifted toward the deepest purples of twilight. They changed now, as she gazed at him, darkened into that secret promise of night. He had touched her heart, he thought with wonder. So he felt, in that magic, timeless moment before he remembered whose face he wore.

The realization made him awkward; he fell short by half a step, which the princess attributed to the exhaustion from his misadventures.

She said quickly, "Please, my lord Ronan, sit." She took his hand, to his astonishment, and guided him to a chair. Then she glanced at her attendants, the guards at the open door. She asked the prince softly, "May we be alone?"

He tried to think; a guard answered for him. "My lady, we dare not let him out of our sight. But if you leave the door open, we can watch him from the hall. He must not go near the windows."

She nodded, gesturing to her attendants. When the watching eyes were all beyond the threshold, and the prince as far from views of water and trees as possible, she sat down beside him. He watched her fingers tighten, twist slightly before she spoke. The callouses were softening, he saw. She had given away her bow, he remembered; caged, she could have only shot at reflections in the water.

"My lord," she said quietly, "do you remember me?"

"I do." Even his voice was not his own, the wizard

thought ruefully; it was deeper, husky, tentative. "You told me your name when we met in the forest."

"I know that you have—that you are still in mourning. I am sorry." She hesitated, loosed a breath, and held his eyes. "I only want to say that you don't have to run from me. I won't ask you for things you cannot give. I only hope that we can become friends. If such a thing is possible in this place."

The wizard hesitated. It does not matter, he told himself, which of us she loves as long as she marries me. A name, a kingdom, the possibility of an heir to his powers and the vast, astonishing powers of Serre, would be his before nightfall, if the wizard himself only relinquished the possibility of love. The true prince, whom he had left without a voice in the deadly house of the witch, would likely be safe enough for a day or two. If he chose, Gyre could rescue him after the wedding, set him free to wear his life to the bone in pursuit of the firebird. He would die or go mad before he found his way beyond the magic and back into the world. Gyre could wear his face forever. If he chose.

At that moment, as he watched the familiar face of the princess with its unfamiliar expressions, as he heard the shift and catch of threads of lace at her uneven breath, forever seemed just long enough.

He heard himself whisper, "You must give me time."

"Yes," she said quickly. "Oh, yes."

"I remember that—you were kind to me in the forest."

A line quivered above her brows. "I threatened to shoot you."

"You gave me your bow."

"I thought you were an ogre."

"And now?"

She hesitated. Her voice grew very soft. "I was as terrified of you as of any ogre before I met you. I am still a little afraid. You are, after all, the ogre's son. But if we can continue to be kind to one another, maybe I will learn to see past your father's face, and you will see past—your past."

He nodded, wordless again, and reached out to touch a strand of tiny pearls circling the sleeve on the underside of her wrist. He heard her breath gather and stop. They both watched his fingers slide from pearl to glistening pearl. "How beautiful you have suddenly grown," he said in wonder, and raised his head confusedly as the breath came too swiftly out of her. "I mean, since I saw you in the forest."

"But you never saw me there," she said, giving him the beginnings of a smile. "You could only see the firebird."

"My lord," someone said stiffly from beyond the threshold. "The king."

The princess's face emptied itself of expression and much of its color. Sighing noiselessly, the wizard braced himself for an explosion because the prince had left his guards in the hall to enter a room singing with water and light. But the single eye seemed placated by what it saw in the prince's face.

Ferus said brusquely, "The queen asked to speak to you alone in her chamber. The princess will come with me." He held out an arm to her on his blind side, riveting her with his puckered, peering eye-socket. "Bring your mother to join us in the hall. Tell her to be brief. We have waited long enough for this moment."

He bowed his head, trying to remember where in the

palace he might find the queen. But the guards did not let him wonder beyond a step through the door; they gathered around him, led him to a small chamber overlooking the crux of separating waters.

The chamber was so full of tapestries, stories covering every stone, in fire and bone and gold, that the wizard felt he had stepped into one of the queen's tales. There was even an unfinished tale at her loom: something with three burly, crowned figures galloping after three bright foxes, who were also crowned. The queen, wearing delicate shades of lavender and grey, said the prince's name as he entered, and took his face between her hands. Startled, the wizard stood very still while she searched his eyes.

Her hands slid finally to his shoulders, tightened. "She freed you, then. You have truly returned."

"Yes."

"How? Brume never gives anything freely."

He hesitated, then decided to tell the tale he knew. He let his eyes slip away from hers, and said bitterly, "I paid her price."

"What was it?" she breathed.

"The firebird." The prince's voice shook slightly. "She wanted it in a cage to sing at her hearth while she boiled her bones."

"The firebird." She stared at him, astonished. "You caught it for her?"

"It wasn't easy."

"No, it can't have been—But how could you possibly—"

"I had no choice," he answered wearily. "There was no other way home."

She was silent, holding him lightly now, a fine line between her brows. "But what made you want to come back that badly?"

"I was so tired . . . I thought—I thought anything must be better than running like a wild thing through the forests after a dream. So I did what the witch demanded. I don't like to think about it."

"No." Her eyes seemed still puzzled, but she brushed his cheek with her fingers. "The firebird will not stay with her any longer than it chooses. Some day, when you can, tell me everything."

He nodded, catching her hand in his. "I will. We must go. The king is waiting for us."

"In a moment." She hesitated, her fingers tight around his, her pale eyes studying him again, trying to see into his heart. "I wanted to tell you that the princess seems to have a kind and loving disposition. How long she can keep it in this crazed household, I do not know. But don't—don't be afraid—"

"I've spoken with her," he said as indifferently as possible. "There's nothing to fear. I'll do all that my father wishes. The sooner the better, for all our sakes."

She loosed a breath. "I never imagined that the witch would lay your ghosts for you. But then Brume has always been unpredictable."

He was silent, trying to imagine Ronan's ghosts. "No one," he said evenly, "will ever lay them. They will stay in my heart until I die."

"I know."

"After my wedding, before the sun sets, I will lay flowers on their graves. Candles will burn on them all night long in their memory."

He felt her hands slacken, then tighten again quickly. She bowed her head; he could not see her eyes. Her voice shook a little when she spoke.

"We must go. The king will be impatient."

"Will you come with me," he asked, wanting to see her eyes. "To light the candles?"

She raised her head; he saw the sheen of grief across them again, the stark grey of winter. She could not speak, but she nodded quickly, and took his arm, clinging to him as he opened the door.

In the great hall overlooking half of Serre, the courtiers had gathered; the princess waited with her attendants. The queen drew the prince to his place in the light. Then she joined the king among his guards. She said something; frowning, Ferus bent his head to listen. The prince waited alone, framed by the sky and the brilliant flare of sun beyond the broad wall of casements. His eyes moved to the golden figure across the hall. Who would marry them? he wondered. Some hermit steeped in lore, so old his body had begun to twist like the roots of trees he lived among? Some good witch, who knew the name of every moss and mushroom in the forests?

No one joined him, he realized, surprised, a moment before the queen spoke again. Then he heard her voice, high and piercing, furious enough, he thought, to shatter glass.

"My son did not bury them!" she cried. "He burned

them, and sent their ashes down the falls! That's why we fear for him near water. You are some spell of Brume's—you are not my son!"

And then the fire came at him, the crude sorcery of the king's, which would never have touched him except that the queen's voice, so unexpectedly powerful in its anguish, held him stunned a moment too long. The wall of glass exploded around him. Every broken shard seemed to call his name as it fell, a rain of glass and Gyre. Stunned again, moving far too slowly, he felt the impetus of fire sweep him through the shattered casements. Fire-blown over an airy expanse of nothing, he heard his name again, a distant and astonishing voice out of the past, it seemed, and calling someone he no longer knew.

Then he began to feel the fire. He changed shape and dropped away from it, translucent as air, mirroring sky. He angled toward the water and fell with it a long, long way before he changed shape again. He crept on four legs behind the thundering water, and hid within the hollow of stone behind the falls until the moon rose. Then the king and the guards searching for the broken pieces of the witch's spell decided that it must have been a powerless thing of twigs and earth, and wended their way back up the cliff.

TWELVE

Sidonie sat in her chamber, surrounded by her attendants. They watched her; she stared numbly at nothing, her face pale and stiff, her hands motionless in her lap. She still wore her wedding gown. Now and then someone ventured to suggest that she let them undress her, put her to bed. She scarcely heard. Two images kept recurring in her mind whenever she tried to think. One was of the prince with his long copper hair and husky, tentative voice, his big fingers touching the pearls at her wrist as gently as if they might grow wings, take flight if disturbed. The other was of the same prince, his weary, harrowed face finally peaceful, looking at Sidonie across the hall just before the queen cried out and the fire picked him up, carried him through an explosion of glass into nothing, flames engulfing him as he began to fall.

It was not Ronan, the queen kept telling her. It was not my son.

Sidonie could not speak. She could not find words. She had never learned words for the sight of the man whom she had been sent endless miles to marry, tossed over a cliff a thousand feet above nothing by his father.

It was not Ronan, they told her. It was the witch's spell. Hours later, the queen had come very briefly to Sidonie's chamber to tell her: they found nothing of him at all. Nothing. Not a scrap of cloth, not even a blackened sword. It was as though the spell had vanished in mid-air.

The spell.

Not-Ronan.

The strange land beyond her windows was black; the moon floated on the swift water, its light rippled, tugged, pulled toward the long straight thundering fall through nothing. So Not-Ronan must have fallen, into water instead of earth; how else could they not find him? That spell that spoke so easily to her of things that Not-Ronan should not have known?

A chilly breeze slid between the casements; she shivered slightly. Her attendants, waiting silently, casting glances at her, stirred as though the breeze had shaken them. Sidonie's stiff fingers twitched. A word or two formed; her brows puckered.

"How," she whispered, and her attendants leaned toward her, listening breathlessly. She cleared her throat, but it had begun to burn painfully; she was forced to speak through fire. "How could Not-Ronan have known that I gave him my bow?" She was seeing her attendants again, their worried, frightened faces. "Do witches know such things?"

They could not tell her.

"My lady," one said, her own voice trembling. "It is inconceivable that the King of Serre would have killed his son."

"So it was Not-Ronan."

"So it must be, my lady."

So the way the prince had looked at her in that chamber, the way his fingers had so lightly touched the pearls around her wrist, had also been illusion. The things she had said to him, the things he had said: time, forest, ogre, bow, past, friends . . .

Illusion.

Faces blurred; again she had to push words past fire. "I could have loved that Not-Ronan." Again he turned his head to find her across the hall; again the deadly sorcery swept him out, away. She blinked, saw her attendants again, one or two weeping silently, the others trying to hide their terror. She gripped the arms of the chair, rose stiffly. They had come too far with her for her to leave them so adrift.

They clustered around her eagerly, unbuttoning, untying, loosening. There was a moment of stillness during which they all looked doubtfully at the wedding dress. The princess quelled an impulse to fling it over the falls. She said wearily, "There must be some place for it out of my sight . . ."

Later, as she sat sleeplessly in bed between a brace of

candles, she felt another thought, urgent, perplexing, and as troubling as anything else, loom into her head.

Where, she wondered, was Gyre?

Death had been a guest at her not-wedding. The wizard should have felt her horror and shock half-way across Serre. Unless he was ensorcelled by the witch, or dead, too. Dead, she amended. The missing Ronan was still a mystery. Now so was the wizard. The peaceful forests she had passed through seemed to have swallowed them both. She slid down beneath the silks and furs, her eyes wide, watching the frail light flutter against the night. Perhaps, she thought in wild hope, the wizard had gone back to Dacia to raise an army to rescue her. If not, what had come so unexpectedly alive within the trees below that could threaten even Gyre?

She caught the noiseless glide of the opening door out of the corner of her eye and went rigid with terror. The queen, still in her lavender silks, the candle in her hand illumining her pale, distant eyes, was not a reassuring sight. Sidonie watched wordlessly as Calandra closed the door softly behind her. She came to the bed, gazed down at Sidonie a moment. Then she put the candle on a table and sat down beside the motionless princess.

"I thought you might be awake," she said softly. "I could not come earlier. The king is deep in his sorceries now, searching for our son." Sidonie, haunted again by the startling image of their son on fire and falling like a star, could not speak. Fine lines of pain and despair appeared and disappeared on the queen's face. Her eyes lost their frozen sheen, became shadowed with memory. She went on, picking up a thread, it seemed, in the middle of a tale. "My son made a pyre on the rock behind the palace at the point where the water divides. He built it of seasoned wood overlaid with fresh boughs still fragrant with pitch and pine. He covered the wood with all the tapestries in their chamber, all the stories. His wife and the child on her heart were also wrapped in rich cloths and tapestries; their faces were hidden. On them, he laid flowers, all the autumn wildflowers that had been gathered that day along the river up here and the meadows below. He stood with them, silent, alone, from sunset to moonrise. When he raised the torch, we went to stand with him. We watched them burn. At sunrise, he gathered the ashes with his hands and let them fall, handful by handful, into the water. We watched him for days, weeks, afterward, to see that he did not follow them." She paused, swallowed. "You see. This is not something my son would have forgotten. Yet when the man who wore my son's face spoke to me alone before the wedding, he asked me to come with him, after you were married, to lay flowers and light candles on the graves of his dead wife and child. There were no graves." Her voice shook, ragged with sorrow. "He should have known. There were no graves."

Sidonie drew what felt like her first breath since the chamber door had opened. She brushed at a cold tear. "He loved her that much."

"Yes."

Illusion turned its face to look at her across the great hall. "Then who was the man I was about to marry?"

"The king believes that he was the witch's spell, sent to

torment us. Perhaps he was meant to entice you also into her hands." But the king's explanation seemed to perplex her; she added, "All of Serre would have suffered from that. It seems unlike Brume. People chance across her; she does not reach out to them beyond her world." She hesitated. "What he—the spell—told me about the firebird troubled me, too, but I let it pass. He was not very coherent about it, and I was too relieved to see that face to question him."

"The firebird?"

"He said that he had caught it in a cage and given it to the witch to gain his freedom. But that is like putting your heart in a cage and leaving it with Brume. Whatever you have gained, it is not freedom."

Sidonie was silent, remembering the true prince's face, spellbound by beauty, turning away from her toward the firebird. She sighed a little, and shifted to sit up. "But how did the man who was the spell know about my bow, and not know about the funeral pyre?"

"Your bow?"

"When I met Ronan in the forest, he had nothing, not even a knife to hunt with. I gave him my bow. I thought he could protect himself from witches with an arrow. The man who was the spell recognized me; he said to me: 'You gave me your bow.' How could he have known about that if he was not Ronan?" She looked beyond memory into the queen's eyes, holding them, and whispered, "That was why I thought he must be your son—I could not understand—"

"I'm sorry." The queen's hand covered hers quickly, closed. "What a terrible—"

"Not-wedding."

"I don't know about your bow. I don't understand any of this. The wizard is still searching for him; perhaps he will bring us some answers."

Sidonie's mouth tightened over that mystery. The queen, she thought, had found and lost her son again; she did not need to lose all hope. She said finally, bleakly, "Thank you for coming. I may be able to sleep now."

The queen rose, looked down at her a moment longer. "At least," she answered more accurately, "you will not lie awake in terror thinking we had killed our son."

Sidonie, buried in a cave of bed-clothes and contemplating her fate until the small hours, came to the only possible conclusion before the dark roaring water surged over her and swept her into sleep: Escape.

In the morning, as she stared out of an open window in search of possibilities of freedom while her attendants huddled and whispered together behind her, Sidonie watched a golden hawk swoop above the lip of the falls and disappear overhead. She saw its reflection in the water as it lighted on the wall, then vanished again. Gyre, she said silently, without hope. The reflection of his face, pale, bruised, hollowed with weariness, appeared in answer on the water below her window.

He sent for her in the afternoon. The king's guards escorted her to his chamber in the back of the palace. She said nothing to him until he spoke to the guards and closed the door. His voice sounded calm as ever, but there was an odd, haunted look in his eyes that she had never seen before. He cradled one forearm as though it pained him; there was a bruise on his forehead that his hair did not quite hide.

"We can speak freely," he said to her. "I wove such a thunder of water into the stones around us that even Ferus could not hear his own name."

"What happened to you?" She felt her eyes swell and burn with unshed tears. "Where were you when I needed you?"

"I was—I could not come. I was caught like a fish by the peculiar magic of Serre; it took all night for me to break free."

He had that look, she saw, as though he had been played like a mouse and barely escaped with his life. "Was it Brume?"

"No. More like one of those ogres in Auri's tales. They are more clever than I thought."

"I told you so," she whispered. "I warned you not to laugh at them."

"I'm not laughing," he said somberly. "The king told me what happened while I was gone. He is furious and desperate—"

"Take me home. You have the power."

He hesitated, gestured at himself. "Look at me. I have the power to rescue you from Ferus, but how can I get you safely out of Serre?"

"I don't care. I don't care. Just get me out of the palace and I will walk all the way to Dacia. The prince has most likely been eaten by Brume, and the queen told me that

Ferus will use me to cause war between Serre and Dacia. I'm very certain my father never intended me to marry a man who could possibly, under any circumstances, get eaten by a witch. If you take me home, my father will have no reason to attack Serre."

"And King Ferus will have no reason to attack Dacia. But he will. And if you don't live with him here, you will live with him on the throne in Dacia."

"But at least I will—"

He held up his hand. "Please," he begged her. "Please. I need to ask you something. I need to know exactly how much trouble we are in."

She felt her face grow tight with apprehension. "Now what?"

"What did you tell Ferus about your magical powers? He said they were locked up in a box somewhere and demanded that I bring them here so that you could use them to search for Ronan."

She opened her mouth; nothing came out. She brought one hand up to cover it and stared at him, appalled. "It was a story," she whispered.

"So I gathered." His own face was suddenly colorless, the bruise vivid on his brow.

"I just—I told him that because I was terrified of what he might do to me—and to Dacia—if I told him I have no powers at all to bring to Serre. I never thought—I thought that Ronan would be found, and then I would be married, and our children might inherit such powers, and so Ferus would never have to know that I—that I lied."

"I see." He didn't seem to; he stared very blankly at nothing for a breath before he asked her, "And did you tell him where this box full of your powers might be found?"

"No. I said that Unciel had advised me to tell no one."

He winced, as at a sudden flare of pain. "Unciel."

"But that you would get it for me when you returned."

"Do I know where it is?"

"I don't remember."

He drew breath, sat down on a casement ledge. Beyond him she saw the broad expanse of granite narrowing to the point where the river separated into its twin strands. There, she realized dazedly, where stone parted water, Ronan had built his funeral pyre.

"Then I'll have to find it," he said simply.

"Take me with you."

"No. It is too dangerous." He thought a moment, his eyes wide, contemplating possibilities. "Then I must find Ronan, too," he added slowly, "whether he is alive or spellbound or dead. And bring him back with a convincing tale about the box full of your magic. What does it look like?"

"I didn't say. The powers themselves are hidden in a jewel in the box. My voice," she added, remembering, "is the key to the box. It will open only for me."

"Inspired," he commented. There was an unfamiliar edge to his voice, but she could hardly blame him.

"What happens—what happens when you don't bring the box?"

"I am hoping that the king will be so overjoyed or so grieved to see his son that he'll forget about your magical powers."

She swallowed dryly. "If he doesn't? Or if you don't find Ronan?"

His jaw tightened, his hand sliding along his arm to ease it. "Someone will have to chance along and steal the box . . . Such things happen."

"What happened to your arm?"

"I came too close to the ogre's fire. Sorcery burns deeper and is harder to heal than fire." He stood up again, and came to her, took her hand gently. "I will find your bridegroom and a tale to explain away your magic. Be patient, and try to stay out from under Ferus's eye." He paused a little, as though waiting for some word from her, something more inspiring than the tale she had told.

But she only slid her free hand tightly over his and said, "Be careful. Please. This time find him."

The wizard was gone by twilight. She watched the hawk spiral into the purple sky, dropping lower and lower above the darkening trees until she could not separate him from the shadows. Much later, in the dead of night and maybe far too late, she woke herself out of a dream of the hawk and remembered that the wizard had watched her give her bow to Ronan; he had heard every word between them; he had been there, silent and unnoticed, from the moment they had met.

I came too close to the ogre's fire, he had said. Sorcery burns deep . . .

"Gyre," she said without sound, and felt as though the entire palace, rock-island and all, were on the verge of breaking loose in the relentless grip of wizardry to follow all that Ronan had loved over the edge of the falls.

THIRTEEN

Heartless, Ronan could not feel the firebird's song.

He noticed that absently as he left the witch's house and began his search for the wizard Gyre. As he walked among the sleeping trees, he saw the firebird in all its beauty, a melting of feather and flame, sitting high atop a tree in the distance. It sang to a setting star. The pure, unearthly voice that had transfixed Ronan, stunned his heart and left him thoughtless, now sounded like any other forest noise: mysterious yet familiar, belonging to the predictable patterns of life within the trees. It made no more impression on him than an owl hooting. The firebird fell silent as he walked beneath it without stopping. He did glance up at it, as though in the hollow where his heart had been, he heard an echo. Its long neck curved; a golden eye peered down, watching him pass.

He had no idea where he was going or how far he was from his father's palace. For his path, he trusted the witch. If she wanted the wizard, she must show Ronan the way home. He walked until the long night bore down on him even as the sun rose. His eyes flickered; he hurtled to meet the dark as it swept toward him. He slept where he fell.

He woke sometime later, his body drenched in hot, late summer noon, his face in shadow. He lay baking on a sheet of dry, prickling needles, a seed cone under one cheek. He lifted his head with an effort, remembering piecemeal: the wizard, the witch, the firebird's cage, what he said, what she said . . . He was on his way home . . . A trickle of liquid fire snagged his eye. He pushed himself up onto his elbows and saw the firebird.

His face had rested in its shadow. Perched on the ground, it loomed over him; its molten eyes, burning like the sun, seemed as alien and remote. He could have reached out and touched that rich tangle of iridescent plumes and what looked like windblown feathers of fire. Its long neck arched like a swan's over its back. Its wings pooled around it in drifting ripples of plumes.

He made a small sound, the beginning of a question. To his utter astonishment, it answered.

"Prince Ronan." Its voice was quite pleasing, he thought; it was as though a flute had spoken. "I have heard tales of your kindness to the owl, the toad, and the wolf. Will you help me?"

They seemed like dreams now, all the speaking animals. He sat up groggily, brushed dust and needles out of his hair. "Perhaps," he said guardedly, for he owed the firebird nothing, and already his eyes were searching above the trees for the familiar face of the cliff. Then he remembered that the firebird had shaded his face as he slept. A small thing, but the forest animals seemed to place great value on such small things. So he brought his attention back to the firebird. "Tell me what's wrong."

"The firebird lays one egg and has one hatchling every seven years. The wind tossed my egg out of the nest. I am afraid that it will slip out of my claws if I try to carry it. Will you put my egg back into the nest for me?"

It seemed a small thing, so he said, "Yes."

He followed the firebird for a long time through constantly changing shadow and light. It waited while he drank from a stream; he could hear it rustling fretfully on a branch above his head. He quelled his own impatience, for one direction seemed as good as another to him; they all looked alike. Finally the firebird stopped beneath a great tree that looked no different from any other tree, and brushed at needles and dry leaves beneath it. Hidden in a cradle of roots lay the most beautiful egg that Ronan had ever seen.

It held all the shimmering hues of fire, webbed with a delicate overlay of gold. He picked it up. It covered his broad palm, and was as heavy as though the shell were carved of fiery jewels and threaded with true gold. The firebird laid her head on it, and he felt, through the warm, glowing shell, the quick fluttering of the heartbeat within.

"It is still alive," the firebird said, and sang something to the dream of itself within the egg.

"Where is the nest?" Ronan asked, glancing through the branches above him. He had whiled away much of the day following the firebird. The slant of shadows began to wear at him; he wanted to find his way out of the forest before dark.

"Climb," the firebird said. "I'll wait for you beside my nest."

It flew away before he could speak again. The nest could not be very high, he thought; the egg would have broken if it had fallen far. After a moment's thought, he pulled off his remaining boot, put the egg gently into it, and tucked the boot into his tunic above the belt. Then he began to climb.

He expected to see the firebird at every branch. But it was always higher; he would glimpse a drifting plume above the next branch, and then above the next. He climbed until, looking down, he could not see the ground through the thick green fans of branches. Looking up, he could not see the sun, only the firebird's eye, blazing down at him. It was just above him, just a little farther. He raised a foot to the next branch, reached high and caught another with his hand, lifted his other foot, reached again, and again, until, half-blind with sweat and locked into the rhythms of the growing tree, he felt that he had been climbing most of his life. The firebird's nest was on top of the world, somewhere in the clouds; at night stars had to veer around it as they wheeled across the sky. He climbed so high that he left everything behind except his name and the egg trembling with life against his breast.

Finally he heard the firebird's voice. "Here."

It perched next to his hand beside its nest. It was a palace of a nest, he saw as he leaned into the amber-scented bark and panted. The nest balanced between two strong boughs, an enormous, broad-brimmed hat fashioned out of spider-web, dried flowers, mosses, and vines. When he had caught his breath, he freed the boot from his tunic and tipped the egg gently into the nest. The firebird nuzzled it with its face, then shifted its body onto the nest, delicately uncoiling plumes and arranging feathers as it sat. Ronan dropped the boot tiredly, looked down to watch it fall.

He saw the whole of the forest laid out like a tapestry beneath him: a background of green in which strange bright figures moved busily through their tales. Witches and hermits, ogres, foxes and languorous water sprites went their mysterious ways, stirring cauldrons, speaking to animals, cudgeling one another. Magic spiralled in scarlet and blue threads from their fingers; song unwound in gold from the throats of birds. Ronan, so high above it that the figures seemed no bigger than stitches in the tapestry, clung like an insect to the great tree, his mouth dry, his blood pounding against the wood. He scarcely knew what he saw, or where he was now, except above it all. He closed his eyes against the terrifying, overwhelming vision of Serre and heard the firebird again.

"Look how far you have come. Don't be afraid. Open your eyes."

He dragged them open to stare incredulously at the firebird and saw his father's palace.

It rose just across from him, its dark towers and flanks burnished with afternoon light. What he had thought must be his own blood thundering in his ears was the churning fall of water hollowing out the stones below and trying to leap back up the cliff. If he had not left his heart with

Brume, he might have wept with relief at the sight of it, or felt his heart grow shriveled and hard with memory and despair. As it was, he only felt his fear go the way of his boot. He was gazing at the palace, wondering how far away it might be on foot, when the wall of windows across the great hall blew apart like a thousand glass birds startled into flight. A ball of fire followed them. It swallowed all the luminous birds, then began to unravel, revealing its heart. Ronan glimpsed the helpless, plummeting body of a man among the flames just before he vanished.

His muscles slackened with shock; he nearly slid out of the tree and fell to earth himself. He gripped the trunk, trembling, trying to make sense of the crazed image in his head. The wizard had killed his father. His father had killed the wizard. His father, deranged with frustration at the loss of his heir, had scoured the hall with his temper and flung some poor innocent out the window. Ronan found himself moving again, still shaken, weak with horror, one bare foot feeling awkwardly for the branch below.

"I have to go home," he told the firebird.

It did not answer, only began what sounded like a lullaby. Ronan left it nesting and descended with the sun into dark. When he could feel no more branches beneath his feet, he closed his eyes and dropped to the bottom of the night.

He woke sprawled on tree roots, thirsty, starving, with a stark memory in his head of the summer palace belching a fireball that turned into a man streaming fire as he began to fall.

Mystified, he stumbled to his feet to search for water. Later, eating early apples in a clearing with the deer, he saw the cliff rising above the trees with its twin ribbons of water spilling down along the dark walls and towers, and the end of the road turning into its gates.

He began the long walk home.

The wizard found him just as he reached the road at the bottom of the falls. The moon would light his path up the steep, dangerous cliff, he hoped, when it got around to rising. He dared not stop. If he closed his eyes, the road might vanish, along with the falls and the palace; he could easily find himself back in the interminable maze of the witch's mind. In the deafening pound of water, he would not have heard a dozen bellowing trolls waving cudgels at him, let alone a wizard who made no more sound than the small bats flitting through the twilight. Ronan had barely taken a step or two beyond the forest, up the sheer ascent of stone, when he heard a voice cut with startling clarity through the thunder of the falls.

"Ronan. I expected to find you with the witch."

He stopped dead, as though the words were a spell. The moon, igniting the water high above, spilled a swathe of light down the cliff, illumining a shadow on the road ahead of Ronan. Gyre, he thought, stunned. But of course the wizard would come to stop him before he showed his true face to his father.

"I expected," he said thinly, trying to think without words so that the wizard would not hear, "to find you with the princess."

The wizard was silent a breath; the shadow, under Ronan's unwavering stare, inched down the road. "How did you get free of Brume?" Gyre wondered. "And you're free of the firebird, as well. What did you do? What did you promise the witch?"

"She flung me out of her cottage when I bit her. The cage broke, and I escaped. I have not seen the firebird."

"You have not answered me at all." The shadow flowed over pebbles, silent and barely perceptible. "She let you see your way home. What did you promise her this time?" He waited; the shadow shrugged slightly at Ronan's silence. "You'll tell me. You'll tell me everything I need to know before I take you back to your father and let him see that I have found you." Ronan blinked. The shadow gave a soft laugh. "And then we will trade faces, you and I. You will leave Serre and all your memories of it behind you forever." The shadow held up a hand at Ronan's sudden movement. The wizard's voice grew very soft, almost gentle. "You can't run from me." His shadow slid closer. Ronan, his eyes wide, unblinking, could only watch it come. Nothing else in the night seemed to move either, as though the world had been caught up in the wizard's spell. Even the roar of water might have been only an echo of itself. "You simply have the misfortune of being in the way of something I want. Without you here, I can take it. And so you must forget everything you ever were . . ."

The shadow flowed over Ronan, hiding even his face from the moon. Staring at the void limned by moonlight into the shape of the wizard's face, Ronan could not move an eyelash; he could not feel himself breathe. He felt the shadow seep, as steadily and persistently as it had crossed stones, through his eyes, his bones, to lie like night across his thoughts.

The firebird sang. Ronan heard it from very far away, as he might have heard a star sing. He recognized it as he would have recognized a star, something incomprehensible but familiar. The distant flame, the distant song, would be all he could ever know about either star or firebird. But for an instant his thoughts, mingling with the wizard's, revolved around that sweet fire; it turned his breath into song, his blood into fire, all of Serre in the firebird's night into poetry.

Then he saw moonlight again on the road ahead of him. Gyre's face was finally visible as he stepped away from Ronan. Ronan stared at him, bewildered, beginning to shake. The wizard, his face taut, dreaming, seemed to have forgotten him. He walked around Ronan and down the road. Ronan turned and saw the firebird.

She stood at the road's end, in all her wild beauty of fire and ivory, bird and human. Her golden eyes, warm and beguiling with light, fixed on the wizard as she sang to him. Gyre went toward her without a word, without a faltering step. As he drew close, she withdrew, slowly, note by note, into the forest. The trees seemed to shift around her. Gyre stepped off the road; they opened to take him in.

Ronan stood alone, stunned. All that the wizard had wanted, he had given away for a song. The prince had heard it once, he knew, but he remembered it only vaguely as he remembered love and loss, something that had happened to him once, but that now seemed as remote as someone else's dream.

He stirred finally, realizing that no distance he put between himself and the wizard would be far enough. The moon would set; the firebird would sleep; the wizard would awaken. All the warriors in the summer palace, all the king's sorcery, would not be enough to keep Ronan safe from the wizard who wanted his face, his name, his heritage, his life. Now, while Gyre was spellbound, lost to the world, was the time to rid Serre of the unscrupulous wizard and drag his bones to Brume to whistle in the wind on her roof.

Ronan picked up the nearest likely stone and moved soundlessly toward the wizard, who was barely more than a shadow again, trailing after the singing woman. Before Ronan could step off the road, something pale and bulky, with a single round eye reflecting moonlight the color of bone, ran up behind the woman. Ronan caught a trenchant whiff of it and stopped. The cottage squatted there. Its door opened.

The firebird, swaying dreamily backward as she lured the wizard forward, stepped across the threshold. Ronan saw her white hand beckoning from within. The wizard followed, bending his head as he walked into the little house of bone. The door closed. The moon, the stars, the wordless prince, stared as the great, splayed feet and burly calves of the witch hoisted the cottage off the ground and ran it back into the forests of Serre.

After what seemed a very long time, Ronan dropped the rock and discovered a coherent thought.

He whispered, "I am free."

No one lured him, trapped him, requested his help, made impossible demands. No one, at the moment, paid any attention to him at all. He could sleep in his own bed that night, if he got himself to the top of the cliff without falling off. He turned, began the climb.

He stopped, after a step or two. There was something he had left to do, something he had forgotten . . . He couldn't remember. Nothing seemed to be missing except his boots. Nothing, then, that was important. He began to walk again, up the road the moonlight carved for him across the stone.

FOURTEEN

Euan tended the wizard for days before Unciel spoke again.

By then, the scribe had gotten used to ideas and images forming in his mind with the random inconsistency of dreams. He interpreted them as best he could, finding odd potions for the wizard, letting the raven out at dawn to feed, letting the cat in and out and in again, trying to keep up with the overladen bushes and vines and roots when Unciel began to fret about them and Euan found a monstrous garden growing in his head. The kitchen became crowded with beans, squashes, cabbages. Euan, kneeling to rummage through cupboards for elixirs and oils, dodged potatoes rambling overhead and fought for space among the beets and carrots piled on the floor. He barely knew how to boil water, which was moot since the wizard refused to eat. He would not let Euan send for a physician. He preferred his own noxiously hued remedies which smelled, Euan thought, acrid enough to dissolve bone. When he was not sleeping, he stared, his eyes feverish and distant, at the milky crystal with the jagged bolt of black suspended in its heart.

One morning, Euan, sleeping on musty furs on the floor beside the wizard's bed, woke with a vivid image of mushrooms sprouting in his head.

He sat up stiffly and cast a bleary eye at Unciel, who looked asleep with his eyes open. Or dead, Euan thought with sudden horror. Then the pale eyes flicked to him, intense, unblinking. Unciel wanted something. Euan waited. But his head was still full of mushrooms; he couldn't see around them. He hadn't been out of his robe in days; his eyes felt as prickly as his chin; he had barely washed. No wonder, he thought mordantly, he was growing fungus. Then he realized what the wizard wanted and blinked.

"Mushrooms?"

Unciel sighed faintly. That shape, he informed Euan silently. That shade of yellow. No other. Along the wall at the back of the garden a patch had finally appeared. Not the ones with specks of white on their caps. Those were poisonous.

"I'm not picking mushrooms for you," Euan said flatly.

Please.

"No."

Euan.

"No."

He felt the wizard's despair then, sharp and sudden as a

blade; the image frayed in his head. Appalled, Euan stumbled to the bedside, looked down at the frail, exhausted figure. "I'm afraid," he whispered, "that I'll kill you."

The mushrooms filled his mind again. Look, they insisted. Look.

"I don't know what I'm looking for!"

Then he saw how long and straight their stems were, how their caps fit close, an even, bright, liquid yellow, like a buttercup. He put his fingers to his eyes, rubbed them wearily. "I never liked that shade of yellow," he said between his teeth.

He turned, trying to empty his head of everything but mushrooms and the sudden resolution to find a physician before he killed Unciel with his own remedies. Euan went to the kitchen, flung the wizard's harvest apron over his head and headed for the back door. The front door opened abruptly. The raven squawked. Euan stopped, blinking incredulously at the king walking alone through the cottage toward the barefoot scribe with his hair in elf-knots, a filthy apron dangling from his neck and mushrooms in his eyes everywhere he looked.

"My lord," he breathed.

"Where is Unciel?" the king demanded.

"He's in—he's—"

"In his garden?"

"In his bed. He's very ill."

The king's brown face lost a shade or two of color. His voice rose. "Why wasn't I told? Why haven't you sent for someone?"

"He won't let me. He said—"

"Take me to him."

"My lord," Euan babbled desperately, finding words suddenly as elusive and exasperating as the fruit flies in the kitchen. "He is extremely weak. He was trying to summon Gyre when something happened—he overtaxed himself."

The king gave an explosive exclamation. He whirled, then stood looking bewilderedly down a long hall, far too long by Euan's estimation, and full of closed doors, ranked like guards on both sides and all exactly alike.

"Which is it?" Arnou stepped forward, flung one open in exasperation to reveal an empty room. "Show me!"

"Stop!" Euan cried in terror, and the king turned, dumbfounded, staring at the scribe who dared command him. The scribe swallowed until words unstuck themselves and said, his voice trembling, "You're forcing him to use magic. He's not strong enough. Please. Let him rest." Arnou turned an interesting shade of plum; Euan braced himself. Then he heard himself speak again, so steadily that he was certain the wizard must have turned him into someone else. "What he needs is mushrooms."

The king's mouth tightened, opened again to expel the word. "Mushrooms."

"Yellow ones. In the garden."

"I came to hear about my daughter in Serre and you are talking to me about mushrooms?"

"They are connected," Euan said, shaken but inflexible. Arnou glanced once more at the impossibly long hallway. Then he dropped his head in one hand.

"You sound like my father."

"Please, my lord, come into the garden," Euan begged,

with an eye on the unyielding doors. "He has been straining his powers to the utmost to help you. He thinks the mushrooms will heal him. I'm afraid that I will poison him."

"Why didn't he — Why didn't you — "

"Because he says no to everything. No and no and no. To everything except what he wants."

The king loosed a breath, stood silently a moment as though he were pleading with the doors. No and no and no, said one shut door after another, and he turned his baffled, troubled gaze to the garden. "I used to know something about mushrooms," he said after a moment. "You shouldn't poison Unciel by yourself."

Euan closed his eyes. "Thank you."

They found the mushrooms near the back wall, a broad patch behind a few squash vines. "No white speckles," Euan said tersely, as they searched through them. "Tight-fitting caps."

"I once thought gold should be this color," Arnou said, picking at them more carelessly than Euan could bear to watch. "Has he heard anything at all from Gyre?"

"Yes. Gyre said that all was well."

The king stared at him. "Why didn't you tell me that?"

"Unciel didn't believe Gyre."

"Why not?"

"My lord, that one is speckled."

The king tossed it into the squash vines, still staring at Euan. "Why not?" he demanded again. "Why shouldn't he believe the man he chose to guard my daughter?"

"I don't know, exactly," Euan answered as vaguely as he dared. "He only said that nothing is ever all well in Serre."

"It's a simple matter of marriage. People marry as often as the sun rises. What could be difficult about that?"

"I don't know. You can put them in here," he added, proffering an apron pocket.

"I wondered why you were wearing that. Show them to Unciel before you cook them; he should be able to see what he shouldn't eat." His face had cleared somewhat; the storm went rolling and grumbling elsewhere. He had found what Gyre had said consoling, to Euan's relief, and the scribe refrained, as they knelt together culling the patch for the brightest yellows, from mentioning blackened crystals or sorcery or anything else remotely ambiguous. The king glanced at the sun after a few moments and rose, brushing at dirt.

"Send for me when Unciel is strong enough to speak to me. I won't be patient long. And send a message to my aunt, Lady Tassel, if you poison him. She's the only one left in the family who can do anything at all with magic." He stopped, his face growing taut again, as he contemplated the princess in Serre. "I hope," he said slowly, "that's not what Ferus was looking for in Sidonie."

Euan felt his own skin chill. "He'll have all of Dacia for magic," he protested, and found himself unconvinced by his own argument.

"He'll have Dacia one way or another," Arnou said pithily. "You must get Unciel on his feet again. If something is amiss and Ferus has betrayed me, he'll face in Serre whatever magic there is left in Dacia. Tell Unciel that he may not have fought his last battle yet."

Euan showed the mushrooms to Unciel, who gave them a

weary, cursory glance and showed the scribe what to do with them. Euan chopped them into tiny pieces and boiled them to a garish stew. Terrified, he held a cupful to Unciel's lips and watched him swallow it. The wizard slept for hours afterward without moving, hardly breathing, it seemed to Euan, who sat up with him for hours. But his cooking did not kill the wizard. When Euan started out of nightmares the next morning, as stiff as the chair he had slept in, he found Unciel awake and gazing into the flawed crystal in his hand.

"What is that?" Euan asked. Unciel looked at him. No and no and nothing, Euan expected to hear again; the wizard's eyes looked veiled, secretive. But to his surprise, Unciel spoke.

"A haphazard way to speak to someone across distances." He paused, resting between sentences. "I was calling Gyre. Something happened." He paused again; his eyes filmed with memory and pain. The crystal slid out of his hand; Euan caught it as it rolled. "The black," Unciel added with effort, "is sorcery."

Euan peered at the jagged bolt frozen within the crystal. "Whose?" he asked incredulously. "Gyre's?"

"No. Someone was attacking Gyre at the moment I touched his mind. I felt the fire."

Euan swallowed. No and no and nothing . . . "Then you were right," he said, his skin prickling. "Something went wrong in Serre. Is Gyre dead?"

"He shouldn't be. Not from this." Unciel stirred a little, restively. "But now we know even less than we did before we knew anything at all. Help me up."

Now what? Euan wondered warily. But the wizard only performed a few ablutions and then crawled back into bed. He fell asleep again. Euan wandered out to the kitchen and surveyed the disorderly profusion of vegetables laying siege to cupboards and chairs and floor. A cabbage fell off the table under the weight of his gaze.

He took up a knife and went to work.

He made a great stew of everything he could possibly fit into the wizard's largest cauldron, including, he suspected, a few beetles and worms. As he chopped, his thoughts kept battering at the door of conjecture. How much danger was the princess in? Who would tell the truth, if not Gyre? And if not Gyre, to whom could the princess turn? His knife slipped off a turnip, stuck in the cutting board. He stared raptly at it, seeing himself riding over the mountains into Serre, seeking the princess himself, finding out exactly what was going on. I could go, he thought, pulling the knife free, then driving it with resolution into the turnip. I will go. The king's physician could take care of Unciel. Someone would surely lend Euan a horse for such a journey. The king's library would have a map. He had money in the box beneath his bed; he rarely bought anything but food and ale and books. Like Unciel, he would write his adventures down as he went. He would have adventures. After climbing the highest mountains, crossing the interminable forests, scaling the steepest cliff, battling witches and ogres, he would appear to the princess as marvelous and unexpected as any magic in Serre. Her violet eyes, drenched with the hopeless tears of many weeks, would turn to him as flowers to the sun.

When the vegetables had simmered themselves beyond identification, he went to see if Unciel was awake. The wizard's eyes seemed oddly bright. Euan touched his face worriedly, felt the fever still warring through his body.

"I should take you to the palace," he said grimly. "Let the king take care of you."

"No." The wizard shifted fretfully at the thought. "You're doing all that the king's physician could do for me. And I don't want to talk to Arnou yet."

Euan was silent, caught in a tangle of impulses. The scribe who was at that moment riding so bravely alone over the mountains looked back at the scribe standing at the sickbed of an aged, weakened wizard, wondering dubiously how to interest him in a mouthful of soggy vegetables. "The king wants to see you as soon as you are strong enough to speak to him," he warned Unciel. "He won't wait long."

"He must wait," Unciel said inflexibly, "until I find Gyre."

"What if Gyre is still in danger? If he can't protect the princess? If he can't even tell you that he can't?" The wizard's pale eyes slid, glittering, to Euan's face, more ice than ash now, but still as opaque. Euan heard himself gabble on, apprehensive and scarcely coherent. "If you can't find him, someone must go. Someone must see exactly what danger the princess is in. The king will go to war to get her back if something has gone wrong. He told me to tell you that. He wants you strong enough to fight for Dacia."

Unciel made a soft, improbable noise, somewhere between laughter and a snort. "Arnou will lose his kingdom along with his daughter if he goes to war with Ferus. And I haven't the strength to deal even with Ferus's crude sorcery. As you see."

Euan's mouth hung; nothing emerged. After a moment he transferred his stare from Unciel to the crystal on the table. "That," he whispered. "That was Ferus?"

"Yes."

"Attacking Gyre?"

"Yes." Euan sat down abruptly in the chair, sending the one-eyed cat scrambling out from under him. "Every spell," Unciel continued, "contains a trace of the maker's heart. If you can look closely enough into it, you can thread it back to the impulse and the mind that conceived it."

"Then someone must go," Euan said, his voice sounding oddly thin, unfamiliar to his ears. "Now. The king can send someone here to care for you if you refuse to go to the palace."

"It may be that all is proceeding as planned for the princess," Unciel said, paying no discernible attention to Euan. "That only Gyre is in trouble. The princess may be happily married by now, for all we know. She may have sent her own messengers back to tell her father."

"Then why—" Euan paused, thumbing his brow perplexedly. He watched the scribe fight his way across Serre to rescue a princess, only to find that the princess did not want rescuing at all, and could not imagine what he was doing there. Too many tales, he thought. Too many possibilities. And Unciel explained nothing, only made matters more complicated. "Why would Ferus attack Gyre?"

"Because Gyre annoyed him, because Gyre has something that Ferus wants, or, just as likely, because Gyre was trying to teach Ferus something and the king was careless. With your help I can find out." He added gently at Euan's silence, "You have no idea how grateful I am that you are with me now. I don't know who else I would be able to trust with such matters. You have been as steadfast and courageous as any great warrior in the face of illness, uncertainty, magic, and even the King of Dacia. And you have taken the time to care for the things that I love as well. Thank you for staying with me. Perhaps, after we have sorted all these matters out, I'll find some way to repay you."

Euan took a final look at the lonely, valorous scribe riding into the unpredictable, the unknown where witches boiled bones and firebirds sang, and a princess fleeing some great evil ran weeping out of the trees into his charger's path. The forest closed around the rider, hid him forever from view. The scribe got to his feet, stifling a sigh.

"I made a stew out of your garden," he answered simply. "I'll bring you a bowl. Perhaps one day you'll tell me a story."

FIFTEEN

Following the firebird, Gyre lost himself in the house of the witch.

One moment, a moment as endless as time, as sweet as anticipation, he saw the warm, golden eyes, the enchanting smile; he heard the wordless song of passion and promise. Come, said the outstretched hand, the slender bare feet taking their slow backward steps toward him and away from him. Come to me.

The next moment, he stood in the stinking, cloying shadows of what looked like the bastard offspring of a hen-coop and a hovel, with smudged, oily flames licking sullenly at a cauldron full of bones, and a monstrous woman making a noise like a chicken being plucked alive. Laughing, he realized sourly. She was laughing at him.

She wasn't a toad-woman this time. She seemed, in what

tatters of light the fire loosed, a perversion of the firebird, a mockery of the heart-rending beauty that had stripped every thought from his head. The witch sprouted bright floating plumes and feathers on her head instead of hair; her long, bony, crooked fingers tapered sharply into golden talons. Her round gold eyes seemed larger than her lenses, and turned a peculiar shade of umber behind the green, as though her perverse fires burned within the gold.

Gyre, feeling like the cold, charred lump of something not even fire could burn, turned abruptly away from her demented jeering. He remembered then what he had left standing on the cliff-road: a mask, a destiny, an entire kingdom. All for a face, he thought incredulously, wanting to weep with laughter himself. For a song.

But it had been sorcery, he reminded himself. And sorcery he understood. "I have no time for this," he told the witch, and stepped through shadows and fowl-droppings toward where he expected to find the door. The prince would hardly have begun the climb up the road. He would not expect Gyre to return so quickly, and would never see him when he did. Ronan would yield his past, his memories and experiences to the wizard as easily as he relinquished them every night to sleep.

The door had vanished. Gyre gave the grisly jumble of bones standing in his way a cursory glance, then became invisible and melted through them.

They rose like trees everywhere around him, stark, weather-bleached bones as thick as the forests of Serre and, as he felt his way through them, seemingly as endless. There, they told him, he would become bone, nothing more, forever. His ribs would frame the witch's window; his thighbones would blacken with her chimney smoke. For the first time since he had trapped himself in the lonely cave in Fyriol, he felt a branch-chattering, wind-howl of panic surging over his thoughts. The bones faded around him. He saw the witch again, with her red feathery head and her enormous, dried-leaf eyes catching fire behind the lenses.

He looked at her silently, this time with more interest. She was, after all, a part of the magic of Serre, the same magic that had created the firebird out of itself and, for better or worse, ignited his heart. It was a language whose rules and logic he did not yet fully grasp. Understanding the witch, he would come closer to mastering the magic.

"I suppose," he said finally, "you want something from me."

She smiled, a beaky smile with corn-yellow teeth. "I want your magic. I'll boil your bones and drink down your marrow. You're that travelling wizard who gave me the prince instead of the firebird. You tricked me. But you paid for it. I heard your heart wailing like a baby among my bones."

"You tricked me," he agreed, glancing around the murky dark for a glimpse of fiery hair. "What have you done with the firebird? You could not possibly have conjured her out of moldering bones and chicken feathers. She was not sorcery but true magic. You tricked her, too, into entering your house. How did she escape?"

"Maybe the firebird flew out the window," the witch answered. "Or maybe it didn't. Maybe these are its bones bubbling over my fire."

"You wanted the firebird badly enough the night I brought it to you in a golden cage."

The witch shrugged. "I have you now. You conjure firebirds out of your head. I'll have your magic out of you and then I'll change all my hens into firebirds."

"It won't be enough," Gyre told her softly. "It will never be enough. Not once you have heard its true voice and seen the face it hides. All the power I possess could not make out of all the white hens in the world a single feather of the firebird."

The bird-woman snorted. "So you say. Your bones will sing a different song."

Again he was silent, studying her, wondering how far she could go with her smelly cottage sorcery. She had been deluded by the firebird he had made out of the prince. She had deluded him with her forest of bones. But perhaps that had only been a matter of an unfamiliar structure of sorcery, the differing languages of their magic. Perhaps her powers resided in her reputation; she was more fearful in tales than in truth. Ronan had believed her dangerous and so, to him, she was. She had trapped him in the forest, he said. But home and marriage seemed the last things he wanted to return to. Perhaps, in some peculiar way, he had used her to trap himself. He had been walking freely enough up the palace road when Gyre had found him.

And must be still walking, alone, unarmed and vulnerable, with no one in the palace aware that he was coming home. Gyre felt his thoughts veer like a compass needle toward that unguarded treasure. But first he had to deal with the witch, who seemed to want to make him into some kind of grotesque supper.

He said to her, "Let me go. I don't want to fight you,"

"Then don't," she suggested unhelpfully, unhooking the steaming cauldron to replace it with another, larger and empty. "You might fit in this one."

"I'll make you another firebird."

"The last you made wouldn't even sing. And it bit me," she added darkly. "Just get in here for a moment and let me see how you fit."

"I've never climbed into a cauldron," he answered, remembering some tale of the queen's. "Show me how."

She gave him a long, opaque look out of her lenses. Then she loosed a burble of exasperation and bundled her skirt around her knees. Her broad feet, splayed like bird claws, seemed almost too big to clear the rim. Somehow, heaving her unwieldy body off the floor, clinging to the pot-hooks for balance, she got both feet into the cauldron.

"There," she said, squatting on the rim. "Now you do it."

"I sit on the edge with my feet in the pot."

Her eyes rolled behind her lenses. "No, you sit all the way in."

"You don't fit all the way in. How could I?"

"I fit."

"You don't fit."

Her tongue smacked off the roof of her mouth; spittle flew. Muttering about wizards from foreign realms who couldn't find their brains with a map, she hunkered herself down into the cauldron, then crowed at him, "I fit!"

Gyre woke the sluggish fire under the cauldron with a thought, sending a curtain of flames so high around the witch that she disappeared within it. He did not bother looking for the door, or trying to melt again through the walls. He turned himself into a gnat and flew to the wall beside the hearth. A speck among the bones, he began to crawl through the chinks between them.

Tiny as he was, he felt the sudden, hot breath that nearly shrivelled his wings. He turned. Something huge loomed over him: a great black circle rimmed with yellow and white, overlaid with a smaller film of green. Above it a jagged red crest shimmered like fire. Beneath it was the beaky profile on which the green lenses rested. The witch had turned herself into an enormous white hen, he realized, even as her beak opened wide. Judging from the noise that made the bone under him tremble, the hen was furious. Her head drew back, then snaked forward, beak plunging toward the gnat, which promptly turned into a flea and leaped from bone to bone deeper into the wall.

As swiftly as it jumped, the hen came after it, tearing bones loose with one twist of its beak. The wizard heard what sounded like an entire skeleton clattering onto the floor. He stopped dead. The ravening beak overshot the flea. In that instant the flea grew pale and melted into bone. The beak stabbed wildly here and there at nothing, then paused. The wizard considered his position in life at that moment. That and the thought of the prince on the palace road sparked a sudden flare of impatience that illumined the bone like white fire.

The hen gave an ear-splitting shriek and tore the bone

loose. Exasperated, Gyre searched his imagination for the most fearsome monster he could remember, the only one that had ever frightened him, and turned into it.

The hen, feeling the bone come alive, dropped it hastily and turned back into Brume. She wore her most hideous, most devastating face, Gyre guessed by the look of it: the one that caused knights riding to battle to faint in their armor and wake up without their wits rather than remember her. He wore the face he had glimpsed on Unciel in his kitchen. Then, it had been little more than an expression, a deadliness in the eyes, a hint, in the flat, scarred planes of the face, of a mercilessness and ruthlessness more savage even than the frozen northern barrens.

He saw himself reflected for an instant in the witch's lenses. Then the floor dropped out from under him. He was dumped, along with stray bones and chicken feathers, onto the forest floor. He sat there, startled, watching the witch, her cottage of bone balanced above her massive legs and feet, running away from him into the moonlit trees, accompanied by the mad screeches of distraught chickens.

He got up slowly, wondering. He touched his face, found it still alien, and shuddered slightly. But he paused before he let the mask fray. It might be useful again, he thought. No one would recognize him, and it would most likely stun even Ferus.

But what had the witch recognized when she looked at it? In Unciel's kitchen, he had seen only the memory of it in the wizard's face, and it had terrified him instantly, though he had no idea what it was. Something in his heart had recognized it. But he had seen it through human eyes. The witch was as old as Serre; what did she need to fear? He puzzled over that, then began to hear the covert steps of animals slinking away from him, others slipping under leaves and brush to evade his eye. Even the trees were silent, not a branch stirring, not a seed-cone dropping. Even the wind was still.

Marvelling at such power, he went to find Ronan.

SIXTEEN

Sleepless in her chamber, Sidonie contemplated the astonishing transformation of the wizard Gyre. Her thoughts, whirling and chattering like the water beneath her window, swerved wildly between memories. Prince Ronan stood fixed at the point of her arrow, talking about witches and firebirds while somewhere, invisible, Gyre listened; Gyre watched as her bowstring loosened, little by little, until finally she had crossed the distance between them herself instead of her arrow to put the bow into Ronan's hands. Gyre sat beside her in the shape of the prince, gently touching the pearls at her wrist, touching her heart with his husky, uncertain words. Barely an hour later, she watched the wizard blown out the window like a burning cinder, only to reappear a day later, slightly worse for the wear, and leave again just as suddenly to find Ronan and bring him home, one way or another, alive or dead.

She lay so still in her bed she might have been entranced. Her fists were clenched at her sides, her skin cold with fear. When she had a coherent thought, it was to hope that Gyre, wherever he had taken himself, was too busy to cast attention her direction. She could hide nothing from him. He could take what he wanted from her; she did not know how to fight such intricate deception. He must have deluded even Unciel.

Escape, the water whispered, demanded, shouted ceaselessly, but it did not tell her how. Her door was always guarded; every door, stairway, passageway around her was watched. She had not seen her own company of guards since she had entered the palace. She could leave either by the door or through the window. She could not take two steps across her threshold before she would be stopped. If she left by the window, the powerful, churning water beneath it would drag her like a twig over the falls and crush her before she hit the stones at the bottom. If only she had learned some magic from her grandfather; if only she truly possessed a casket full of power . . .

She was conjuring up an image of herself disguised as one of her attendants, sent on an errand—what?—slipping down a side-passage, finding a door warped with disuse at the bottom of a stairway everyone had forgotten but the spiders, a strangely empty yard beyond the door, the gates wide open, guards busy watching a hawk or a cloud or something trapped in the relentless grip of water when Ferus's voice, a full-throated rumble that swelled and broke into a roar, seemed to come out of every stone around her. For a moment she thought the falls had poured through the casements. She clung to the bed as though it were about to float. And then she heard the answering shouts through the halls, the running boots, the chaos beyond her door.

She rose shakily and opened it, peered through a crack. Darkly dressed figures were running everywhere, bumping into each other, pointing, brandishing swords at shadows, and yelling at one another. In the next moment they had all spilled up and down various stairs and passageways. A door slammed. The hallway was suddenly empty.

Sidonie stepped out cautiously, her bare feet soundless on the stones. She closed the door softly behind her and ran.

She bumped hither and yon among the walls like a moth, ducking from one shadow to another, taking the darkest stairwell, slipping behind tapestries when noises came her way. She passed clusters of frightened faces, heard their whispers. The startled, conjecturing eyes did not recognize the barefoot girl in her nightgown, her hair loose and disheveled, flitting along the edge of torchlight like a stray dream. The princess never walked unattended, and certainly not without her shoes. Even though she had spent only a scant handful of days in the palace, she would know enough by now to huddle in her chambers with her attendants when Ferus let loose with a cataract like that in his voice.

Sidonie found the abandoned stairway by accident, pushing through the nearest door when she heard steps. She felt her way down in darkness. The stairs and walls spiralled; the old stones were worn smooth, hollowed underfoot. The tower smelled of damp and mice. Now and then, a long narrow window suitable for shooting arrows into the woods across the river loosed a shaft of moonlight to illumine her path. At the bottom of the stairs, she felt at a grainy, pocked door until she found the latch. It dragged across dirt and pebbles when she opened it. But there was no one in the yard to hear. And there ahead of her, she saw the open gates through which she had ridden a lifetime ago. The guards were standing outside the gates at the far edge of the road, their backs to her, looking down at the forest as though they expected the peaceful, moonlit trees to start marching suddenly up the cliff road. That close to the water, they heard nothing but it and their own voices. Sidonie, little more than a smudge of moonlight in her pale nightgown and her skin shocked colorless with terror, ran noiselessly down the road behind them to where it turned its first abrupt angle and disappeared behind the falls. There, in a wet, pounding dark so loud that she seemed to breathe sound like air, she stopped for a moment, feeling safe for the first time since she had left Dacia.

But she wasn't, she knew. At any moment the king and his guards might take it into their heads to come riding down the road; at any moment Gyre might appear in front of her. The guards watching the forest might notice the movement along the cliff and come after her. They would drag her back to Ferus, who would drown her in his torrential bellow and then lock her back in her chamber. She would rather take her chances with the ogres in the forest, who might at least be more careless and stupider than Ferus. Wet from hair to hem, she emerged on the other side of the falls, and clung to the moon-shadows the cliff cast along one side of the road. The moon, drifting across the sky, peeled away shadow as it moved, illumined the entire face of the cliff, until it seemed that she ran down a waterfall of light.

But no one rode after her. She must have been the last thing on Ferus's mind. What, she wondered starkly, had been on his mind when he had shouted like that? Ronan, she guessed, and put both hands to her mouth as she ran. Ronan's death would tear a cry like that out of Ferus's granite heart. And if he were dead, Sidonie would mean nothing any longer to the king except an excuse to goad her father into war. He would bury her in the depths of the stone palace and throw away the key. And if she was of no value to Serre, she would mean nothing to Gyre, who would not bother to rescue her. Perhaps, decades later, someone would chance upon the white-haired crone in the dungeons, and remember the lost Princess of Dacia, daughter of a vanquished king. Only then might she be permitted to live her final days in unfamiliar light, bewildered by freedom, among strangers who did not know her name.

She was so convinced that Ronan had died that she did not recognize him when she ran into him.

He did not recognize her at first either. Careening headlong in her frantic flight down the cliff road, she smacked into something tall, sturdy, and breathing audibly. She took him for a troll. He grunted when she hit him, and caught at her. She flailed at him; he lost his balance and pulled her down with him. They slid a little along the steep road and separated. She sat up, at once frightened and incensed. Her damp hair was tangled over her eyes; she could not see the troll. She brushed at it wildly, trying to drag herself away from him even before she could get to her feet. He did not touch her again. She pushed strands of hair back and saw him finally, clearly in the moonlight.

She stared, astonished. It was not a troll. It was the missing prince, walking barefoot up the cliff road, his lank copper hair littered with bracken, his grey eyes no longer haunted, but very tired, and beginning to blink at her incredulously.

She whispered, "I thought you were dead."

He tried to speak, cleared his throat. "Is it—It is the Princess from Dacia?"

She got to her feet then, backed a step warily. "Are you Ronan? Or Not-Ronan?"

His mouth tightened a moment before he answered. "Ronan. Despite that wizard you had travelling with you."

She closed her eyes, felt a long breath ease out of her, and realized then how much knowledge could weigh until it was shared. She looked at him again. "I almost married him two days ago. Your father threw him down the cliff." She stopped, bewildered suddenly by their twin faces. One had made her feel his longing, his trust of her. This Ronan's eyes saw nothing when they looked at her; they did not know her at all.

But they had glimpsed something familiar, in memory. "So that's who it was. I saw him fall. How did my father recognize him?"

"He didn't. It was your mother who recognized him as a spell. He said something to her about graves, she said, when he should have known—he thought you had buried your wife and child. Instead of—Instead." She finished with a gesture, appalled at the sudden turn of their talk. But Ronan's eyes remained cool. She added quickly, dropping down beside him again, "They thought it was some spell of Brume's that your father's fire had blown out the windows. They don't know that it was Gyre. I only guessed it myself."

"How?"

"I could not figure out how the spell I nearly married knew things that you and I had said and done when we met in the forest. Then, earlier tonight, I woke myself up suddenly remembering that Gyre had been there with us in secret; he saw and heard everything."

Ronan was silent. He glanced behind him down the road to the deep shadows around the foot of the falls which the moon had not yet touched. Sidonie felt her skin prickle again, as though the invisible wizard had trailed a finger down her arm.

She shifted more closely to the prince and asked softly, "Is he down there?"

"The last I saw of him, the firebird had enticed him into the witch's cottage. She told me that she wanted his bones for the magic in them."

Sidonie blinked at the idea. "Gyre's bones? Can she really do that? Surely he wouldn't let her have them."

"I think not." The prince's head was still turned away; she couldn't see his face. But she heard the sudden tautness in his voice. "He told me he would take my face. My name. My memories, my heritage. And you." He turned to look at her finally, his eyes clear as glass and as expressionless.

"Did you plot this together, you and the wizard? To take Serre for yourselves?"

Stunned, she sat down hard on the road again. She felt the blood streak back into her face. "No." Her voice shook badly. "I came here in good faith to marry you. You were the one who ran from me."

He shrugged slightly. "I was bewitched. I had to ask you."

"No. My lord Ronan, you did not." She stood up, brushed her nightgown straight around her, and started down the road again, so furious she could barely see.

He called after her, "Where are you going?"

"Home."

"We are betrothed. This is your home."

"I find, my lord, that I do not wish to marry you. I'm going back to Dacia."

He caught up with her. "In your nightgown? In the middle of the night? Why," he added, when she only strode down the road without answering, "were you running down the road in the middle of the night in your nightgown?"

"Because," she answered between her teeth, "your father keeps me prisoner. It was the only chance I had to escape. I am terrified of Gyre and I thought you were dead. There was no reason for me to stay."

"But I'm alive."

"I am not going to marry you just because you're alive."

"But you are." His hand closed above her elbow, but not tightly; it was the certainty in his voice that stopped her, held her motionless, staring back at him. "According to such agreements as our fathers negotiated, that's all I have to be to marry you: alive."

She saw every nightmare she had had of him standing in front of her. She pushed her hands against her eyes and cried at him, "I liked that other Ronan so much better. The one who was not you."

She felt his hold tighten. Her hands slid down; she looked at him again, bewildered at where they had suddenly found themselves, somewhere on a precarious road between love and hate and no clear sign in which direction either lay. His face had shut like a door. Only his eyes, hard and suspicious again, warned her that she did not know this prince at all; he had thrown off all enchantments, even those of memory.

He only said, "You will have to make the best of me. My father wants heirs." He turned her, not roughly but inflexibly, led her back up the road toward the summer palace.

"I have no powers," she told him desperately, trying without success to twist free of his big fingers. "No gift for magic. I was born without it."

He paused only briefly before he answered. "Our children may inherit what you did not. One way or another, all the powers of Dacia will belong to Serre." He stopped walking when she still struggled, and turned her to face him again. "It could be worse," he said with chilling simplicity. "Unlike my father, I am not violent. You will be Queen of Serre one day, and all I will ever ask of you in return is that you bear my children. Nothing more." He sighed a little as her tears ran suddenly, noiselessly in silver streaks across her upturned face. "Most women would be grateful."

Sidonie felt the cliff road tremble beneath them then, and saw, rounding the higher curve of road, what the shouting falls had hidden: a small army of the palace guards riding too fast for safety down the cliff, led by the one-eyed king.

Ferus reached them in another moment; the guards pulled up raggedly behind them, shouting with surprise, one or two nearly sliding over the cliff. The king drew his sword as he reined in front of the prince. The blade stopped an inch from Ronan's eye.

"Are you my son? Or are you some trick of the witch's?"

"He's yours," Sidonie said succinctly. The king's eye rolled at her, startled, then back to the prince.

"The wizard Gyre is with Brume," Ronan said. "She gave me my freedom in exchange for him." Sidonie, still in his grip, felt him shaking; he looked too worn suddenly to stand.

Veins surfaced and throbbed in the king's face; he roared incredulously at Ronan, light shivering down the sword in his hand, "You gave Gyre to the witch?"

The prince's voice remained remarkably even. "If there is justice in the magic of Serre, he'll be nothing more than soup stock by now. Who did you think wore my face to that wedding?"

The king, swallowing words, looked as though he might choke on them. He let the sword fall finally and managed, "Then how—Then who will fight for us?"

Ronan, his eyes locked on his father's, swayed a little on his feet as though some force behind the words had struck him. "Fight what?"

"That thing. That thing out of Dacia." The sword swung

again, this time at Sidonie. "Ask her what she was on her way to meet at the end of the road."

She felt her mouth go dry; her skin seemed suddenly too small, as though it were trying to disappear under the king's wrath. "I was running from you," she told him, her voice trembling. "All the guards left me when you shouted like that."

"What thing?" Ronan asked. His haggard face looked moon-pale, but he still spoke steadily. "What were you shouting about?"

The king began to answer; again his voice failed. The sword moved away from Sidonie, pointed down the side of the cliff to the road below where it began, a hollowed rise carved out of the barren face of the cliff. "I saw it," Ferus said raggedly, "in my mirrors."

Something stood there in the moonlight, its face turned toward them. Even from that distance it seemed huge. It did not move, it simply looked up at them. Sidonie felt something sweep through her like the coldest of winter wind, hissing and stinging with snow, that killed everything it touched, and then laid waste to the earth beneath the dead.

She felt Ronan's fingers slacken, grow cold around her arm. "What is it?" she breathed, her lips numb with the fear she felt all around her, even from the king. Nobody answered. It melted away under their eyes, left a frozen memory behind.

"To the palace," the king snapped. A guard leaped down to give Ronan his horse, then heaved himself up behind another. Ferus reached down for Sidonie's wrist, hauled her ungently into his saddle. The king fumed at her all the way up the cliff for trying to run away, for bringing Gyre into his land, for all the useless powers she had carelessly left locked in a casket and hidden even from herself. Still numbed by the terror the nameless stranger had cast about him like a mist, and by Ronan's even colder heart, she scarcely heard a word he said.

SEVENTEEN

In the king's mirrors, they watched for monsters.

Ronan, so exhausted he could have dropped then and there to the stones and slept, managed to stay on his feet with his charred eyes open. The half-dozen mirrors blinked through images of a dark and tranquil forest; even the trees seemed to dream. Now and then something moved. But it was always named, recognizable: a hunting fox, an owl, a very old woman picking flowers opening under the touch of the moon.

Ferus, muttering and growling with increasing impatience, snapped finally at the princess, "We could have used your powers. If you had brought them with you instead of hiding them."

Ronan woke a little at that, looked at her curiously. "I thought you said you had none."

The king whirled at her, his single eye fulminating. She answered Ronan icily, "You misunderstood me, my lord. I said I have none here."

He had not misunderstood; on the cliff road she had made herself as clear as possible. But he let it pass, presuming that she was tired of the king shouting at her. As Ronan had pointed out to her, it did not matter anyway. She was very angry with him for some reason or another. But her anger would pass; his mother's had. As Calandra crossed his mind, a guard opened the door.

"My lord," he said to Ferus, "the queen."

Ferus grunted, still searching the mirrors. Calandra entered, her own gaze caught and held by the face of her son. Ronan saw the uncertainties, the fears, the questions in her eyes as she came toward him. She did not touch him; she stood in front of him, studying him, and asked a question like a test. Vaguely, through his weariness, he sensed its importance. But he could not care. He was her son. He could only tell her the truth; if that did not convince her, he did not know what would.

"How did you escape from Brume?" she asked.

He tried to remember; it seemed a season or two since he had left the witch. "Gyre," he answered finally. "He turned me into a firebird and gave me to Brume. He left me trapped in a cage in the witch's house, while he left wearing my face. I guessed then that he intended to return here and marry the princess in my place. I bit Brume when she tried to feed me, and she threw me out the door. The cage broke. When I freed myself, the wizard's spell over me was gone. But not the witch's, because I had failed to bring her the firebird. She told me then that she would set me free if I brought the wizard to her, for she had seen enough of his powers to want them for herself.

"But Gyre found me before I found him. He caught me at the bottom of the cliff road and told me that he would take me to you and my father to convince you that I was truly your son. Then he would leave Serre because his work here would be finished. But in truth, it would be I who left Serre behind forever, while he stayed wearing my face, taking my name, my memories, my past, and marrying in my place."

Ferus, who had turned away from his mirrors, made a guttural sound; his single eye had gone flat black with a deadly fury, as it did when he fought.

"How," the queen whispered, "did you escape the wizard?"

Ronan paused, rubbing his eyes tiredly as he wove threads backward. "Earlier that day, the firebird came to me and asked me to help her return her fallen egg to its nest. So I did that. Hours later, when I finally found the palace road, the wizard found me. I remember standing there, frozen in the grip of his mind like a hare under the fox's eye. I could not move, I could not speak, I could not think . . . And then I heard the firebird sing. I saw Gyre walk away from me. She sang to him in her woman's shape; she lured him back into the forest; he followed her without a thought." He hesitated again, unable to comprehend or quite believe what he had seen. "While I watched them, I saw the witch's cottage of bone run up behind her, open its door. Still singing, the firebird stepped across the witch's threshold. The wizard followed her. The door closed behind them both. Brume ran back into the forest. She had what she wanted and I was—I was free."

He stopped. The word sounded odd as he said it, as though it did not quite mean what he was. But free meant free; it was a simple, unambiguous word, and there he was, Prince Ronan of Serre, back in his father's palace, owing nothing to the witch, and safe for the moment from the wizard.

After a moment, the king said to the queen, his voice harsh with hope and dread, "Well? Do you challenge this one?"

Her face, usually so stiff and drained around Ferus, seemed to be choosing and discarding expressions like jewels. Blood warmed her skin; her eyes glittered as with tears; a corner of her mouth crooked toward laughter. "The firebird herself saved your life? Because you rescued her egg? And now Brume has the wizard?"

"Or he is the wizard," Ferus breathed, "with all my son's thoughts?"

"But what a tale you brought out of the forests, my son," the queen said with wonder. She was raising one hand toward Ronan at last to touch his face when Ferus struck.

He gave Ronan little more time than the blink of an eye to evade the sudden flare of power that seemed to come out of the ruby eye in the skull. It slammed into Ronan with all the force of the water pounding down the cliff. It spun him like a leaf, dragged him across a table, and then swept the contents of the table on top of him as he fell. Blinking dazedly in the aftermath, with the skull on his chest and the poisonous toad on its back hissing furiously in his ear, he thought: A wizard would have fought. The room grew dark; he felt himself begin to slide over the falls. He cried out in terror, felt his hands caught, held tightly. When he could see again, he found himself still on dry stone, the queen kneeling beside him, gripping his hands. Her face looked wintry again, bloodless and pinched; her eyes, on Ferus, seemed cold enough to burn.

"I told you that I knew him," she flared.

"Now," the king said without compunction, "so do I. A wizard would have defended himself."

"You might have killed him to prove a point!"

"I did what I thought best," he answered, his voice rising dangerously. "Don't question me." He reached down, hauled Ronan to his feet. The prince caught a glimpse of Sidonie, frozen across the room with both hands over her mouth. Then, abruptly, he was on the floor again, with the one-eyed skull grinning at him.

He pulled himself up this time, beginning to feel now that the numbing shock of the power was wearing away. He might have run headlong into a stone wall, his stunned bones told him. He said calmly to his mother, who seemed unaccountably willing to drive the king to further violence, "I understand. It was a test. Like yours."

The blood streaked into her face; she seemed suddenly close to tears again. "Not like mine," she whispered. "Not like mine at all."

"But it worked," he said inarguably. "Now you are both certain." He limped to the nearest chair, sat slumped, his elbows on the table, his hands over his eyes. He dropped his hands at the silence, dragged his eyes open again, and found them both gazing at him oddly, as though they recognized him as more or less their son, but what was more and what was less, they did not have an inkling.

"My lord," the queen pleaded finally. "He must rest. I will watch with you."

Ferus nodded. "I want you to see this monstrous thing for yourself. You might recognize it from some tale." He threw open the door, spoke to the guards in the hall. "Bring a pallet and blankets for the prince; I do not want him out of my sight tonight. Take the princess to her chamber. She is useless here. Bring her company up to stand along the walls outside the gates. If they begin to fall, we'll know the monster has found us."

"Should we give them back their arms, my lord?"

"No. If they argue or try to run, throw them over the falls."

The princess turned as white as bone; for a moment she seemed to waver on her feet. But she said nothing, just put one foot in front of the other until she reached the door. There was nothing to say, Ronan thought. She seemed to be learning that. The king spoke again before she crossed the threshold; she stopped mid-step at the sound of his voice, her back and profile rigid.

"You will wed when my son and my house are safe. I will not have another ill-omened disaster on my hands."

The princess could not seem to find her voice, so Ronan answered for them both. "Yes, Father," he said mildly. He remembered the toad then, upside down on the floor and vulnerable to a careless boot, because such small details seemed to matter. He picked it up and put it back on the table. Then he laid his head down beside it and went to sleep.

When he woke, the tower room was flooded with light. He stirred on the pallet, aching in every bone and muscle. The king, gazing into the mirrors alone, turned as Ronan struggled to sit. The sound of cool water rushing uselessly past him seemed suddenly unbearable; he reached for the nearest pitcher.

Ferus growled, "Don't drink that." He raised his voice, sent a servant running for food and wine, then handed his son another pitcher, from which Ronan drank noisily and sloppily until he could finally speak.

"Did you see it again?" he asked the king.

"No."

"Do you want me to go—"

"No," Ferus said tersely. "You will stay here under the queen's eye. She was first to recognize the imposter, and first to be certain of you, despite her confusing ways. I'll take a company into the forests. If the wizard wants to wear the ruling face of Serre, let him look out of mine. Let him try." He paused, his single eye dubious, as though he were studying the face of Serre himself. "The witch," he said abruptly. "How powerful is she? Can she keep the wizard in her cottage?"

Ronan, considering the witch, dipped a hand into the pitcher, dragged wet fingers through his dusty hair. "She said she wanted to boil his bones for broth and drink the magic in them."

The smoldering eye contemplated that with interest. "Can she do that?"

"I don't know. At times she seems almost stupid, at others . . ." He remembered the astonishing sight of the firebird singing the wizard through the open door of the cottage made of bone, its round green window, silvered with moonlight, flashing like an eye as it watched. "In the end she got them both. At such times, she seems almost subtle. But subtle enough to deal with Gyre? I don't know. Don't ride down any white hens while you're in the forest."

"I'll give her all the white hens in my kingdom if she kills that wizard," the king said grimly. "I wanted Gyre to help us fight that monster. Now we may be faced with fighting both of them at once."

"Maybe my mother can remember some way in a tale to outwit the monster."

"She doesn't think such a thing belongs to Serre."

"Dacia, then?"

"The princess did not seem to recognize it. And why would the King of Dacia send that for a wedding gift? He might have sent it instead of his daughter. But not with her."

"He sent the wizard," Ronan said evenly. "Perhaps that was the king's plan all along: to marry his daughter to Gyre and take Serre for himself."

Ferus's empty eye swung toward the casements, contemplated the invisible land beyond the distant mountains. "You'll marry her," he said tersely, "if I have to drink the wizard's marrow myself to defeat him. What possessed you to go chasing after firebirds and letting Gyre into your place, and your face, and nearly into your bed?"

Ronan lifted a shoulder. "I was possessed," he said simply. "Now I hardly remember why."

"You were possessed by ghosts," the king reminded him harshly. "Past as well as magic."

He remembered the funeral fire burning all night long, illumining the dark, swirling water, eating at his heart until there was nothing left at dawn but ash. It seemed something that had happened to another man, a sad tale his mother might have told him long ago. "Yes," he said, and pulled himself painfully to his feet. "But past is past. The Princess from Dacia is the future of Serre. The sooner we can safely marry, the better. I need a bath."

The king seemed to be gazing at him out of both eyes, then, the blind eye trying to see what the seeing eye missed. "What," he wondered, "did that witch do to you?"

"What do you mean?"

"I never saw myself in you before."

He sent Ronan to wash and dress, accompanied by a dozen guards and as many servants. When the prince returned to the tower, he found his breakfast and the queen. He stood beside her, eating bread and cold meat, while they watched Ferus lead a heavily armed company out of the gate. When the riders disappeared behind the falls, the queen turned to Ronan.

"I have sent for the princess," she said. "I thought that this might be a good time for you to talk."

Ronan settled himself to watch the mirrors. In one a bluebird flew through a brilliant shaft of light to a high bough. In another, the king's standard-bearer appeared from behind the falls, the standard limp with spray. "About what?"

"About—" Her voice faltered. "About yourselves. About your marriage."

"What—" He paused as the door opened. The princess entered, more sedately dressed than he had seen her last, her eyes oddly swollen and wincing at the light. She greeted them courteously and expressionlessly, then stood gazing blankly at a mirror.

"Sit down, my lady Sidonie," Ronan said as politely. "My mother thinks we should talk."

She brushed a few dried moth wings and an old bone off a stool and sat without taking her eyes from the mirrors. "What is there to talk about?"

"Exactly," he began with relief, "what I—"

"I am a prisoner in this palace, my guards and servants stand outside your walls as bait for that monster, and as your wife I will have no choice but to do what you want. What do you want me to say?"

Ronan opened his mouth, paused, and scratched one brow with a thumbnail. "My father isn't using them as bait," he said reasonably, tackling the easiest argument. "Only as a kind of warning signal. Someone must do it."

"He makes them stand unarmed! They'll be killed! I travelled for weeks with them—they are not only guards but my hunters, my cooks and drivers—they brought me here safely and now they must die? Because the king is afraid to give them weapons?"

"Well. It's likely that weapons would be all but useless anyway. So why—" He stopped as the princess flung herself off the stool to stand at the window, her eyes reddening as she stared across the forests to the high, jagged peaks awash with light. Ronan said patiently to her back, "I am trying to be fair. You'll get used to my father's ways."

"Ronan." The queen's voice cut sharply at him, cold and edged with astonishment. "What is the matter with you? You came out of that forest as heartless as your father."

Ronan looked at her. He drew a long breath as her eyes held his. It seemed as though that wintry light in them unburied memory like something lost amid a shower of leaves. "Yes," he said slowly, seeing it finally, clearly. "I remember. I had to leave something with the witch, so that she would show me the road home, and I could find Gyre for her. It must be something, she said, that I would find worth returning for."

"What did you leave with her?"

"My heart."

The princess turned, stared at him. The queen closed her eyes.

"No," she whispered. "You are not free. But you cannot go back into the forests—you can't! I will not lose you again!"

"But you see I tricked the witch," he said, surprised that he had to explain. "She really believed that I might return for it. I could not, at that moment, think of anything I wanted less." He saw the women, their faces stunned, give one another an incomprehensible look. "It's not important," he told them. "Let the witch keep it. I can live without it."

He heard the princess make a small mouse's squeak in the back of her throat. But she said nothing; neither did the queen. In silence they watched the tranquil, deadly forests within the mirrors.

EIGHTEEN

Euan stood beside Unciel's bed, watching the wizard watch his shadow in a bowl of water. The bowl, a plain, serviceable wash-basin, was balanced on a tray across the wizard's knees. Euan, more experienced now with the vagaries of magic and with Unciel's frailty, flicked a dubious eye at the water. It did not so much as tremble. Unciel was as motionless, gazing without a blink at his sunlit reflection. Such simple magic, he had explained to Euan, required light. They would not be able to hear Gyre, but they would see him. He would move across the face of the water as easily as a dream across the eye of night. They would at least know where he was, if not why.

Why might easily prove self-explanatory, if Gyre happened to be standing in a palace talking to Ferus or Sidonie. Things might be that simple, Euan thought, daring for the moment to hope. All might be peaceful in Serre: so they could tell the king, and then all would be peaceful in Dacia. He blinked as color seeped across the water, staining it with sudden swirls and clouds. Colors massed themselves into the greens and browns of enormous trees, the forest floor, gilded here and there with a sudden splash of light that had slipped past the massive boughs. Euan glanced at Unciel. The wizard, his eyes wide, blind to Dacia, seemed undisturbed at the sight of trees instead of palace.

Perhaps, Euan conjectured with wild abandon, Gyre had finished what he had been asked to do and was on his way back to Dacia.

Unciel moved.

The movement was little more than expression trembling across his face, a line or two deepening. He seemed to be gazing at the water now instead of into his private vision of Gyre. He made a soft sound. Euan shifted weight from one foot to the other, disturbed without knowing why. The water, images still drifting across it, had begun to quiver slightly, as at the wizard's heartbeat. A flock of yellow birds swarmed suddenly out of shadow, burned into light, then swooped away beyond the rim of the bowl. A wolf, shoulders sunken inward, tail down, slunk like smoke around a trunk and vanished.

Someone moved through the shadows into light, turned to glance out of the water at Euan.

He found himself sitting on the floor, clinging to it as though for an instant the world had rocked like a boat. He had to grope for breath. His face felt wintry, bloodless and scoured. For some reason, he was dripping. He wiped at water on his face bewilderedly, before he realized where it must have come from. Then he felt his heart, which had stopped for a moment, leap painfully to life, and he pushed himself to his knees to see the wizard.

Unciel was still sitting upright, though the tray was askew on his knees, and the bowl of water had flung itself over the side of the bed. He was frowning deeply. His breathing sounded like a bird trapped in a wall, flurried, erratic. Euan touched him after a moment. The eyes that turned to him belonged to a stranger, no one he knew, or ever wanted to know, in any world.

Then they changed, became Unciel's again, grim and very troubled.

Euan whispered, because that seemed safest, "Who was that?"

Unciel drew a deep breath, calmed the frantic wings in his chest. He pushed the tray off his knees wearily and dropped back. "It was Gyre."

"Gyre." The name came out in a sheep's bleat. The wizard looked at him again, seemed to see him this time. "You're all wet. I'm sorry."

"I'll dry," Euan said tersely. "That wasn't Gyre. That wasn't what you sent to guard the princess in Serre."

"No. The thing itself is dead. I killed it. Gyre is wearing its face."

"Gyre," Euan said. His voice had vanished again; he had to push it out in dry pebbles, in hollow reeds. "Is wearing the face of the monster you killed. The one whose heart he stole."

"Yes."

"The thing that came so close to killing you, that turned you into a crippled recluse in Dacia. Gyre is wandering around in the forests of Serre scaring birds with its face." Water was runnelling into his eyes; he pushed trembling fingers through his sodden hair, drew it back. "Could we venture a guess why? Perhaps he's lost his mind?"

"Perhaps," Unciel said faintly, "he's lost his heart."

Euan swallowed drily, his eyes clinging to the wizard's frail face, with his skin like old parchment and the lines running like scars down the sides of his mouth. "Now," he heard himself say abruptly. "Now would be the time to tell it. What exactly is that thing? It looked at me across Serre, out of water, and I knew I was dead."

"It is Gyre," Unciel insisted. "Not some nameless thing."

"If you die in this bed, it will be some nameless thing alive again in the world, and none of us knowing what to call it. What if it forgets that it is Gyre? What do we do with it then?" Unciel was silent. Euan turned, slid down to lean against the bed, staring numbly at the overturned bowl, waiting. After a moment or five, he closed his eyes. "Please," he begged. "If you want me to help you with this, then help me to understand. What is ghost and what is Gyre and what about him makes you care so?"

He heard the wizard draw a cobweb breath, and opened his eyes. Unciel spoke finally, his voice even, distant. "Write it down."

"Yes." He looked around quickly, before the wizard changed his mind; his eyes fell on the little leatherbound book on the table with the quill marking a page. He reached for it, his hands shaking again. "In this?"

"Anything. That will do. It is my garden record."

Euan fumbled for a blank page among the lists of herbs and sketches of vegetable plots. He pulled himself back on the chair, opened the ink jar.

"You're still wet," the wizard said suddenly. "You should—"

"Later," Euan said tersely. He wiped a stray drop of water from his cheekbone, sucked the quill nib clean, and dipped it. "Tell me."

"I went north," Unciel began, "after I stole the heart back from Gyre. I felt it follow me, even when I flew in bird shape, or travelled for days as invisibly as cold. It knew me always. It recognized its heart."

Hours later, Euan still sat in the chair beside Unciel's bed. The light had faded; he could barely see the words he was writing in the wizard's book. His hands were cold; his nose was cold; he kept expecting his breath to come out in a mist above the pages. The wizard, hidden beneath bed-clothes, was little more than a ragged, halting, unfamiliar voice, and a vague face in the dusk. Deep in his tale, he scarcely noticed the difference between day and night. Euan dipped his pen; it shivered in his fingers, dropped a pearl of ink on the paper. He left it there, scrawling past it, hunched and miserable, and wishing with every word he wrote that it might be the last.

"The way to destroy a heart," the voice said, "is to make it unrecognizable to the one possessing it. I know that now. The creature who fought me so furiously for its heart nearly destroyed mine."

Euan huffed a breath at his chilled fingers and wrote

grimly. He tried not to think about what he wrote. Words were words, he told them: patterns in ink on a page; as such they were powerless, they meant nothing to him. They could not heal, they could not harm, they could not live or die. If he stared them down until all meaning wore away, then he could keep writing.

He had thought the wizard's last battle would be a tale of terror and courage, feats of unimaginable magic performed with heart-stopping skill and passion, good and evil as clearly defined as midnight and noon, a heroic battle for life and hope against the howling monster that left death in every footprint and ate life to fill the unfillable void where its heart had been.

Instead he was trapped in the middle of something grisly, ugly, dreary, that ate into his own heart word by word until he could scarcely stand to look at himself. He could not bear looking at Unciel. So he left the candles unlit for as long as possible, preferring a twilight world where he did not have to watch the terrifying changes in the wizard's face.

"How can I describe what it did? Think of the known monsters in the world. The dragons with their fierce and deadly beauty. Their fires destroy the body but not the mind. The ogre who has torn his children apart does not become you when you fight him. He may tear at your body, but he can only kill you, he cannot change you. The renegade wizard is a subtle, dangerous force whom you must outwit to stay alive. Your heart is challenged, but not corrupted. A cherished innocence might be lost, but knowledge and experience which might be of far more value take its place. The knight battling the seven-headed serpent or the army of trolls may have to face his own cowardice as well. He changes the way he sees himself; the serpent does not change him, nor the trolls. Do you understand that?"

Euan grunted. I've never fought a troll, he wanted to say to the wizard. I've never faced a dragon. But mostly he wanted the wizard to get on with it; he wanted to understand as little as possible. Unciel took his noise for assent and got on.

"This monster, when it could not kill me, reached into me and broke my heart.

"We had been battling one another in the coldest, northernmost parts of the world for days. Years. I had drawn it even deeper into those remote realms where there was not much alive for it to kill. Someone watching would have seen us as little more than wind-whipped snow and the wake of bloody, frozen animals. I kept the stolen heart close to me, as close as bone, as my own heart. I had to kill the heart before the monster would die. It was like trying to kill stone, or dark. How can you kill something that has never been alive?

"It gave me a clue when it tore my own heart in two. Why don't you light the candles?"

Why don't you light, Euan wrote, then stopped reluctantly. He was hunched over the book, seeing little more than straight dark lines of words.

"I can see," he said shortly.

"So can I," Unciel said. "You're trembling."

"It's cold. I mean, your tale is."

"You're afraid of me."

Euan was silent, gazing down at the pages. He raised his

head finally, hesitantly, and saw with relief how dark it had grown. The wizard's face was as formless as cobweb in the shadows. The cobweb spoke when he did not.

"Do you want to stop? Should I leave it unfinished?"

Yes, I want it to stop, Euan pleaded. Then he heard himself say, horrified, "No, you can't leave me here."

"Where are you?"

Lost, he thought, in some bloody, frozen waste. The last thing alive, watching a pair of monsters battle each other and hoping that neither one looks in my direction.

The wizard made a soft sound, as though he had heard. Euan put the book and pen down, stood up stiffly. "You should eat."

"I'm not hungry."

"Neither am I. But you need your strength for this."

"When it's finished, I'll eat."

"Is there an end to it?" Euan breathed.

"Soon," the wizard said, as he had each time Euan had asked. "You can't write in the dark."

Twin flames sprang from the brace of candles on the table. Euan sat down again, trying not to look at the wizard. But the face on the bed, divided raggedly between flickering light and shadow, haunted his thoughts. What could be worse, he asked himself, than what he imagined? He let his eyes be drawn. He felt his skin grow icy, his blood run cold, as though the raging winter winds were suddenly in the room, and he was something pale and small in the snow, transfixed and utterly helpless. The stranger in the bed looked as if it ate snow-bears whole. The bones of its face were broad and flat like slabs of stone; its eye-sockets were empty pools of dark. It moved restlessly beneath the covers, struggling against its shape. If it breaks free, Euan thought numbly, I'm dead. A scribe from the king's scriptorium, frozen to death by a tale.

But it was already dead, he reminded himself. It was past. Memory. So he hoped. The wizard's face began to surface, molding bone into more familiar curves and hollows. The darkness drained out of his eyes, left a hoarfrost behind, cold and barren, but remotely human.

"Where were we?"

Euan, freed, ducked back behind the thicket of words. "It tore my own heart in two," he read tonelessly, and dipped the quill.

"Every memory, every scrap of power, every word I ever learned spilled out of me. I tried to hold them; they were birds, blood, sand, swirling endlessly away from me in that dark power, until I could not remember even the names for snow, or eyes. I could cling to the only things it could not yet take: my name, and its heart.

"So I put its heart where mine had been, and gave it my name." The stranger's voice, thin and dry as the scratching of words between nib and paper, paused. Euan lifted the quill, waited. He did not dare look up. Whatever lay there on the bed swallowed once or twice, then spoke again. "I looked out of its eyes. I knew all its past, its powers. I became it. And so I knew how to destroy it."

He paused again. Euan waited, staring at the candle flames. The silence stretched, became unbearable. I will not look at him, he thought. I will not look . . .

He turned his head slowly, his eyes strained wide,

unblinking. A frail, aged wizard lay quietly on the bed, his eyes open but unseeing, expressionless. Looking inward, Euan guessed. He still breathed, so he hadn't died. On impulse, Euan glanced behind him to where the wizard gazed.

He saw what stood in the shadows.

The book leaped off his knee; the quill went flying. He slid out of his chair, crouched, ostensibly feeling around him for book and quill, but shifting to put as much furniture as possible between himself and the monster that had come out of the wall beyond the bed. "Memory," he whispered, trying to convince himself. "Illusion." But as he stared at it, he felt himself begin to disappear into the dead void of its eyes. Flesh and bone seemed to be melting into air; all his thoughts shrivelled, rattled like seeds in a dry pod.

Then Unciel spoke and Euan heard his own breath again, felt his shuddering bones.

"Write," the wizard said.

Euan pulled the quill out from under the bed, opened the book again, and drew the next word in a tear of ink out of the jar.

NINETEEN

Gyre watched the one-eyed king hunting through the forests of Serre for the monster more terrible than himself. His warriors were armed from head to foot in silver and steel. Some carried weapons so old that Gyre could not put names to them. His wizard's eye saw the secret fires of magic within the massive blades, the painted, barbed spears, the studded balls and cones of iron. The warriors gathered closely beneath the tree where Gyre sat, then fanned out into smaller companies, each with a trumpeter to speak to one another at need. Gyre, invisible on a branch so high it seemed to overlook the entire forest, saw the birds wheel, startled, beneath him, marking the warriors' paths.

He had no interest in them; they would circle themselves into a labyrinth before they laid eyes on him. His own eyes rose, turned to the dark palace on the cliff just across the air from him. The tree, jutting impossibly high out of the forest, was magic, illusion, someone's secret. He had glimpsed the spell that made it, and had climbed it out of curiosity. That high, he could see the glaziers and glassblowers rebuilding the shattered wall of glass in the great hall. Below them, lined along the outer walls, a motley, unarmed guard stood watch. He could sense their terror, a roil of broken thoughts, nightmare images, regrets and longings for Dacia. He recognized them. I will not, he promised silently, let anyone harm you. Least of all the ogre who rules Serre.

All his thoughts turned then to the ogre's son.

He nearly took the shortest way, a sparrow's flight from the tree to an open casement in the palace. There, invisible, he would simply wait until he found the prince in an unguarded moment, trade faces with him, and send a bewildered and harmless wizard on his way out of Serre. But something caught his eye before he changed shape: a brush of fire, a glint of gold. The tree's secret, he guessed, shifting a branch to see more clearly. A great, crazed nest fashioned out of vines and spiderweb and drying flowers hung across the crook of two boughs. The egg within it seemed to illumine the air around it with its jeweled, glowing hues.

The wizard's throat closed; he swallowed dryly. Such beauty, such magic, must have come out of the very heart of Serre. He felt his hand warm as at the touch of that raw gold, those sweet fires, even before he thought of reaching out to it. What bird, he wondered dazedly, forming within that glittering shell could match its beauty? Then he knew, and felt his heart move, reshape itself at the memory of its song.

The firebird's egg lay there at the top of the world, alone and unprotected. Where, he wondered, was the firebird, abandoning its egg to any passing predator? His mouth tightened as he remembered the bird-woman who had sung every thought out of his head. When last seen, it had crossed the witch's threshold. Surely Brume, avid for firebirds, would not have let it escape easily. But Gyre had seen no sign of it, not a burning feather, not a hair. Even the voice that had melted the wizard's power into dross had not left so much as an echo within Brume's bones. Perhaps the firebird had hidden itself within the witch's fire. Wherever it had gone, it was not in its nest, guarding its egg from rain, or snakes, or from the man crouched on the branch above it, staring at the egg and remembering what other mysteries and beauties he had reached out for in his life. A heart. A princess. A man's name. A kingdom.

Because it is so beautiful, he told himself helplessly. Because if the firebird cannot return, it will die. Because if it dies, the firebird may never sing again in Serre. Because it melts my heart even now with its unborn song. Because I want.

He reached down and took the egg. He had time to hide it like a jewel within an invisible casket lined with a nest of warmth and power, and to slip that nest into his tunic over his heart, before the great tree shuddered and tossed him out of it like a bad fruit. Curious again, he kept his shape, but fell to earth gently and on his feet. Standing in oddly moving shadow, he looked up to find an enormous hand descending over him. It seized him by the hair, raised him with a sickening swoop through the air, and dangled him in front of what looked like the one-eyed King of Serre, but even uglier and multiplied by three.

"I saw the egg first!" the middle head shouted furiously at him.

"No, I did!" argued the head on the right.

"I did!" the left head wrangled, turning a pale, heated eye on its middle self. "And you got the last treasure."

"That was only a book," the middle head grunted disgustedly. A second hand caught Gyre's boots and shook him upside-down over a huge and dirty palm, open to catch the egg when it fell. "And it wouldn't open—I couldn't even read it."

"You can't read," the right head muttered.

"It was magical," the left head fumed. "It was the oldest book in the world and it was magical and you could have kept the jewels on it. You just tossed it away instead of giving it. I would have taken it, lock and all, it was that beautiful. So the egg is mine."

"What about me?"

"The jewels wouldn't come off," the middle head protested, shaking Gyre aggrievedly.

"Just bite his head off," the right head said impatiently, "and give me the egg."

"Wait!" Gyre shouted. His voice boomed and echoed through the trees; the heads went still, staring at him. "Wait," he repeated more quietly, hanging limply with the blood singing in his ears. "What book?"

"What?" one of them ventured finally.

"What book? I might," he suggested, "trade you something for the book."

They considered themselves. The left head produced a verdict. "Just eat him."

"Maybe I can open the book. Maybe I can show you its powers."

The middle head snorted. But its eye wandered uncertainly, from right to left, then back to Gyre. "What are you, besides a thief?"

He paused, surprised at the word. "I suppose I am a thief," he said slowly, trying to explain himself to a three-headed ogre as he dangled upside-down in its grip. "I've only tried to take what looks like my heart."

"I wouldn't touch what your heart must look like by now," the middle head said fastidiously. "Stealing the likes of the firebird's egg. What more have you stolen? Maybe we'd like that even better?"

"I'll show you, if you tell me where the book is. The oldest book in Serre would contain secrets, powers, wonders greater than all the jewels covering it."

"Tell him where you left it," the right head said. "He can't open it anyway. Then we'll bargain."

"I threw it in the cave behind the waterfall in the grove of the oldest trees in the forest. Where the hermit's hut is. Him, I stole the book from. He couldn't open it either. He's dead," the head added.

"Did you eat him?"

"No." The head made a face. "He was too scrawny. And he was already dead."

"Which way?"

"Oldest trees are tallest," the right head said briefly. "You can't miss them." His mouth stretched in a lipless smile, revealing gaps Gyre could have crawled through. "Now give us the egg. Then show us what else you've stolen."

Gyre twisted free, hit the earth again, and changed shape as he rose. This time, he was tall enough to look the ogre in all three eyes.

What had worked with the witch worked for the ogre. He saw stark horror multiplied by three. Then he saw the backs of the ogre's heads as it lumbered away, trying to shrink into its bulk and put trees between itself and the dead-eyed monster as quickly and noiselessly as possible. The monster patted its tunic over its heart, feeling for the egg. Then it stood still a moment, thinking, while birds swirled out of the trees around it and fled.

Kingdom or book?

Ronan, he decided at last, could wait a little. There was nowhere the prince could hide from Gyre and the king would not give up his search for the monster until nightfall. The palace would be quiet and relatively empty until then. Gyre could spare a moment or two to find a book. After he became Ronan, he guessed, he would have few moments to spare for some time, especially for a book hidden within a cave within a waterfall within a grove of the oldest trees within the forest.

He turned himself into one of the fleeing birds and went to look for it.

The oldest book in Serre, he mused as he looked for the tallest trees, might explain the origins of the peculiar magic of Serre. Understanding it, he would possess it; possessing the magic of Serre, he would possess Serre itself, as though he had taken its heart. All its beauty would be his, its mystery, its treasures and secrets. He felt his own heart try to change shape again, grow to encompass such marvels. An echo of the firebird's voice drifted through him then, as though the bird forming within the egg had begun to sing in its dreams.

He saw the huge trees below then, a cluster standing high above the younger forest, and he dropped.

He took his own shape beside a little waterfall as wide as he was tall, and barely twice as tall. A tiny, moldering hut stood near the stream below the falls. The hut was so overgrown with moss that it had begun to resemble an old stump. Its door hung open. Something wafted out of it like a good smell: a hint of power, beckoning, inviting. Gyre eyed it speculatively. In a moment, he answered, and went to investigate the waterfall. It had a silvery exuberant current that pounded over him as he ducked behind it. Clambering over broken slabs of slate in the hollow behind the falls, he saw a smolder of damp blue fire in the shadows.

He pulled the book out of the puddle where it had been tossed, and slipped through the falls again into light. He dried himself with an absent gesture, and studied the book. It was thick, heavy, and unmarked by water, mold, or age. Uncut jewels inlaid in melted pools of gold crusted its binding, front and back. It had no title. The words engraved on it in gold ink said only, succinctly: DO NOT OPEN ME. Gyre could see no lock, but the pages refused to part.

He took it with him into the hermit's hovel. Perhaps the hermit had discovered some way to open it before he died, and had written it down. The hut, dropping a mossy tendril here and there between the ceiling slats, was damp and silent. The skeleton of a raven tied by one leg hung upside-down from its perch near the table. The hermit had died in the chair beside it. His hair, long and silver, still clung to what seemed more like tanned hide than moldering skin. His eyes, a milky blue, startled Gyre. Surely something should have eaten them by now?

Then the hermit spoke and he nearly dropped the book.

"It didn't get far, then."

Gyre swallowed, feeling his heart thwanging like a bow string against his ribs. "It was just behind the waterfall. I thought—the ogre told me—"

The hermit shook his head, one eye narrowing in a smile. "I just pretend, sometimes. It makes living easier, especially when you're visited by an ogre."

"I see."

"Or a stranger." He rose creakily, still looking dead despite his movements, dried and brittle and full of dust. "What," he wondered, "do I have to offer you?"

"What happened to your raven?"

"It died one winter. I forget which. I kept its bones for company." He opened a cupboard; the door fell off, clattered to the floor. "A nice rosehip tea?"

"No," Gyre said, uneasy without knowing why. "Thank you. I cannot stay. I only came in to see if you might have left some clue about how to open this."

The hermit looked at him, surprised. "It says not to."

"So you didn't."

"No. Do you go around opening things that you shouldn't?"

"How else can I find out what's in them?"

"It's very dangerous," the hermit said. His shaggy brows, either of which could have lined a bird's nest, tried to weave themselves together. "That's why it says not to."

"Where did you find this book?"

"It's been here as long as I have," the hermit answered vaguely, and kicked a three-legged stool beside the cold grate. It walked across the stone floor to the table, its sharp, precise steps hitting the slabs in wordless rebuke. "You have to," the hermit whispered to Gyre, "sometimes, to get them started." He cleared his throat, added normally, "I might have a key around somewhere."

"A key?"

"To open the book. That's why you came in here, isn't it? Sit down. I'll look for it."

Gyre glanced uncertainly at the stool. But it was that or the hermit's chair, which wore a dry whitewash of raven droppings. He put the book on the table and sat carefully, expecting the stool to pull itself out from under him and stalk off. It stayed put.

"The book," he said, examining it again, "has no lock."

The hermit stopped clattering through oddments on a shelf. "Oh. Then maybe I don't have a key."

"But," Gyre breathed, inspired, "perhaps the key is in a jewel. If I press the right one, or the right pattern . . ." His fingers slid lightly over a small treasure of rough-hewn jewels, trying to shift them in their solid splashes of gold.

The hermit watched over his shoulder, his finger-bones knocking hollowly around each other. "Can't you take it outside?" he pleaded. "I don't want to see."

"See what?"

"Whatever it's hiding. Look at those jewels. You're waking them. They're seeing you."

So it seemed: Gyre saw his face reflected in sapphire, in emerald, in diamond as clear as water. The gold letters among them seemed to burn more brightly, insistently, warning.

"But I want to know," he told it, stretching his hand to touch five jewels at once, one beneath each finger, each finger covering his intent, curious, fearless face.

The book opened. Steadily and firmly, it pushed its cover back and separated its pages, chose one in the middle for Gyre and the hermit, breathing heavily in Gyre's ear, to gaze at. The page was blank except for a single line of fine gold script across the middle of the parchment.

You have opened your heart, the book said. *Now what will you do?*

The hermit swallowed with a click of bone. Gyre felt his shock like a cold splash of water. The old bones sagged down in the chair, became still again, the filmy eyes wide and staring at what had come to visit him.

Gyre turned and saw the monster he had brought with him into Serre.

TWENTY

Sidonie sat in her chamber, ripping scallops of lace off a skirt. She had sent all her attendants away except for Auri. The girl stood mutely in front of her, thin face pinched with the habitual fear of the past days, her eyes enormous as she watched the princess ruthlessly parting threads, the lace coiling onto the floor at her feet.

"Tell me," Sidonie commanded, "everything you know about Brume."

Auri's eyes grew impossibly larger. "My lady," she whispered, "she is a terrible, ugly witch who eats people."

"She didn't eat Prince Ronan."

"She can be outwitted," Auri conceded reluctantly. "But only if you are very lucky."

"What if I bring her something? Does she like presents?"

"Nobody ever—You must want to find someone, if you

think to bring them a present. Nobody ever wants to find Brume."

"I do," Sidonie said tersely, and ripped an arm's length of lace free with one pull. She heard Auri swallow and scrutinized her suddenly, silently a moment, her eyes narrowed. Auri wore her pretty chestnut hair in an untidy bundle at her neck; a ribbon here and there at wrist and pocket were her only adornments besides the brightly embroidered cloth that her mother had given her. She wore that around her neck, sometimes over her head. It reminded Sidonie of the tapestries on the palace walls, all golds and reds and forest hues. Auri shifted under Sidonie's gaze, beginning to look panicked, as though she expected to be sent on an errand to the witch.

"My lady?" she queried nervously, and Sidonie loosed her, gave another pull to the lace, then shifted her attention to Auri's feet.

"Take off your shoes."

"Yes, my—" Her voice died before she finished; she reached down with shaking fingers to untie a pair of satin ribbons around her ankles. She stepped out of the slippers; the princess, kicking off her own shoes, stepped into them.

"Good," she said, and stepped back out. "The boots you travelled in—I want them."

"Yes—"

"And your scarf."

Auri touched it speechlessly. The touch was gentle, a caress; in the girl's silence Sidonie heard a reluctance to argue. She sighed, her own white, stiff face loosening; she dropped the skirt and put both hands on Auri's shoulders.

"I know that your mother, who is far away in Dacia, made it for you. I'll bring it back to you. I promise."

She felt the girl tremble in her hands. "No, you won't. Not if you're going to look for Brume. You'll never come back."

"She has something I need. She stole it from the prince."

"Let him get it back—he knows how to deal with her!"

Sidonie picked up the skirt again. "He didn't bargain any too well when he saw her last."

"But how can you talk to her? You're not from Serre. You won't know how to speak to her, or what's dangerous and what's not. You don't know not to go into her cottage, or not to drink or eat anything she offers, or not to touch her chickens even if they're tangled in brambles, or not to trust the witch even if she looks like the most beautiful woman in the world. You're a stranger here; you weren't born to deal with the likes of Brume."

"Everyone," Sidonie said between her teeth as she bit through a knot in the thread, "is a stranger when they're born. Tell me what else I don't know."

"My lady, the king will be beside himself if he finds you gone. And what will the prince say? And how will you get out of the palace anyway?"

"What you don't know you won't have to tell. Go on about Brume. How should I speak to her?"

"Just say no," Auri answered miserably, "to everything she wants."

"But I have to give her something in exchange for what I want." Auri didn't answer. Sidonie watched her raise both hands, cover her eyes with them, as though she were already envisioning an absence of princess. "That bad, is she?" Sidonie guessed.

"Yes," Auri whispered.

In spite of all her resolve, the princess felt her hands chill; a tiny, viper-strike of terror bit deep within her. But which, she asked herself, would she rather face? Brume at the end of a very brief life? Or a long and loveless marriage to a man who gave his heart away because it was too much trouble to keep?

She said firmly, tearing a lace bow off the front of the hem, "Auri, go and get your boots, and then help me with my hair. Leave your scarf here. I will bring it back to you. I am going to write a note to the queen. You will give it to her several hours after the king has returned. Not before, and not until dark. Do you understand?" Auri nodded wordlessly, untying the cloth. "And don't tell anyone," Sidonie added fiercely. "Not until you have given the note to the queen. Then, you can say whatever you want if you are questioned."

"I can tell the King of Serre that you have gone to be eaten by Brume."

Sidonie paused at that. "Or," she suggested, "you can hide under my bed."

"Thank you, my lady."

Dressed in the rumpled, laceless dark skirt, her plainest bodice, Auri's boots, and Auri's scarf over hair wound ruthlessly into a knot, she looked at herself in the mirror, and then at Auri. "What do I look like?"

Auri eyed her glumly. "Like a princess in scuffed boots.

Whatever it was the prince left with Brume, let it stay there. It can't be worth—"

"Oh, it's worth," Sidonie said, her voice shaking. "It's worth, to me. I am not doing this for Ronan, but for myself."

The door opened; both their faces went blank with apprehension. A guard threw the door wide for the prince who, appearing so suddenly, startled even Sidonie with his broad, muscular bulk, his face so ambiguously like his father's. Belatedly, Sidonie thought to curtsey; she nearly fell over in Auri's boots.

He gave her frozen, downcast face a cursory glance and asked, "Where is the princess?"

"My lord," Sidonie said gruffly, since Auri seemed incapable of speech, "I believe she is with the queen."

"I have just left the queen."

"Then she must be with her attendants in their chambers. I will summon her for you."

"No. Tell her to remain there until my father returns. I'll come for her then."

"Yes, my lord."

Sidonie curtsied again. He left in a cluster of guards; she made her escape, turning the opposite way down the sparsely guarded hall, while Auri, left in the empty chamber to her own devices, made herself, the princess guessed, as scarce as possible.

With the luck that sprang out of desperation, Sidonie found her way again to the unused tower, spiraled down the steps to the bottom, and hid there until dusk.

The torches along the walls had been lit against the night

before Sidonie felt the pulse beneath her feet of many horses moving quickly into the yard. In the turmoil of dark and fire, of sweating animals, weary warriors, servants and stablers, one plainly dressed figure clinging to the shadows along the walls went unnoticed. The guards were watching the company filling the yard; they did not see what they did not expect: someone going instead of coming. The princess did not stop where the road ran beneath the falls. The rising moon had not yet illumined the face of the cliff; she wanted to reach the bottom before it stripped the shadow off her and gave the watchers on the wall something to see.

She remembered, half-way down the road, what else she had to fear besides the witch.

There was Gyre, the renegade wizard who had tried to steal Ronan's life. And there was the strange, nameless apparition suddenly haunting the forest, frightening even the King of Serre, invisible as wind when it chose to be, whose glance was like a raw, blinding weal left by a shard of ice. Sidonie felt her skin shrink; she wanted to make herself small, creep behind something, under something just to avoid the memory of it. Of the three, witch, wizard, and monster, she decided that she would prefer encountering Brume. She could not outwit the wizard, or outrun the monster. The witch, with her chickens, her stew pot, and her unending hunger seemed at least remotely comprehensible.

The princess met none of them along the road. Standing at the bottom of the falls with the moon looking over the cliff at her and the impenetrable dark within the trees beginning to fray into a lace-work of moon-shadow, she wondered which way to go next.

Anywhere, prudence warned her, rather than stand there at the end of the road waiting for an enraged Ferus to catch up with her. She forced herself toward the huge, ancient trees, motionless and frosted with moonlight. What, she mused, did it mean to lose a heart? To leave it somewhere, walk away from it, find no reason to return for it? She remembered the disheveled, wild-eyed young man who had run out of the trees into her life so long ago. The grief and torment in his face had been the measure of the burden he had yielded to the witch.

No wonder he refused to go back for it.

"I am sorry," she whispered to the prince in the palace high above, who even now must have that cold, stubborn look dawning in his eyes of a man determined not to be thwarted by a recalcitrant possession. "But I cannot live without your heart."

Something moved in a cross-hatch of moonlight and shadow ahead of her and she froze. Pale light struck a star of gold, and then pelt as bright as Ronan's hair. And then an eye and a sharp tooth and Sidonie breathed again. A fox. Two foxes—no three—were padding through the trees ahead of her. They scented her, stopped to look. Her breath caught again. They all turned toward her, as though they had been searching for her, and all of them were crowned.

She closed her eyes, opened them, but the small gold crowns, tilted rakishly behind the pricked ears, had not vanished. They came up to her, sat together in a row, gazing at her. After a moment, she curtsied, so not to offend them in case they took their crowns seriously.

They did, apparently; three heads nodded simultaneously

back at her. Then the one in the middle spoke in a courteous, mellifluous voice, and she resisted an impulse to sit down suddenly in the bracken.

"We are three princes, my lady, who have been turned by fate and the misfortune of our careless lives into foxes. To break the spell and atone for our foolishness, we must stop each human we meet in the forest and ask in what way we might serve."

"How did you—how do you know—"

"In our spellbound, magical forms we see what in our earlier lives we would have been blind to. Worn boots and simple dress do not disguise you. Tell us how we can serve you."

She caught the undertones of eagerness and desperation within the dulcet voice, and could not help asking, "How many humans do you have to help before you regain your true bodies?"

"We do not know, my lady. Every human we meet might be the one who turns us human again. Please tell us what we can do for you."

"You can help me find Brume."

They gazed at her silently again, eyes dark and moonshot. Then they looked at one another. One loosed a strangled whimper and they all sprang up and then away, slinking low to the ground, noses toward the nearest pool of darkness, tails between their legs.

She stared after them, dumbfounded and suddenly overwhelmed with the temptation to turn and slink back to the palace herself, rather than face what they feared more than the spell that bound them. But she heard herself cry, "Wait! Come back! I might be the last! I might turn you human!"

"They panic so easily," someone commented behind her. "Feckless men make feckless foxes." Sidonie jumped, and nearly took off after them. "Don't be afraid, child," the voice added. "I'll help you."

She turned slowly, looked this way and that and then down. A tiny, bent old woman, made of twigs and spiderweb it seemed, smiled up at her. Her eyes looked the color of the moon, so old they were. She held a basket filled with some strange, pale, pungent flowers. "Moondrops, I call them," she explained as Sidonie sneezed. "They only bloom at night, and for only seven days a month. They keep ogres away, and sprites and trolls, such things that might disturb an old woman alone in her cottage."

"I can understand why," Sidonie said stuffily. "Do they guard against witches?"

"Nothing will guard against Brume when she's of a mind."

"Was it Brume who turned the princes into foxes? Is that why they ran?"

The old woman shook her head. "Brume wouldn't work such a spell. Why would she bother to reform anybody?"

"Then who did?"

"I don't know. Those foxes have been around as long as I have." She dropped a bloom into her basket. "I should ask what dire straits a young and unprotected maiden might find herself in to go seeking that abominable witch."

"I—"

"But I won't. I'll only ask you for something in return for my help." The crone paused, still smiling, head crooked expectantly for Sidonie's reply.

"What?" Sidonie asked cautiously, wondering if she might be asked to sneeze the night away picking flowers.

"That lovely scarf you wear over your hair. My daughter has so few bright things of her own. Let me give it to her. I'll take you to Brume. I know where she likes to sleep; I've seen her cottage many times."

Sidonie's fingers closed on the knot at her throat. "I wish I could give it to you, but I can't. It isn't mine to give, and I promised to return it."

The sudden bark of laughter the woman gave startled Sidonie; it sounded like a fox's noise. "Return? From that witch's house? She'll make a quick meal of you, and why should she have the scarf as well?"

Sidonie swallowed, her fingers tight around the knot; she backed a step. "I'm sorry—"

"If you won't, you won't," the woman said shortly. "Mind your feet, you're stepping in the flowers."

Sidonie shifted hastily, smelling them. "Is there anything else you want?"

"No."

"I didn't promise to bring the boots back."

"No."

"Can't you just point me in one direction or another? Please?"

The old woman, bent over the crushed moondrops, pointed in one direction, then another. Sidonie sighed noiselessly.

"Are you certain—"

"Nothing," the woman said without turning. She said nothing more. Sidonie left her finally, a smell acrid enough to discourage the King of Trolls wafting from her boot soles as she walked.

It seemed to discourage the entire forest; nothing accosted her again for a very long time. She walked for hours, it seemed, though the moon hardly seemed to move. The forest's night must be longer than the moon's, she thought wearily. She paused to scoop up a handful of water that tasted of frogs and moss and wondered if she were walking in circles through the unchanging trees. If not, she must be half-way to Dacia by now. Surely a witch with wits enough to trap a prince would know when a meal was trying to put itself under her nose. Maybe, Sidonie thought finally, the witch knows that I'm searching for her. Perhaps the cottage of bone was running silently away from her at every step she took toward it. Perhaps Brume did not want to give up Ronan's heart.

She slumped against a tree, cold, hungry, and exhausted; she saw with despair that the moon, its face tilted to one side, was peering down at the other side of the forest now. It would set and plunge the trees into deep night, leaving Sidonie with nothing to do but wait for sunrise. She would be forced to search for the witch and elude the hunting king at the same time. And Ronan, too, very likely; she would have to find his heart before he found her. She would never get another chance, if they found her first. She would become queen of her own prison, like Calandra. She would forget that once she had glimpsed the love and sorrow, the despair and wonder that Ronan had abandoned to the witch; she would come to think, like he did, that she could live without.

Tears scalded her eyes, glittered in the dying moonlight as they fell.

A sweet, haunting voice said above her head, "I will take you to Brume."

She looked up and saw the firebird.

TWENTY-ONE

The queen sent for her son some time after supper. One thing and another delayed Ronan: his father's return, Ferus demanding his son's immediate presence, renewed suspicions for no reason other than that the king had not laid eyes on Ronan for a day and in a day anything could happen. Nothing had that Ronan could see. King and warriors had come back unscathed; the terrified company from Dacia ringing the outer walls remained unmolested. Even so, the wizard had once blinded the king in his remaining eye, and the king no longer trusted it. The test he devised for Ronan left the prince limping. But Ferus was satisfied and Ronan held no grudges: in matters concerning Serre, better to be safe than sorry.

So it was nearly midnight when he finally went to see

Calandra. He expected her to be asleep, and would not have wakened her. But she was pacing among her bright tapestries, her long hair unbraided and rippling down her silks, her eyes as wintry as he had ever seen them.

She saw the hesitation in his step; her mouth tightened.

"I'm sorry to be so late," Ronan said. "I have been with my father."

"So I see."

He waited politely for her to sit so that he could rest his aching leg. But she only handed him a note in passing and continued pacing.

"Read it."

He opened the thick paper with the broken seal he did not recognize.

I have gone, it said without preamble, *to find Brume and persuade her to return the prince's heart*. The prince blinked. It was inconceivable; therefore it could not be true. *You will not receive this until I have been gone for many hours*.

He glanced up bewilderedly. He had not seen the princess at supper, but then he hadn't come for her, either, as he had said he would. He assumed she would be with her attendants, waiting for him.

"No one," the queen said, "can find her in the palace. Read."

"Preposterous," he breathed, but finished the note. *Ronan may be able to live quite happily without his heart, but I cannot. If I do not return, I will be sorry, but not as sorry as I will be if I return without. My attendants can tell you nothing. No one knows how or where I have gone. I will try to come back. Sidonie.*

Ronan stared at his mother. "I don't believe this," he said blankly. "Do you believe this?"

"Yes."

"That she went off on her own looking for Brume? Nobody goes looking for Brume! Most certainly not a princess from Dacia who wouldn't know Brume from a goose-girl. And how could she get out of the palace again? She's hiding somewhere. Question her attendants. Who brought this to you."

"Sit down," the queen said, and he realized that he was trembling, precariously balanced on his injured leg. He sat a moment before he might have fallen.

"Does my father know?"

"Have you heard him shout?"

He remembered then that he had been with the king himself all evening. "You didn't tell him," he breathed incredulously. "Why didn't you tell him? We could have gone after her immediately; how far do you think she could have gotten, alone in the forest?"

"I don't know, Ronan. How far did you get?" The odd impatience in her voice, verging on exasperation, puzzled him. He opened his mouth; she did not give him a chance to answer. "You have grown as blind as your father, seeing the world out of one eye and missing it entirely with the other. What exactly do you think she has gone to look for? And why do you think she cannot live without it?"

"She has gone looking for my heart," he said, for that much was clear. "I have no idea why she can't live without it. I can."

"She may die, and all you can do is sit there wondering who in the palace to punish for the fact that she is gone. Perhaps—I know this is a foolish thought and I am equally foolish to consider it—you are to blame?"

He studied her, trying to understand. She did not look foolish. She looked furious, grim and formidable, ready to bellow herself, if he could not make himself immediately comprehend what he had done wrong.

"But I've done nothing," he told her, and forced himself to stand. "Neither have you. You should have told us as soon as you received this."

"I tried."

"You sent for me. You didn't tell the king. It's late now; we'd have to ride with torches, search the forest in the dark. My father will be—"

"Ronan." Again her voice stopped him. It seemed gentler now, as though she spoke to someone else, another Ronan she once had known. "Do you trust me with matters of Serre? Its tales, its history?"

The matter of Serre was all around them, in her lively tapestries, her books. "Of course I do," he told her, for it was true. Even his father trusted her in such matters, usually without question.

"Then go." She held his eyes. "Just go and find her. Alone. Now. Because all I can tell your father, if you don't, is that you belong to Brume, you have never truly left her, and the King of Serre's only son and heir is still imprisoned in one of the witch's spells, still doing her bidding in spite of all your protests that you are free. Go and find that princess before Brume does. And don't come back without your heart, because if you do I will not recognize you as my son."

She left him, he realized, with not a word to say. So he said nothing, simply bowed his head before he turned, limping unsteadily, feeling oddly bruised again as though, like his father, she had tested him, only she had seen what the one-eyed king had missed.

So he rode back down into the forests of Serre, carrying a torch to see the road and well aware that the fire which might draw the princess to him could also attract the monster even his father feared. It might also catch the king's eye as he watched his mirrors. But Ronan was fairly certain that his father, worn with long days, longer nights, and constant worry over his son, was sleeping for once. Gyre crossed the prince's mind. He reined, nearly turned back at the memory of the wizard who had waited for him at the bottom of the road. But even if the wizard had escaped from Brume, which seemed more than likely, he couldn't take much more from Ronan than Ronan's mother would if the prince returned without whatever it was he had left with Brume. If the queen refused to recognize Ronan, neither would the king, and Ferus would show no more mercy to his true son than he had to the false bridegroom.

The prince reached the forest without drawing the attention of anything beyond the eyes of a few night-hunters, who kept well out of his torchlight. He stopped among the trees to think. If he found Brume first, then he could retrieve his heart as well as rescue the princess if she managed to find Brume's cottage before him. If the princess had not yet found the witch, so much the better. From what Ronan remembered of Brume, he might have to leave an eye or a hand behind in return for Sidonie's life. If he chanced across the princess first, he could send her back to the palace on his horse, along with a solemn promise not to come home without his heart. That should satisfy her. And his mother. He could remind Brume that she held his heart hostage in return for the wizard Gyre, and she had already captured him. She had no further use for it; in all fairness, she should give it back to Ronan. He had no idea if Brume had ever been fair about anything in her very long life. But that heart was worth a kingdom now, instead of nothing, and he would do what he had to, if not what she demanded, to get it back.

He rode into the heart of night. The moon grew distant and cold, and even the hunters slept. In the barren clearing where he had first crossed the witch's path, he saw her cottage. Its round window was dark. The hens were silent. He dismounted wearily, as the cottage loosed a breath of rotting bone over him. Armed now with sword and fire, and prepared to kill if he had to, he drew his blade and pounded with the hilt against the door.

"Brume! I am Ronan of Serre and I have returned for my heart."

He had to pound and shout a few more times before he heard the chickens cluck. Something hit the floorboards hard; an incoherent grumbling followed. The door opened. The witch appeared, scratching an armpit and yawning hugely. She was quite lovely, which caused the sword to falter with a blink of torchlight before Ronan forced it forward to touch the pearly skin in the hollow of her throat. Her hair drifted past her knees, a rich, tangled gold. Above the green lenses sliding down her nose, her eyes were blue as cornflowers. She squinted at him, then pushed the lenses up with a slender finger.

"Oh," she said. "It's you."

"I have come back for my heart."

She seemed oblivious of the sword at her throat, only argued, "You didn't bring me the wizard."

"I was watching," he said evenly, "when Gyre walked into your house. You shut the door and ran away with him. If I had not been there for him to trap, he would not have been there for you. What did you do with him? Is he dead?"

She shrugged a little; a lacy sleeve slid off her shoulder. "He was too much trouble," she answered vaguely. "So now I have neither my white hen, nor the firebird, nor the wizard. I have only your heart, for what it's worth, to repay me for the hen you killed."

"I want my heart back."

"I want my hen back."

"Enough," he said between his teeth. A streak of fire ran down the blade as he readied it. "Give me back my heart or I will kill you here and now and burn your house and all your hens when you are dead."

She gave him a long look out of the corners of her eyes, down the length of the blade. The steps he stood on vanished suddenly and he fell with a thump that jarred all the drowsing pain awake in his leg. He swallowed a cry, dropped the torch, and caught his balance on the blade, desperately reaching out to catch hold of her threshold with his other hand before the door slammed and the cottage began to run.

But the door stayed open. The witch spat on the torch to put it out, and turned back into her house, grumbling. "Well, you'll have to come in and find it. You're not the only one to leave your heart with me, but you're the only one who has ever come back for it. I can't be expected to tell them all apart."

She waited expressionlessly, her arms folded, not giving him a step to climb on. He hoisted himself up across her threshold, gritting his teeth and bearing the pain rather than lowering the blade between them and helping himself up with it. The chickens muttered anxiously on their roosts on one side of the tiny cottage; sullen embers in her hearth pulsed and snapped on the other. Beyond the witch, the shadows gathered like folds of heavy, dark fabric.

On his feet finally, he asked her tensely, "Where is it?"

She gestured, yawning again. "Back there. In the dark. Go on, choose one so I can go back to bed."

He shook his head. "You go. Find it for me."

She rolled her eyes and heaved a sigh. Then she faded where she stood. He was turning edgily, his sword cutting a swathe through the rank smells, when she reappeared carrying what looked like an armful of glittering starfire.

"Here," she said crossly and tossed it at him. He raised one hand awkwardly to catch it; it melted into him and vanished. He took a breath or two, wondering if it would try to tear him piecemeal, like one of his father's spells. Then he found himself thinking about goats.

There seemed to be an entire herd of them in his head,

along with the goatherd, a barefoot, comely boy picking flowers on the slope where the goats fed. The goatherd held the flowers out, smiling, his eyes streaked with summer light, opaque as the golden eyes of the black goat behind him.

"I don't think," Ronan heard himself begin breathlessly, as the heart within him opened like a flower.

"No?" the witch said, and drew the heart back out of him in a long scarf of sparkling light. She vanished again, returned with another armful, her pipe lit now and adding to the stench. "Try this one."

This time, he heard a voice after what seemed an eon or two of some hushed, tranquil darkness, a night without stars, without sound, or deep motionless water in which he lay without thought, without dreams. "I think," the voice said, far above the water, beyond the night, "I'm dead."

"Really?"

He blinked and saw the witch again, expelling little, rapid clouds from her pipe as she frowned at the gleam in her arms. She tossed the heart into the fire. Ronan watched it burst in a dazzle of stars, then melt into a hard, black lump among the coals.

He closed his mouth. The witch appeared again, threw a third heart to him.

"Take all night," she said peevishly. "Don't choose just any heart. You must want the one badly that you left here with me, thinking you'd get the last laugh at the old witch and her bones."

It was true, so he did not answer, just took in the stray heart in dignified silence.

He saw a face on a bed, so beautiful in its pale, dreaming stillness, that all he could imagine was how much more beautiful it would be awake and smiling into his eyes. He was reaching out to it when he felt the heart without him swell to unbearable dimensions and then break, spilling love and grief, pain and bewilderment everywhere through him. He fell to his knees, half-blind, every breath aching, a sound coming out of him like the keen of wood in the flames.

Dimly, he heard the witch speak. "I'll take it back, if you don't want it. In return for a small favor, of course."

"No," he whispered, between breaths of fire, "I want it."

"Why? Why would anyone want such a terrible thing?"

"I don't know, but it is mine and I must take it." He got to his feet somehow; still racked, barely able to walk, he stumbled to the door. He tripped on the bone that was the witch's threshold, and fell headlong back into night.

He lay there on the forest floor, dazed and half-dreaming, while his life pieced itself together with a needle as sharp as sorrow drawing threads of every color from gold to blood to bone. He gazed at every memory out of his heart's eye, relearned all the words he had forgotten, including wonder that such enormities could be contained in such small, brief sounds as love, grief, life, death. Such words grew out of the wordless, wild language of the heart. That, he realized finally, was what he had so carelessly given to the witch: without that wordless language, he had left himself mute.

He raised his head finally, wearily, and relearned more words: beauty, magic, peace. The firebird had flown soundlessly into the barren clearing. It came to rest, its plumes of fire gathering and settling around it, on the line of bones along the witch's peaked roof. Transfixed, wordless again, he watched it. Its gold beak opened; it did not sing, but spoke in a clear, tender human voice.

"Here," it said to someone entering the clearing. "She will wake when you knock."

Ronan brought his gaze down from the roof, stared in astonishment at the young woman trudging up to the witch's cottage. It had shifted a step or two toward the stranger, and its steps had reappeared. She was simply dressed; her bundled hair was hidden beneath a scarf; her thick soles clumped up the steps. She raised a fist at the door of bone. Ronan heard her breath catch shakily, and he opened his mouth to cry a warning.

But the witch spoke first, screeching over his voice at the knock on her door. "Now what?"

"I am Sidonie of Dacia," the young woman said, "and I have come for Prince Ronan's heart."

The cottage door flew open, snapped up the princess like a pecking beak, and swallowed her.

TWENTY-TWO

Euan sat at the wizard's bedside, watching Unciel while Unciel watched nothing at all. His eyes were open; he still breathed. By that, Euan concluded that he was still alive, though the wizard had not moved or spoken for hours. The last word he had said was "finally." Euan had written it down with a silent groan of relief. Finally the wizard did whatever it was he had to do to kill the monster. Finally the bleak, endless tale was coming to an end. He waited, pen hovering impatiently. But that, it seemed, had been the wizard's final word on the subject. He simply stopped, left his frail, weary, helpless body behind, and went elsewhere in his mind. Euan called to him, pleaded with him, read the gardening records aloud until his voice was hoarse. Not even his garden could coax the wizard back.

The scribe slumped sleeplessly in his chair, his eyes gritty, burning candles through the night while the wizard lay in his strange trance. The tale had drained his strength, Euan guessed. The harrowing memories, the unpredictable shifts the wizard's body made between man and monster had worn him down to little more than a heartbeat weak as a moth's flutter and just enough strength to take the next breath. He had fought the monster again in his telling; this time, Euan thought starkly, it might be the wizard who lost his life.

He replaced a guttering candle. The monster still haunted the shadows around him, but the thought of the wizard's death was beginning to out-loom the unfinished tale. It would be a hideous mockery of fate for Unciel to be slain by the story of his own victory. And, Euan thought miserably, it will be my fault. He leaned over the wizard, spoke gently, clearly, around the tightness in his throat.

"If you don't wake by dawn, I must tell the king that you need help."

But not even that roused the wizard. The raven, perched on the carved wooden bed frame above the wizard's head and gazing darkly down at Unciel, did not make matters easier. The one-eyed cat watched as well, sometimes on Euan's knee. Euan, wrapped in a blanket against a cold that seemed to have taken up residence in his bones, waited and wondered how much to tell the king.

Slowly the long night frayed, turned silvery beyond the windows. Euan blew out the candles, stood up stiffly. The wizard did not move an eyelash. The broken thread in the blanket near his face, which Euan had been staring at for the last hour, still quivered under the wizard's faint breath.

"I'm going now," Euan told him, "to the king. I'll be back very soon. Wait for me."

He fed the raven and the cat in the kitchen before he left, and closed the door to Unciel's room so that the raven's plunging beak would not be the last thing the wizard saw. The raven gave a cry at that, but only flew to its perch and ruffled its feathers, regarding Euan dourly as he left.

He had flung his scribe's robe over his disheveled clothing. But his limp hair and blood-shot eyes, he realized, would not charm those guarding the palace gates. They would recognize the robe, however, so he went into the gate nearest the king's library. It was early for the usual stream of scribes into the scriptorium. A proctor might be there, though; they seemed to live among the worm-eaten scrolls. He drifted, dazed and forlorn, into the scriptorium, feeling that years had passed since he had left it to find the wizard's house.

To his relief, Proctor Verel was there, sitting at his desk and rubbing his bald pate absently as he read. He blinked at Euan.

"I have to see the king," the apparition said. "I think Unciel is dying."

"Dying!" The proctor bounced to his feet, eyes narrowing with bemusement as they took in the unwashed, exhausted scribe. "Of what?"

"I was writing down the story of his last battle. He

couldn't finish it. Now he won't speak or move—he only breathes. It was my fault—I persuaded him—"

"You persuaded him to let you write that tale?" The proctor navigated his circular body around his desk, staring at the scribe. "The king himself asked him to tell it and he refused."

"It's a horrible tale," Euan said bleakly.

"Of course it would be. Look what it did to him. Were you expecting poetry?"

"I suppose I was."

"It'll get turned into that soon enough."

"He hasn't finished it."

"Then we cannot let him die, can we? I'll get a message to the king. Wait here."

But Euan, feeling lonely among the empty desks, like something dark, unrecognizable with portent in the bright, tranquil room, did not wait. He walked blindly back through the streets, worried that Unciel might wake suddenly to no one, and decide to die alone. The raven gave its usual cry as he entered and fluttered toward him, a confusion of claw and beak and rattling feathers, before it settled itself on Euan's shoulder. The one-eyed cat ran ahead. Euan opened the door, holding his breath. Then he breathed again. So did the wizard. Euan sank down in the chair and closed his eyes.

He was asleep when the raven cried again. The sound seemed to come from Euan's heart, as though it had split itself in two and hatched the raven's child. He jerked himself awake, heard footsteps in the hall. He cast a bleary eye at the wizard as he stumbled to his feet. The little fiber still quivered; Unciel still gazed expressionlessly at nothing. Euan opened the door, found the King of Dacia pushing doors open at random down the hall.

There was a woman with him. She did not bother to glance in the rooms the king searched. Her eyes were on Unciel's chamber door when Euan opened it. Intent, somber, they melted into a smile at the sight of the scribe. Heliotrope, he thought, remembering the pale purple wash of color and scent from Unciel's garden. It seemed a very long time since anyone had smiled in that house.

He bowed his head to the king. Others had crowded into the outer room; he heard murmuring, floorboards creaking. They had come for Unciel, he guessed, and felt a numb despair that things had gone so terribly awry.

"In here, my lord," he said to Arnou. He ducked his head again, shyly at the king's companion.

"Euan Ashe. Lady Tassel," the king said briefly. "My father's sister. She inherited some of the powers of Sailles's line. She may be able to help the wizard."

Lady Tassel was a tiny woman with great, sunken lavender eyes and a pale, pointed face full of constantly shifting lines. They rearranged themselves as she cast a veiled glance at the king, who seemed, even to Euan's distracted attention, to be tense as an unsprung trap and inwardly fuming.

"My lord," Euan began, hesitated, then took a blundering step toward the truth. "Unciel did not want to tell you, but—"

He felt flingers slide around his arm; Lady Tassel interrupted gravely. "He was far weaker than he let us know.

True? And so he had some difficulty speaking to the young wizard in Serre."

"Well. That, too, but—"

"One thing at a time. Let me see if I can wake him. Maybe then I will be able to help him."

"Maybe," Euan sighed, evading the king's suspicious eye. But none of them wanted to bring the unspoken tangle into the wizard's chamber. They stood silently while Lady Tassel, her eyes hooded again, saying nothing, studied the wizard. Something of the tale must have lingered in the room, or in the wizard's mind, Euan guessed; he saw her eyes widen suddenly. She dropped down into the chair, the lines suddenly harsh on her blanched face.

"What is it?" the king asked sharply.

"I don't know," she answered vaguely. "I've never known the like . . ." She glanced at Euan. "Where is the tale he has been telling you?"

"What good will that do?" Arnou demanded. "He must be moved immediately, he must be watched by a physician—"

"My lord." She patted his hand. "If you cannot be quiet, go away. You promised that you would let me do as I see fit."

"Yes, but—"

"I don't think he is dying."

"You don't?" Euan breathed.

"I think he has summoned a memory or fashioned a dream and gone into it. You'll have to wait until he returns to ask him anything." She turned again to Euan, holding out her hand insistently. "The tale?"

He gave her the little leatherbound book full of gardening notes and an unfinished battle. "Be careful," he warned. "The tale has a life of its own."

"So I see."

"What does that mean?" the king asked edgily. Euan shook his head wordlessly, chilled at the memories. Lady Tassel, glancing with interest through the wizard's sketches, answered gently.

"Perhaps, my lord, you should leave us for a while. I will call you the instant we need you. Whatever danger Unciel might be in, it's nothing a physician can remedy. When he can speak again, of course I will ask him first about Sidonie."

"It might be faster," the king said impatiently, "if I just send an army into Serre to ask Ferus."

"It would certainly make most other matters irrelevant," she murmured, and found the beginning of the tale. She added to Euan, without looking up, "Go and eat something. Take a nap. Wash. I will watch him very carefully, I promise." Euan, hovering, reluctant to leave her, found the old eyes on his face again, cool and startlingly perceptive. "Don't worry. I'll call you if it comes to an end."

He left her. Arnou, after a word or two, followed; he found Euan in the kitchen, pouring water into a kettle over the fire.

"What," the king asked explosively, "is going on in Serre? Has there been any word at all from Gyre since he told Unciel that all was well?"

Euan opened his mouth to answer, saw again the monstrous face in the bowl that was Gyre, and closed his eyes. "No, my lord. Not a word."

A voice drifted out of a half-open drawer. "Arnou. Go home."

The king tossed his hands. "You'd think that my daughter could pick up a pen and write."

"Yes, my lord."

The king, still simmering, finally took most of his men out of the wizard's house, back to the palace with him. Euan washed himself in the kitchen, put on clean clothes, listening tensely all the while for sounds from the wizard's chamber. It was very quiet. He made a cup of something hot to keep himself awake. Half-way through it, he laid his head down on the kitchen table and went to sleep.

The raven woke him again, crying as it floated down the hall in front of Lady Tassel, who seemed to be lighting candles with her fingers as she walked. She disappeared. Euan heard her speak to the men who had remained in the house. She sent them away, apparently; the door opened and closed again. Euan, his head and mouth full of wool, took a sip of cold, bitter tea, then rose as the lady and the raven joined him. Candle stubs sparked on the table. Lady Tassel sat down slowly, very carefully, as though her bones were made of glass. Her face under its lacework of lines seemed also to be made of glass, too brittle for expression.

Euan asked huskily, apprehensively, "Is he—"

"As he was."

"Did you see?"

The old eyes shifted to him, still stunned. "I was able to go a little way into his thoughts. My brother, Arnou's father, had a great gift for that. It's an enormously valuable skill for a ruler to possess, and we are fortunate that Arnou inherited nothing of it, or Dacia would have been at war with Serre by sunset today. That would be his only possible response to the danger in Serre: that it must be Ferus's fault."

"What is Unciel doing?"

She put a slender, bony hand over her mouth a moment, her eyes filling with what she had seen. Then she reached for Euan's cup and swallowed the dregs. "He seems to be fighting again. But whether he is battling memories or something real, I can't tell. It seems to have a name, though. The other one—the one he killed—he didn't name, when he told you the tale."

"No."

"Don't you have anything stronger than tea?"

"I think there's some old wine."

But he did not move; neither did she. "This wizard," she said finally, "whom Unciel sent to guard Sidonie through Serre."

"Gyre."

"What possessed Unciel?"

"I don't know." Euan's voice caught. "I have never understood that. It's as though he sent them off to Serre together, but to different places and with different expectations. I can love him and care for him and write whatever it is he wants to tell me, but don't expect me to understand him. All I know is that if he dies and that monster still lives, no matter what its name is, we are all in trouble."

"Its name is Gyre."

"And its name is Unciel," he told her, and rose to get the wine.

TWENTY-THREE

"You're dead," Gyre whispered to the flat-faced, slab-muscled monster standing where the hermit's threshold had been. The front wall of the hovel looked as though it had been slashed away by some inhuman claw. A broken slat swung crazily from the ceiling overhead. One side of the rough stone hearth had crumpled to the ground. The hermit, collapsed in his chair, seemed to retreat farther and farther into himself. Gyre heard the breath trickle out of him, and then silence; even the waterfall seemed to be frozen within that suspended breath of time.

"Gyre," said the face of his heart, and the hut exploded. Stones, boards, cupboard doors, hermit, book, and raven bones spun upward in a wind so cold that Gyre felt his body fray into it rather than endure it. All around him a terrible winter seemed to be stretching across the forest. Trees groaned and buckled; panicked deer bounded past wolves running in the opposite direction. Birds wheeled together and scattered, windblown and helpless. Gyre heard a distant, fiery cry, like a splash of liquid gold, as if, far away, the firebird had been finally touched by cold.

"What have I done?" he wondered, too incredulous even yet to be terrified. A faint, sweet voice echoed the firebird; it seemed to come out of Gyre's own thoughts. Then he remembered the egg encased in magic and hidden in the secret place over his heart. He had time for nothing more than that moment's worth of memory. Then the monster, which had faded behind the howling, biting wind, shaped itself out of it, skin pallid as winter and impervious as stone, eyes that stripped the name out of everything they saw, until nothing recognized only itself. Gyre felt the stunning blankness of its gaze, the power that might have renamed him nothing because nothing was all it understood.

But it knew him. Its voice was deep and raw, a roar more like storm than wild beast. "Give me my heart," it demanded. Gyre, confused by the sweet murmuring of the firebird disturbed within its shell, wondered for an instant exactly what he had stolen out of the nest.

Then he remembered the dark cave in Fyriol, the dragon within the dark, the casket within the dragon's heart, the heart within the casket . . . He felt his face grow slick with horror before the cold sweat froze into that expression.

"You. I took your heart." Wind ripped the words out of him before they sounded. But he was telling the waiting monster nothing it did not know; it was he who had not known. "And then it vanished. I thought it vanished. I thought it had faded away, something long dead, too ancient to live any longer in light. But all that time you were alive. You had begun to search for your heart. It didn't vanish—Unciel must have taken it from me. And then he fought you alone on the edge of the world. But he killed you." He felt himself trembling badly, from horror as much as from the raging winds. "You're dead."

It did not seem to realize that. It took a step toward Gyre, reaching for him to pull its heart out of wherever Gyre had hidden it. But there is no heart, Gyre thought confusedly as he put the grove of oldest trees between himself and the monster. There is only the firebird's egg. The trees were suddenly flying around him like a handful of wildflowers uprooted and tossed into the wind. Gyre, making something very small and very fast out of himself, ducked into the cave behind the frozen waterfall.

He remembered then that the King of Serre was riding through his forests, hunting that monster.

Another roil of comprehension and dread surged through him. The one-eyed king, with all his careless, obstreperous magic and his fierce love of Serre, would not survive one glance from that bleak-eyed death that had followed Gyre into Serre. His men would meet the fate of the forest dwellers, hermit and fox and bird, whose distant cries the wizard's heart picked like threads out of the howling wind.

What have I done? he asked himself bewilderedly. I borrowed a face. I opened a book. Unciel thought it had died but he couldn't kill it. If he could not kill it, with all his immense powers, how can I?

"Where is my heart?"

The ribbons of ice shielding Gyre snapped, rained in pieces around him. Gyre made himself even smaller, hid within a cracked stone. He was pulled ruthlessly out and into his own shape by winds that cut like knives across his skin, whittling the living, breathing, shuddering human thing out of themselves.

"Give me my heart."

"I don't have your heart!"

"I saw it in you."

The wind with the face of the monster and fingers of ice seemed to rifle through him, flinging thoughts, powers, memories along with torn pieces of clothes and shoe leather and buttons piecemeal into the storm. Gyre felt himself begin to disappear; a sound tore out of him. Then he was running again, maybe a snow hare, maybe a silver fox, trying desperately to hide from the winds within the wind.

Something was falling. He saw its pale shadow on the white ground, looming larger and larger as it came down, seeming to come down forever because it had so far to fall. He gave one desperate surge of speed, leaped from under it just before it pounded down across his last footprints. The earth shuddered. Branches whipped across him, throwing him down. Something collapsed on top of him, buried him in light, rustling fragments.

He felt the earth thud again, and pulled himself out of the tangle. He glimpsed, just before he changed shape again, an odd jumble of vine and wildflowers, cobwebs and twigs, that the relentless winds were busy picking to pieces. He recognized it as he flew.

The firebird's tree had fallen.

Too stunned for coherent thought, his mind crowded with images: trolls and magic stags, ogres, water-sprites, hermits, wood-witches, the firebird itself, all fleeing the incomprehensible killing storm. As though his fears had summoned her, Gyre saw the cottage of bone running through the forest ahead of him. Trees broke like broom-straws around Brume as she passed, their ancient hearts groaning, streaking the wild winds with the scent of resin as they died.

Then he was dragged out of flight, pulled again into the shrieking snarl of wind to stare into the empty eyes of the monster that saw nothing everywhere it looked, except when it looked at itself.

"Give me my heart."

Gyre was silent. He was still alive, he guessed, for no other reason than that the monster had recognized something of itself in him. He was allowed to contemplate that bitter thought for an instant. Then he felt a bone twist as the monster probed for the marrow. The wind tore away what might have been a scream. He saw the palace then, through the flurrying winter the monster seemed to carry with it. The twin falls had frozen. The dark palace seemed to float on a river of ice, high above the ravaged forest. He could no longer see the helpless company from Dacia ringing it. They had fallen where they froze, or had fled across the ice into the wood whose pale, slender trees, stripped of leaf and bird and bent nearly double, streamed bare boughs like hair in the wind.

Sidonie, he thought. The name sparked a rill of power that the monster batted away like a leaf. He had sworn to protect her from all the unpredictable magic in Serre. Not even Unciel had guessed that the most unpredictable magic of all would be her protector. And now her protector was being probed in mind and marrow for something he had taken that seemed to belong to no one, because of a face he had borrowed, a lie he had told. As the monster tore apart the wizard to find its heart, so it would tear Serre apart around them, until like a book with all its tales and history ripped from it and tossed to the frenzied wind, there would be nothing left of it but a name.

The winds shrieked suddenly as the monster wrenched something out of Gyre. For a moment, feeling suddenly hollowed, empty without pain, he thought he must have lost his life. Then what the monster had found became clear in its hold, as it unravelled Gyre's careful spell. Gold warmed the merciless wind, colors and shapes of shell like cut jewels glittered wildly at every shift of light as though the egg were trying frantically to make itself more beautiful still, to attract the firebird's vanished eye.

Gyre heard the cry within the egg, the night-music of the firebird, calling to the magic of Serre.

"No," he gasped. "No. It is not your heart. It is the heart of Serre and you are breaking it."

The monster did not answer. The fires within the net of gold, within the jewels, began to fade as the empty eyes gazed at it, seeing nothing. Gyre tried desperately to snatch it, all his powers, his own fires, swirling around him to break the relentless hold over him. All he had left within himself he turned to power: words, knowledge, memory, love, longing. That and whatever he found still alive around him enveloped him in white-hot sheets, swirling plumes, and feathers of fire. He came to the end of it finally, blind, drained; he had nothing left but the cold, charred ember of himself. He felt the winds again, saw the empty eyes. He could not move.

He found a few stray words in him, as all the beauty left of Serre dimmed and frayed before his eyes.

"If you cannot find your heart, take mine," he whispered. "But let the firebird live."

The flat, barren eyes held his for a very long time, it seemed, before he received an answer.

"Give this to Brume," the monster said, handing him the firebird's egg before it wandered away into the green and suddenly peaceful trees.

TWENTY-FOUR

Sidonie, inside the witch's house, saw nothing at first but chickens: ranked on their roosts, turning a black, glittering eye at her in the sullen light, shifting a feather, loosing a cluck over yet another disturbance. Their acrid smell nearly overpowered the stench of rotting bone. She pushed Auri's scarf over her face, trying not to choke, her eyes watering as she looked warily around for the witch. A pot of something oily and dark above the fire formed slow bubbles that belched wetly as they broke. A shadow moved above the pot. She saw a hand crooked and skeletal as a hen's claw pick up a wooden paddle and stir the pot.

Then she saw the eyes above the pot.

They were entirely round, enormous, and shimmering with fire. Sidonie inhaled a bit of scarf in terror. Then the fire slid across the eyes and out, and she realized that they were lenses, perched on the most hideous face she had ever seen in her life. It looked so wizened that all its parts were melting together, eyes lop-sided and sliding toward a jutting, bony beak of a nose that was sagging to push the lipless mouth into the chin, which seemed to be buried half-way down the wrinkled neck. Hens, fuming coals, the green lenses began to eddy gently, as though they were all being stirred in the stinking cottage by another witch, an even bigger paddle.

Sidonie pulled her whirling thoughts together. This was no time to faint; the witch would surely eat her if she did.

She said again, her voice shaking badly, "I have come for the heart of Prince Ronan of Serre."

The witch took a spoon, filled it with her brew, and raised it to her nose. She sniffed, then spilled it back into the pot. What looked like a fingerbone surfaced, sank again. Sidonie stared dazedly. Surely there had not been a wedding band on it.

The witch spoke finally, her voice like the creak of tree limbs swaying in the wind. "So? It's his heart. Why should I give it to you?"

A pounding began somewhere, sporadic, muffled, like a shutter banging in a distant room. Sidonie, trying to hold a thought in her head, found the sound perilously distracting. A few hens protested peevishly. The witch, waiting for an answer, ignored the thumping.

"Well?"

"Because he doesn't want it—"

"I'll keep it, then. It's worth something to me."

"But I need it! He needs it, I mean. He doesn't know that

he needs it. And anyway," she added, inspired, "if he doesn't want it, there's no reason you shouldn't give it to me. For a price. A small price. Since it's worth nothing to him."

The witch sniffed again, drew the length of her forearm under her nose. "A princess, are you? You're not dressed like one. You've nothing worth it to me—no jewels, no hairpins of gold, not even a satin ribbon in your hair, just that ugly scarf. Take it off." Sidonie pushed it back wordlessly. The tilted eyes, sunk like old nails in a post, swam with fire again. "Let down your hair."

Sidonie unknotted Auri's plain dark ribbon; the untidy bundle of hair fell loosely; the heavy strands uncoiling like honey in the firelight.

"Oh, yes," the witch muttered. "Oh, yes. I'll have that from you before you go into the pot."

Sidonie felt her heart lurch, toad-like, into her throat. She pinched her lips, swallowed it, and whispered, "There must be something I can—"

"Stop that!" the witch bellowed, and Sidonie froze. Then she heard the faint shouts mingling with the annoying thumping. It seemed to be coming from behind her, and had gotten louder.

"Who—what is that noise?" Sidonie asked tremulously.

"Nothing. The wind," said the witch. "You were saying?"

"I'll do—Ronan said that you asked him for things, in exchange for—"

The lenses sparked again. "Ronan. He killed my white hen."

"I could get you another white hen. In exchange for his heart."

"His heart?" The witch's sparse brows went up. "That's a different matter entirely now. Now you are bargaining for your life. What's that worth?"

"My—" Words dried up; she closed her mouth, staring at Brume. In the sudden silence, the din behind her took on a frantic tone. Why are you so desperate to come in? she wondered numbly. Go home. Stay indoors. Never, never come looking for the witch . . . She cleared her throat. "You can't—you can't seriously want to—"

"Put you in a pot, boil you to a stew over my fire, and have you for supper? What else did you think I would do when you came here? Put Ronan's heart in a box for you and send you on your way? A young, well-fed princess with that hair? Which reminds me." She turned, glancing here and there. "Where did I put those scissors?"

"But don't you want—Can't we bargain—"

"You haven't offered me anything." She waited, bony hands on her enormous thighs. "Come, girl. Make me an offer. What's your life worth to you?"

Sidonie considered her brief life bewilderedly. "My father is King of Dacia. He could give you—"

"The moon and the stars and the firebird? He could, couldn't he? But would he, once you're out my door and down the steps?" She bent, scrabbled through a jumble of cooking utensils and hearth tools. "Where could they be? How about your firstborn child?" Sidonie gaped at her. "Now that would be something for the pot."

The princess heard words she had never said before suddenly spilling out of her mouth. "You wicked—you evil, despicable, curdle-faced—"

"Ha!" the witch said, brandishing shears so big they might have bitten an ox-bone in two.

"You can't just kill me! My father would go to war with Serre!"

"What's that to me? I've seen wars come into the forest, and I've seen them go." She snicked the giant shears open and shut a few times. "Give me your hair and your life, or give me something worth your life. One or the other. Surely you must know what your life is worth by now."

"I'm thinking!"

"Don't take all night about it. It can't be a very long life."

"It's not," Sidonie said tightly. "That's what makes it difficult. How do I know what I'm worth? I know what I'm worth to my father, and to King Ferus, and to Ronan, but how do I know what I'm worth to me? What would you be worth to you?"

The tiny, skewed eyes behind the lenses peered at her, black and bright as a hen's eyes taken aback by a peculiar insect. "I'd be worth what I could get," Brume said pithily. She plucked a few of her ashen hairs and tested the scissors' blades on them. "Which is rapidly becoming a moot point where you're concerned."

"Ferus would probably give you gold for me," Sidonie suggested desperately. "We could send him a message."

"What if he won't?" The witch's head cocked suddenly, at a thought. "You know what I've always wanted, though? I've always wanted one of those hens that lays golden eggs. Do you have one?"

"No."

"Oh." She gave a meditative grunt. "Well. I guess that's

that, then." She started to heave herself up, then sat back down again, panting. "Look at me. I'm weak with hunger. You'll have to come to me so I can cut your hair off."

Sidonie's eyes flickered down to the scarf hanging loosely around her neck. A scene from one of Auri's tales had been embroidered on it: a young girl, who had tricked the witch, watching Brume climb into her own stew pot. Sidonie had outfaced Ferus with a tale once; perhaps she could do it again.

She said carefully, "Those scissors are enormous. They must be very heavy in your small hands."

"They are, but I'm used to them."

"My hands are very strong. I can cut my own hair off for you if you'll show me how."

"That's easy enough. You just snip," the witch said, shearing a lock from her balding head.

"I'm a princess. I've never cut my own hair. Show me again. I'll watch carefully this time."

"You take," Brume said with exaggerated patience. "A lock." She held one out, on one side of her skinny throat. "Then you open the shears. So." They gaped wide in her other hand. "And then you. Snip!"

She finished in a strangled squeal as Sidonie, leaping at her, gripped the witch's matchstick wrists and pushed her backward off her stool. The witch hit the floor. The scissors in her hand, still open wide, split the floorboards on either side of her throat, pinning her within the broad angle of the blades.

The witch screeched. So did the chickens. Sidonie, having no wish to upset Serre by doing away with its oldest witch, scrambled to her feet and ran to the door. She flung it wide. A burly figure, pulled off-balance by the impetus of the opening door, reeled toward her, blocking her way. It was faceless against the stars. Sidonie shrieked. The figure toppled and went down, dragging her with it. The scissors shot over her head as she fell, and smacked against the door. It slammed shut again, bones rattling. Then it vanished.

The witch, pulling herself out of the shadows, gave a sudden cackle. "Welcome back."

Sidonie, scrambling in terror away from whatever it was that had fallen over her, made a desperate grab for the scissors along the way. She put her back to the wall, and opened them menacingly, one long blade pointed at the witch, the other at the sprawling figure on the floor. "Stay away from me," she warned tersely. "I'll cut you both into very small pieces and boil you in the pot."

The witch snorted. The figure on the floor shifted, raising a fire-streaked, coppery head. Sidonie, staring, slid down to the floor again; the shears slipping from her lax grip clattered beside her.

"Ronan?"

He sat up, wincing as he uncrooked one leg from around a hen's roost. "I saw you come in," he said. His voice sounded strained, raw as though from shouting.

"Was that you making all that noise?"

"I was trying to get back in."

"What for?" she asked incredulously.

He eyed her wordlessly, pulling himself up the roost. "To rescue you," he explained finally. "It's what I had in mind, anyway. You wear the strangest things to escape in."

"Do you expect me to run down that cliff road in my wedding gown?"

"I would have expected you to run all the way back to Dacia in your wedding gown," he said grimly. He draped himself over the roost, ignoring the hen pecking indignantly at him, and looked at Brume. "Well? What have I got left to offer you for the Princess from Dacia?"

Sidonie closed her eyes, banged her head against the bone wall. "I was nearly out the door! You got in my way."

"I'm sorry."

"We both would have been free!"

"Yes. I didn't know you would deal so easily with Brume. I couldn't."

"She wanted my hair," Sidonie explained. "She showed me those huge shears and I remembered a tale." She remembered the witch then, and turned her head hastily. Brume was sitting on her stool again, applying a burning broom-straw to the bowl of her pipe.

She puffed a few times, then said quizzically around her pipe, "Go on. Don't mind me."

Sidonie looked uncertainly at the prince. Out of tales for the moment, she took hold of the scissors again. He had been armed, apparently, but his sheath was empty, and he was using the roost for balance, letting his weight fall on one leg. A brawl, she guessed, with one of the forest-dwellers.

Then she thought twice, and asked in sudden horror, "Did Gyre do that to you?"

"No. My father."

"Why? He recognized you—he trusted you—"

"That was yesterday," he said, so dryly that even she

barely recognized him. His eyes went back to Brume, who was stirring her cauldron, and puffing sparks into it at the same time.

The witch said as though she felt Ronan's gaze, "Leave the princess here and I'll let you go free."

"No," he answered without surprise or hesitation. "Let her go free and I will stay."

Sidonie hesitated, tempted for an instant to leave the ogre's obnoxious son to Brume. "No," she sighed, getting to her feet again. "We are trapped here together. We will find a way out together. I will not leave without you. Unless," she added, desperately, remembering what she had come for, "you try to leave without your heart. Then you can leave without me."

He looked at her silently, his eyes heavy, but oddly clear. He listened, she thought with astonishment. He heard me. He gave a nod that might have been, to a watching eye, only the shift of light across his face.

Then his attention went back to Brume, who remarked querulously, "Well, by yourself you couldn't find me the firebird, or give me any recompense at all for my white hen. I got nothing out of the wizard, and nothing from you either but what you thought you didn't want in the first place, and was worth nothing to me anyway—"

"Oh—" Sidonie gasped, shocked by the lie. "You would have made me pay for his heart."

"What did you offer for it?" Ronan asked curiously.

"I—She didn't give me time to offer, before she started asking me what I was worth to myself."

"And what did you say?"

"I couldn't think of anything. I'm worth heirs to you, and power to Ferus, and peace to my father, but I couldn't think of anything else. So I attacked her with the scissors instead."

"You're worth my heart," Ronan said simply. "That's what you risked your life to get."

She stared at him. For the first time, she saw him smile. In the face of the witch, she thought dazedly. In the house of bone without a door, he could smile.

"Ronan," she said, feeling that she had met four of him by now, and the fourth Ronan was by far the most bewildering. "What are you doing here? Surely the king didn't let you come alone. Would we be right in telling Brume that your father and his warriors are outside waiting for us, and that if we don't come out, he will come in and rescue us?"

"We could try," he said, and Brume laughed, an unpleasant noise like a hen with a grain caught up its beak.

"Try," she suggested, and rapped her pipe suddenly, sharply against the side of the cauldron, spilling her foul leaves onto the flames. "Enough. You both either go out the door together, or into the pot together. Which is up to you. You have just time enough for me to rekindle a fresh pipe to persuade me to set you free. After that, I'll use those bone-shears on you. Choose."

Someone knocked on the door, which suddenly became visible.

Brume flung her spoon and the pipe furiously into the pot, splashing her noxious brew into the fire. "There is no such thing as a quiet night in the forest anymore!" She pushed between them, wresting the scissors from Sidonie as she passed. She threw open the door. Sidonie, gathering her breath to scream for help above the shrill, startled clamor of the chickens, felt the sound vanish in a wordless rush of air.

Gyre entered the witch's house.

TWENTY-FIVE

Not even Brume wanted to see him.

"You!" she snapped and tried to slam the door in his face. But he threw up a hand and left Brume wrestling with a door that refused to budge as the wizard passed her. Ronan's reclaimed heart leaped like a startled hare at the sight of Gyre. He backed a step, glancing around swiftly. Nothing in the house to fight with, it seemed, but pot hooks and scissors. He felt the princess shift close to him as he angled toward the hearth. Her face looked waxen in the sparse light. The prince wondered if his last experience of life as Ronan of Serre would be trying to limp surreptitiously across the crazed cottage of bone under the wizard's eye while disturbed chickens screeched around him and the witch snarled futilely at her door.

The wizard seemed astonished at the sight of them. He

looked, Ronan realized suddenly, as though he had been battling a whirlwind. His clothes were shredded, his skin bruised and torn, his face harrowed. Something had shattered the opaque calm in his eyes. He had crossed paths with some strange magic, Ronan guessed, and it had left him dazed, cudgeled, vulnerable. Then Ronan, who had thought he was facing the worst when the wizard came through the door, remembered what even worse was roaming the forest, and he felt the blood drain out of his face.

The princess remembered it, too. She put both hands to her mouth and whispered, "Gyre. Did that monster find you?"

"Yes."

Behind him, Brume gave the door a frustrated kick. It slammed shut abruptly, startling her, and sending chickens flailing into the air. Annoyed, she kicked it again. Then she turned, said crossly to Gyre, "You were the monster. You showed me your face."

"You?" the princess said faintly. She took one hand from her mouth, reached out to grip Ronan's arm. Ronan felt her trembling. "That—that thing was you?"

The wizard hesitated. "In a way. Not exactly."

"You were, too," Brume argued, going back to the hearth to fish in the pot for her pipe. "You scared all my hens."

"I was, then. Yes. But not—" He gave up on words, gestured at his battered self.

The princess closed her eyes tightly, opened them again. "Then there are two of them? Of you?"

He shook his head. "It's gone now," he answered elliptically. "You will never see it again." His eyes went to Ronan, who felt himself freeze mid-step, the hare in the fox's stare. "There is no need to be afraid of me. I won't harm you."

"That's what they all say," he answered tersely. "All the foxes. If you didn't come looking for me, then why are you here in the witch's house?"

"I came to see Brume. What are you both doing here? I didn't expect you to be anywhere but safe in the palace."

"Nowhere," Ronan reminded him bitterly, "is safe from you."

"No," the wizard answered softly. "You were right about that. But why are you here?"

"I came to get Ronan's heart back from Brume," Sidonie said, her fingers still locked on Ronan's arm. "Ronan came to rescue me. But now we are both trapped in the witch's house, and I haven't got so much as a gold hairpin to offer her for his heart, and I am afraid to ask you for help—I don't know any longer who or what you are, or what you might do to Ronan."

Gyre was silent a moment. "I can't ask you to trust me," he said finally. But maybe I can persuade you to stop fearing me." He didn't wait for Ronan to answer. He turned to the witch, who was blowing liquid out of her pipe, and said, "I will give you my heart if you let the princess and the prince go free."

Brume dropped her pipe in the pot again, her eyes growing enormous behind the lenses. Ronan, blinking, tried to speak, couldn't. The princess could.

She cried, "The last thing we need in the world is you without a heart! Gyre, if you cannot do better than that with Brume, then keep quiet. It's difficult enough to rescue

Ronan's heart, and if we get out of here alive, I don't want to be forced to come back for yours."

"Oh, you keep quiet," Brume said. She took a step toward Gyre, her hands clasping. "I'll take it."

"No," Ronan pleaded. "Sidonie is right. She came here because she could not bear to live with the man who had abandoned his heart to Brume, and I came here because the queen could not bear to live with me, either. She told me not to bother coming back without it or she would refuse to recognize me as her son."

The princess was giving him a strangely skewed look. "I'm right?"

"What?"

"You said that I was right. You listened to me."

He hesitated, feeling off-balance, though she seemed to be holding both of them upright. "Yes?"

"You have already taken your heart back from Brume," she said around her knuckles. "That's why you seem so— You were already free, and you came back in to rescue me."

"What was I supposed to do? Explain to my mother that I left you to be eaten by Brume?"

"But you didn't tell me!"

"I was hoping," the prince admitted, "that you might notice. That it would make a difference."

"Never mind," Brume shouted, startling them, "about your heart!" The lenses swung at Gyre. "What about yours?"

"There's a difference," the wizard said, holding his hands together and open, as though he were about to receive something, "between giving up something you cannot bear to live with any longer, and giving something you will love for the rest of your life."

A shimmering of gold and jewelled fires began to form in his hands. Ronan watched breathlessly, wondering how such beauty could come out of anyone human, let alone the wizard who had lied to him, and caged him, and threatened to steal his life. Then he realized what he was seeing and he felt his own heart try to break again.

"No!" he cried, stumbling between wizard and witch, trying to reach the egg before she did. But she only nudged him out of the way with a thump of her shoulder, sent him sprawling among the roosts. "Take it," he pleaded to Sidonie. "Don't let him give it to Brume!"

She was moving to help him, though she could not take her eyes from the glowing thing passing from Gyre to Brume. "Why?" she breathed, tugging at his arm. "What is it?"

"It is the firebird's egg!"

She let go of Ronan, straightening incredulously, but the witch had already taken the egg.

Brume turned away from them immediately; they could only see the reflection of its fires leaping and glittering all around them on the walls. Ronan, his breath catching harshly, pulled himself up painfully, took a step, and caught his balance again on Gyre, gripping the wizard with both hands.

"Why?" he whispered, holding the bruised, haunted, incomprehensible eyes. "Why have you given the most beautiful thing in the world to the most hideous thing in the world? You have perverted all the magic in Serre."

He heard an answer then, but not from the wizard. It was as though one of the sweet, brilliant shafts of light from the jewelled egg had found its way into his heart. The firebird answered, her song falling through him like a bright, private shower of fire. The stark walls of bone, the rank, rustling shadows, the foetid cauldron, even the wizard's face faded around him as he found his way into a timeless place where the firebird and the woman and the egg all sang to one another peacefully, endlessly, weaving a magic around them that nothing could ever destroy.

How long he listened, he had no idea. When he saw the wizard again, Gyre was holding him. In those moments, Ronan realized dazedly, the wizard might have done anything at all, taken anything, everything. He had only waited until the prince could hear him again. And then he said simply, "I had no choice."

Ronan shifted out of his hold, looked bewilderedly for the witch. She was fading into her shadows, nearly invisible now. He could only see the faintest glimmer of her hair, the suggestion, as an ember popped out of the grate and tumbled after her, of what might have been a drift of stray pinfeathers illumined red by the fading ember, or a glimpse of a fiery plume.

He closed his eyes, and saw his life, like one of his mother's tapestries, patterned with the busy, colorful magic of Serre, the witch in her bones, the firebird in her tree, wearing one another's faces, both taking the fragments of his broken heart and making a trail for him to follow of song and bone until he pieced it back together again, and their faces became indistinguishable in his heart's eye.

"I want one more thing before I set you all free," said the witch in the shadows. "Promise me this, Ronan: You will tell your father that he will only recognize his true heir when he brings me a white hen to replace the one that you killed." He stared wordlessly into the shadows, trying to see her face. He heard the smile in her voice, and wondered if it was the witch's twisted smile or the firebird's magic. "Promise me."

"I promise," he whispered.

"If he doesn't come to me, I'll find him. It's high time he met me. Now all of you: go away. Go home."

The door of bone opened to the roar of water. They saw the road up the cliff unwinding just ahead of them, a spill of gold at the end of it that was the rising sun.

Ronan turned as they stood once again among the trees, to watch the astonishing sight of the witch picking up her cottage and running back into the magic of Serre. But the little house had already vanished. He stood dazed a moment by the familiar, prosaic world. Birds chattered in the sunlight; the tree boughs swayed gently in a passing breeze. His horse stood drinking placidly at the river's edge.

Ronan looked at the wizard, who was looking at Sidonie, who was facing the breeze and tying her hair back with the cloth full of tales. Go home, the witch had said. But where was home for Gyre? Ronan glimpsed something then of the wandering, questing, boundariless life that wizardry demanded, and felt the beginnings of an understanding of the man who had relinquished all claim to history, and then found himself perilously drawn to it. Gyre felt his eyes, turned swiftly.

Ronan held his gaze without flinching, said after a moment, "You wouldn't have liked my life. You would have been convincing maybe for a year or two. But then what? You would have found Serre, as vast as it is, too small a world, and even ruling it, having to hide your powers, would have been a very tiresome task. You could never just go off on your own and learn something. Or whatever it is that wizards do."

"I know," Gyre answered, his bruised face rueful. "I haven't been thinking very clearly."

"What happened with the monster? I didn't understand. Can I tell my father that we don't need to fear it any longer?"

"Yes. You can tell him that."

Sidonie drifted closer to hear. Her eyes were on Gyre, Ronan saw, but whatever inner compass she was following drew her to a stop beside Ronan. For some reason he thought of the owl and the little toad who had come to him for help. And the firebird. And now the princess, the stranger in his land, homing into his burly morning shadow as though she felt most comfortable there. For the first time in a very long time, he remembered what peace was, in that brief moment before they started back up the road.

The wizard seemed to sense his thoughts. Some of the strain, the grimness of whatever he had gone through, eased in his face.

"Brume was right," he answered Ronan. "I did take that monster's shape, a time or two. I came far too close to the power it had over every living thing. It was a useful disguise in the forest. I just never expected that it would come alive again and confront me, demand that I give back its heart because I had stolen it, and it saw itself in me."

"Is that true?" Sidonie demanded. "Did you steal it?"

"Some time ago. I thought it had been dead for centuries. I finally recognized it, as I battled it, as the monster that Unciel had fought, which nearly drained him of all his powers and his life."

Sidonie's face turned the color of cream. For some reason she moved even closer to Ronan, who had no conception of such powers and no more defense against them than a water ouzel might have had.

He said, appalled, "That was the monster running loose in Serre?"

"I thought," Sidonie whispered, "it was dead. Unciel killed it."

"It was. He did."

"It was what?" Ronan demanded. "Here? Or dead?"

"Both." Ronan stared at Gyre silently. The wizard rubbed his face wearily, and gave them a hint, when he dropped his hands, of the ruthless, relentless fury in his memories. Then his face quieted; he gazed over Ronan's shoulder, as though he could see through the trees, across the high western peaks, into the peaceful land beyond them. "Unciel killed it. But the only way he could have done that was by knowing it better than it knew itself. He became that monster and more, to kill it. I was not fighting the dead. I was fighting Unciel."

Sidonie put her hands to her mouth. "He was too ill—Gyre, how could he—"

"How could he not," the wizard said evenly, "when he

guessed what harm I might do in Serre? I think he sent his memories into Serre and let me battle them."

Ronan asked confusedly, trying to fit the odd assortment of pieces together, "Is Unciel dead, then? Did you kill him?"

"I don't know," Gyre said tightly. "I may have, forcing that battle on him. All I know is that he seemed alive when he freed me."

Ronan groped for another piece to the puzzle. "But the firebird's egg—what were you doing with it?"

"I stole it. As I tried to steal Serre itself. Because it was so beautiful, and held such ancient and innocent powers. I loved it. So I—" He stopped to draw breath, looking past them again into the heart of the battle. "When the monster found it and began to destroy it, I offered my life in exchange for the firebird's life. Because I could not bear to be the death of it."

Ronan stared at him. "What is it," he cried suddenly, incredulously, "you have been looking for in Serre?"

The wizard gave him a brief, tight smile. "What have you found, pursuing the firebird and contending with Brume? You are not the same man who crept into my firelight, starving, half-mad with love and grief, who would have relinquished his own name to any passing stranger. I was the passing stranger. We both got ourselves tangled in the magic of Serre. So Unciel must have done once, long ago, because he knew to tell me to give the firebird's egg back to Brume."

"Back to Brume." Sidonie's brows crooked. "Back—Gyre. What are you saying? That that filthy old witch who talked about making a stew out of my firstborn child could have anything at all to do with the firebird?"

"It's possible," Ronan said, hearing an echo of the magic that had burned through his heart in the witch's stinking cottage. "Anything is possible."

"Does your mother know this?"

"I doubt that Brume herself would encourage such speculation. She has a reputation to uphold." He looked at Gyre, the renegade wizard in his tattered clothes, with his battle-worn face and scarred heart. "What will you do?" he asked softly.

"What do you want me to do?"

Ronan raised his head, his eyes on the dark palace at the end of the road, and considered the matter. "Do what the witch said," he suggested finally. "If you can find a home. My father would never understand any of this."

"I could return to the palace with you first," Gyre offered, "to convince him that you are yourself and not me."

Ronan shook his head. "Leave my father to Brume," he answered pithily. "Maybe she'll find his missing eye for him. Or take the other one so that he'll have to see out of what he's got left of a heart." He turned to Sidonie then, who was eyeing him with wonder. "What do you want to do? Gyre could take you back to Dacia, if you want."

"And then what?" she asked him steadily. "We wait in Dacia for your father's armies to come over the mountains and take us by force instead of on paper?"

"So I take you by force instead?"

She regarded him silently again, the princess from Dacia in her plain dress and thick-soled boots, and tales knotted around her hair, who had gone alone into the house of the oldest witch in Serre.

Tall as she was, she had to reach up to lay her hand on his shoulder. "Perhaps now we can get to know one another," she suggested. "Before the king comes down the cliff road looking for us. I have met the prince in love with the firebird, the prince who was Gyre, the prince who had no heart, and now you. The fourth Ronan. Do you think you might be the last?"

He smiled, remembering how she had stood beside him against the terrors and confusions of the night. "I hope so," he answered.

He went to get his horse, then turned to watch her for a thoughtless, tranquil moment as she bade farewell to the wizard, who vanished, as the witch had, into the light of day.

TWENTY-SIX

Euan Ash was standing in a strange little house full of birds, all white hens except for one the color of fire that was laying golden eggs. It sang each time it dropped an egg into its nest. Euan could not hear its voice, but he knew that that was because its song was so beautiful no mortal could imagine it, even in dreams. Each time it laid an egg, the egg would break in two and his name would come out of the gold shell. No yolk, no chick of white or fire, just a word in that unimaginable voice.

Euan. Euan. "Euan."

He woke with a start and found a stranger at Unciel's bedside.

Unciel still slept, looking so frail he might have floated away if the blankets weren't weighing him down. Euan had never met Gyre. The young wizard had come and gone in

Unciel's cottage one evening in early summer after Unciel summoned him. But enough power had loosed itself in that bedchamber in the past days for Euan to recognize it in the lean, haunted face, the still eyes gazing down at Unciel.

Euan, waking in the chair as usual and feeling molded to it, leaned forward stiffly to study Unciel. He still breathed, apparently. The stranger gave one brief glance at Euan, taking in the unshorn scribe with the reddened eyes, the wrinkled clothes, the gaunt, colorless face.

"I'm sorry," the stranger said.

Euan blinked. "Gyre," he said after a moment. "You must be."

"Yes."

"How is—how are things in Serre?"

"When I left, they seemed unusually peaceful."

Euan, remembering his dream, sensed a tale tangled somewhere within the flock of hens and the lovely, secret voice that perhaps told the tale from beginning to end, but which he could not yet hear. He rubbed his eyes wearily.

"You should tell that to King Arnou."

"I spoke to Lady Tassel, who was strangely unsurprised to see me appear in Unciel's kitchen. She went back to the palace to tell the king that all is well with his daughter."

Euan pulled his hair into spikes and slumped back in the chair. "What about Unciel? Will all be well with him?"

"He's not dead yet," the enigmatic Gyre answered. He shifted the blankets a little, pulling them closer to the wizard's face. "How long has it been since you've eaten?"

"I don't remember. There's some limp cabbage soup hanging over the ashes."

"I'll see what I can do with it," Gyre said. Euan stopped him before he made it through the door.

"Wait—" He paused, trying to drag his thoughts into some coherent form. "Wait." Gyre did so. "You just—You and Unciel—You were just roaming around Serre wearing that monster's face, terrifying every living thing—Now you're going to warm up some old cabbage soup? Is that how life normally is for a wizard?"

"Some days you battle yourself and other monsters. Some days you just make soup. You'll both need to eat, after all that."

"After all what?"

"After all you did for him. After all he dreamed for me."

Euan sat back with a sigh. The raven, perched on the chair back behind his head, picked through its feathers in search of something moving. The one-eyed cat on Euan's knee closed its eye and went back to sleep. So did Euan.

This time his name was written in elaborate, elegant script in the midst of his dream by what looked like a burning finger. Euan, the fire said, and he woke himself answering.

"Yes. Where were we?"

Unciel was looking at Euan, his eyes open for the first time in days, and strangely clear. They had lost that ashen mist of memory; fire had rekindled itself behind the blue.

"Finally," he said, and the scribe, still moving out of dreams, reached for his pen.